THE DIRT BEAT

Venero Armanno is the author of a book of short stories and seven critically acclaimed novels including *Romeo of the Underworld, Firehead, The Volcano* and *Candle Life*. *Firehead* was shortlisted in the 1999 Queensland Premier's Literary Award for Best Fiction; *The Volcano* won that award in 2002. His fiction has been published in America, France, Germany, Switzerland, Austria, Holland, Israel and South Korea.

Also by Venero Armanno

Jumping at the Moon
The Lonely Hunter
Romeo of the Underworld
My Beautiful Friend
Strange Rain
Firehead
The Volcano
Candle Life

THE DIRTY BEAT

VENERO ARMANNO

Venero Armanno

UQP

First published 2007 by University of Queensland Press
PO Box 6042, St Lucia, Queensland 4067 Australia

www.uqp.uq.edu.au

Typeset in 13.5/16 pt Spectrum MT Regular by Post Pre-press Group, Brisbane
Printed in Australia by McPherson's Printing Group

Cataloguing-in-Publication Data
National Library of Australia

Armanno, Venero, 1959–.
The dirty beat.

ISBN 978 0 7022 3614 3

1. Jazz and rock musicians – Fiction. 2. Funeral rites and ceremonies – Fiction. I. Title.

A823.3

CONTENTS

PART 1
I FEEL SO STRONG

I

If you can keep yourself from becoming too anxious when you wake to discover someone using an electric power tool on your head, then you're on your way to making peace with your new circumstances. With an odd sense of detachment I take note of the way these two attendants work methodically and fast, sawing my skull open and creating a flurry of bone-dust as they go. Their Perspex goggles fog up with the fine spray but they don't stop until the job's done – out comes the brain.

The two boys handle it with plastic-gloved hands. I can hardly call these two individuals 'men' for they must be all of twenty years apiece, but they seem to be skilled apprentices in the little-discussed mechanics of a death's investigation. Their boss will come and check their work as soon as he finishes his coffee and Danish in the staff room, but he's got no need to worry: the intensity and curiosity in their faces is exceptional. They love their job. In fact, they make me feel special, though there's nothing too special about dropping dead days shy of your fiftieth.

The extraordinary in this situation doesn't have to do with birthdays or these boys. Instead, it's my sentience. Is it like this for all fresh cadavers? I have no idea. None of the other stiffs in here is talking. For me, though, my body might be finished but my mind is as alive as it's ever been. Possibly more so because I feel free from quotidian responsibilities. Nothing remains undone or half-done, as is usually the case in the ongoing frustrations of our daily lives. I don't have to fret about getting myself ready for work, finding a mechanic to fix that new knocking sound in my truck's transmission, buying groceries and eating more fruit and vegetables, or where and how will I go about getting some girl to sleep with me. All that's left, really, is to drift off into the white forever – but it doesn't happen.

Now these two young students of mortality and its limits carefully transfer my brain into a glass beaker. Awareness doesn't follow that slide into glass; it stays here with my body. I guess this is where I am, then, attached to a corporeal self that was – for the most part, barring the encroaching decrepitude of middle-age – the fun part of me.

Back in my primary school days of the sixties, the nuns believed they had a good grip on the mysteries of the great beyond. Heaven, hell, purgatory and limbo – each has its membership rules, though I remember hearing recently that the Pope, whatever his name is, might rescind the antiquated idea of limbo. Everybody gets to go somewhere; no one will go nowhere. This is good of him.

The nuns told us that there's no definite span of time defined for exactly how long the soul will remain with its body upon physical expiration. If the death is sudden and unexpected, say a stroke, car accident or gunshot, then it might stay where it is for a day or anywhere up to three or four. If the death is long and drawn-out, something like an octogenarian succumbing to a long bout of disease, then the soul will probably slide on out and be on its way almost immediately. In other words, it has been primed for departure and is absolutely ready to go.

Where the good nuns of the Holy Mother primary school got their information, I don't know, but everything they said was reinforced by the Christian Brothers.

'Your flesh is weak,' Brother Collins told us in a Religious Instruction class, 'but your soul is forever. That means this—' and he took a chunk of chalk and wrote a '1' on the board, then with a sense of theatre followed that number with zeros scrawled all the way off the chalk board. He went across all four walls of our school room, then he went around again, and again, and again, and again, without stopping. The chalk was worn down to a nub. It took him the better part of the lesson to get all the hundreds and hundreds and hundreds of zeros he wanted. When the bell rang, he surveyed his handiwork.

'And even *this* will be the blink of an eye when it comes to the neverending life God has blessed his children with.'

Without warning, and with the force of an expert pitcher, he then hurled his chalk-nub at the side of the head of a boy named Lawrence English. Laurie was languishing at the back of the class-room picking his nose and staring at the pigeons cooing in the playground. The chalk hit him square in the temple. The boy started to cry.

'Try crying to the Lord!' A red, thick vein had appeared in Brother Collins' brow. 'Try crying to the Lord when your time comes!' He paused for effect, then dropped his voice to a whisper, 'So why not pay attention to your soul from now on? *Can't you see it's the you that God is going to judge?*'

We strained to hear that spooky voice and he terrified all the nine- and ten-year-old boys in his school room. Except for me. Why? Because I thought he was a clown. His sense of theatre was for the theatre of the absurd. He knew nothing. A year hadn't quite passed since the morning I went to wake my mother and discovered I couldn't. From that moment on nothing much had the power to scare me, and certainly not a buffoon in a cowboy's black clothes, a white inverted collar yellowing with age and a zealot's belief in things that simply could not be proven.

Still, maybe I could have paid more attention. Maybe mad belief is proof enough of the existence of things: such as souls, eternity and the afterlife. I'm trying to remember if the nuns or the brothers ever said what your soul was supposed to do while it was still stuck to its cadaver or if there was some purpose to being trapped that way.

Whatever. Life – or maybe I should just call it Existence now – never stops throwing challenges at you. I find myself in new terrain and I don't have a map. I don't know if I'm going to heaven, hell, in-between, or even – despite the Pope's promise – absolutely nowhere. No matter. I'll deal with whatever does or doesn't happen. At the moment my biggest task seems to be to keep any rising apprehension and disquiet at bay. Which is of course a little more easily said than done: I'm all too aware that the most pimple-faced of the morgue attendants is idly using a sponge to wipe the skull cap he's helped saw off. He's humming a tune. Tufts of my hair are matted and moist. He peers into the empty cave of my head and I also get a glimpse.

Let me tell you, there are some things you don't want to see, dead or alive.

II

Another sterile room; time has passed. I've slept, at least in the metaphoric sense. It could be a day or two later, but these are the sorts of measurements that mean nothing now.

Today I've been dressed in the clothes the boys from the band put together out of my closet at home. They chose a typical look: black t-shirt, jeans and lace-up hiking boots. If not for the fact that my blood was pumped out and my brain extracted, I'd almost be my old self.

Here's a memory: the embalming fluid that went in had been cold and dry, like a wind whistling through my veins. After a while that wind died and the fluid set like concrete. Now there's a thoroughly unfamiliar sensation. Something's in my stomach and it isn't some delicious meal. Ah, that'll be my brain. The cavity in my head has been stuffed with surgical padding – a nice enough term that really means they've wadded up the inside of my skull with lumps of those paper towels you take from a roll to clean up your kitchen messes. Then, because even the most devoted necromancers like shortcuts, and this has become the burying trade's conventional practice, the two morgue boys deposited my brain into the slit they'd made when they dug out my guts to see what was inside. Sewed up my head and sewed up the smile in my belly – all is well.

None of these physical misfortunes should mean very much, but I seem to retain enough human frailty that I wish my regular GP, Dr Bailey, had said something like, 'Yeah, I saw this guy often. His heart wasn't going to last much longer. Had a balloon fitted eighteen months ago. I'm happy to sign the death certificate.' Instead, he'd come to see me on the morgue slab and declared, 'Lot of musicians around Max, better open him up and make sure this wasn't drug-related.'

It wasn't and now they know it.

I understand that my friends haven't arranged an open-coffin visiting session, so the stitching these two young apprentices made didn't need to be too perfect. No makeup required either. What I've got to look forward to is the farewell ceremony itself, at which time the coffin lid will be as tight as my sutures.

My mind, my glorious undead mind – or maybe I should give in to the nuns and brothers and call it my soul after all – tells me I should be cold on this table, but no, whatever sensation I have, none of it's really all that physical. Just the recollection of how things used to feel against my skin. Instead, I seem to be a floating ball of emotions and memories and moods. I'm not so anxious any more, just sour. Sour because my veins have been filled with concrete, my skull has been stuffed with paper towels, in the place where glorious food and drink used to go I now have my dissected brain, and someone is using a dry razor, no shaving foam, to scrape the whiskers off my face.

I'm in a different place. It's no longer the morgue, but a funeral home. The person shaving me is the other end of the spectrum to those apprentices. He's a wizened old man with a forest in each nose hole. What indignity to be toyed with by an individual who owns such fertile nostrils. Maybe he'll have an assistant in a slinky nurse's uniform, zip down just a little too much and a nice healthy cleavage. Maybe Father Concrete here dreams of allowing his hairy nose to rove over those merciless hillocks, taking in the perfume of young flesh after the iniquities of being the handmaiden to death day in, day out, no respite till the weekends.

No.

His assistant wears a green cardigan and is as old as he is. She has a limp, thanks to a titanium hip installed less than a month ago. Actually, she's feeling better than she has in thirty, thirty-five years. I'm happy for her, yes I am – wish I could say the same for myself.

III

Thirty, thirty-five years: that was when a black-haired hippie named Maree came into my life. So long ago, but who'd ever forget? It was November 1973 to be precise.

I turned seventeen years of age on the twelfth of the month and was already something of a drummer by then, my jazz-loving new stepfather teaching me just about everything I needed to learn. I met Maree at a friend's place while a little practice band I was in trashed surf music tunes like there was no tomorrow.

The first days of being seventeen and the last days of school; I lost my hated virginity and betrayed my best friend, Davey, at the same time. She was going out with him and he was foolish enough to bring her to the practice session, showing her off. Dave wasn't a musician, just one of the gang of useless Christian Brothers' teenage boys we all were. He should have had the presence of mind to stay home that day. We went to a bum of a school, but that didn't stop him from discovering Dvořák and the cello by himself; Maree couldn't get enough Hawkwind and drugs. We talked for about fifteen minutes. I was the only person she'd met who knew about a poet and performer named Bob Calvert, an

American counter-culture figure she idolised. I only knew about him by chance. A couple of weeks earlier I'd stolen a new live Hawkwind double album from the local record store, and this nut called Calvert screamed maniacal lyrics and monologues all over the spacey music. To me it was all thoroughly awful – but why tell a pretty hippie that?

Maree stood a little closer while everyone else talked about whatever. I was already dying for her to touch my cock. Soon enough, she did.

She left Davey to eat his heart out and in the way of selfish young boys I felt guilty for less than a week. By the second week that troublesome lump of human metal of mine was raw with the quick, furtive, soundless fucks Maree and I had in my bedroom while my by-then-widowed stepfather watched television in the lounge. I didn't feel so guilty about my ex-best friend any more. Sex makes you heartless. It also makes you want more. When we weren't at my place, Maree and I had long horny sessions in her older brother Michael's flat.

We'd go for hours at Michael's place, at the same time working our way through his knee-high stack of LP records. There I learned about women, lovemaking and rock music. For the rest of my life, in my mind, the three would remain inseparable. *Led Zeppelin II* was perfect for the things Maree taught me. We'd take a minute's break when the end of side one started ticking, then get going again with the wintry fervour of *Immigrant Song* at the start of side two.

Another break, what's next? *Who's Next*. We'd have it so loud Keith Moon's drum skins might as well have been my shoulders and back, as if he was wrenching his rolling beat out of my young muscle and flesh. We'd scream with Daltrey after that long synthesizer break in *Won't Get Fooled Again* and still not come. Eyeball to eyeball, staring straight into one another, we breathed each other's expirations and ground pubic bone against pubic bone. That's where the human soul starts, that's what we learned, in the raw aching pubis of sex-mad teenagers. Away from one another we were young, bored and stupid, but together the world was one long, loud song – with many more to come.

I'll ask her this from the coffin: 'Stick on another album from your old collection, won't you do that for me, Maree, if you're still alive somewhere? Bob Dylan said it better than me on that album *Blonde on Blonde*. We used to eat each other up to: "Where are you tonight, sweet Maree?"'

She was younger than me but smarter and better read. Maree introduced me to even greater pleasures by channelling Bobby Zimmerman, Marc Bolan and David Bowie. Her taste was eclectic. Alice Cooper was getting big in Australia so Maree would copy his death's mask makeup, wearing little pink hot pants and long silver boots with spiky heels. Somehow she'd have a fluffy feather boa to wrap around herself. She lived in op-shops, spent all her money on outrageous clothes. At sixteen she was already doing her own writing and I'd take her raven hair in my fist and push my nose into her unshaved armpits, breathing the sweaty stench and silk of a poet.

Panting. Stop.

Then what?

Get shoved onto my back and Maree would say, 'Don't come. Do not come. Please don't,' and she'd grind her hips down into me. I only came as required. In his green days, a young man can do just about anything with his body. 'Whew,' she'd say. 'Fantastic. Okay, another album.'

'You choose this time,' I'd tell her, 'I'm very busy.' Her fingers would leave wet fingerprints on Michael's much-adored record sleeves and vinyl. 'That new one, *Billion Dollar Babies*, put that on.'

Naked, she'd crawl off on all fours, and while she was digging for it I'd take her from behind.

'I'm going to make it so loud,' I remember her telling me, her white rump in the air, her small breasts shaking and vibrating, flushed-pink face pressed down over her forearms. 'Wait. Just for a second, let me get the needle down on this one, it's my favourite. Then you fuck me all the way and you don't stop. You finish me off with Alice.'

Alice Cooper would sing, *God/I feel so strong/I feel so strong/I'm so strong/I feel so strong*, and for the first time in my life I knew exactly what that felt like, tingling gooseflesh covering my body at the raw power my Maree had led me to.

More weeks and more months and more records devoured like meat. Michael was a hospital wardsman and kept strange hours. He didn't mind what his little sister was up to, so we had his flat all the strange hours we wanted. The only thing he asked was that we should sometimes vacuum his carpets. Small price to pay; Maree and I practically wore holes in it. He didn't want us to use his bed and he expected that we would always restack his LPs in alphabetical order. Sometimes I'd leave a pot of soup on the stove for him, ready to heat when he came home to empty rooms still thick with sex. In those days I was already a pretty good drummer and an even better cook. It's not so bad to have an Italian stepfather: he could have a quick temper but he loved Miles Davis and John Coltrane, strongly flavoured food with a bottle of red wine, and an artichoke-based liqueur called Cynar that he had his friends in Italy send over. There were times we fought like hyenas but I ended up following him in almost everything.

I'd like a drink now, truly I would, a nice aperitif of iced Cynar.
They ought to serve it in Heaven.

Anyway, if Maree and I could scrape some cash between us,
sometimes we'd buy exotic stuff and she'd make her brother
some special delicacy, leave it in a casserole dish in the oven for
him. Ham hocks with cannellini beans. Baked chicken breasts
with rosemary and sweet potatoes. A dish she called Mongolian
lamb. For a hippie, she was quite the gourmet. In Brisbane in 1973
you had to look hard to find interesting epicurean ingredients;
we weren't quite aware of it but we were in a complete cultural
desert, and things wouldn't change for fifteen years. That didn't
put Maree off. Thing was, the hippie era was already years out
of date, so she could reinvent the sensibility in any fashion she
wanted. She hated vegetarians, daisies and the acoustic guitar in
the hands of any sensitive soul. The music of Simon & Garfunkel
made her want to scream. The new era of the vulnerable singer-
songwriter brought tears of exasperation to her eyes. Poor James
Taylor, Donovan and Elton John, they couldn't know what vit-
riol they inspired in one sexy, crazy, antipodean pseudo-hippie
named Maree Kilmister.

God, I was crazy about her. Anything she did or said was fine
by me. Whenever we cooked for Michael, which was often, it gave
us a break from our sexual proceedings. We'd get back to the real
stuff soon enough. Near the end of one of Maree's favourites, Jef-
ferson Airplane's *Surrealistic Pillow*, we'd start shaking one another
like skeletons dancing over gravestones, and then we'd come, but
it wouldn't be an explosion but a sort of melting, young bodies
dripping like wax.

Later we'd dab our knees with Michael's Mercurochrome.
He stole things from the hospital; his medicine cabinet was like
a well-stocked Emergency Ward. Our generation believed it was

only fair that the world should give us whatever we wanted, and we took it all like greedy young dogs.

Maree Kilmister, outlandish poets, neverending pleasures.

That was 1973. Go on, try to tell me you had a better year.

IV

What's this magic?

It's not nearly thirty-five years ago, but tomorrow. I might be dead, but a few walking rock-and-roll cadavers have come out of the woodwork. To tell the truth, I don't think I could be looking as bad as some of these mummies no matter what's been done to me. There's not much that's less attractive than musicians in their fifties and sixties still trying to look like teenagers, but it is funny to see how startlingly black or blonde or red their hair is; how wide their eyes; how taut the facial skin. How absolutely white and perfectly formed their teeth have become. A lot of expensive work has been done to hold Father Time in check, but He's the one laughing; his children are comical and scary, surgically conserved testaments to His absolute claim.

And now, oh God, listen to this.

Some well-meaning soul has ordered up a dose of Pink Floyd for me. Here's a bet: any minute now everyone'll be getting misty to *Wish You Were Here*, perennial song of funerals, wakes and farewells to just-been-pensioned-off factory workers. People will be shaking their heads that I went too young. I did. For now we're treated to the interminable suite called *Shine On You Crazy Diamond*, and it must be a little more *a propos* than I can imagine. People are smiling and nodding in recognition. I'm their Crazy Diamond.

Oh well, if it makes them happy to think so.

Truth is, I had more common sense than the lot of them put together. So many tried to hold onto the past, to keep their glory days going, or to reinvent failures as successes, miseries as triumphs. The rose-coloured glasses syndrome married to the natural human desire not to have to tell your children – much less yourself – what a waste your life turned out to be.

Not me. My little hippie-chick Maree taught me the value of veracity early on in life. It went like this: she used to compose love poem after love poem in my name then read them out while I lay spent on the floor. Tears would well in her eyes as she declared neverending fealty. Her whole body used to respond to her appeal: eyes would shine, nipples would grow hard, colour would spread like a burnt-orange stain all across her sternum. She meant it all and it came from her heart, until the day I found her on the balcony of Michael's flat tearing her love-poetry out of her special diary and burning the pages one by one.

'What are you doing?'

'Forgetting you.'

Why, how? I never really understood, but I learned something else: some things you build just to watch fall down, there's nothing you can do. Face the truth of that and life gets a little easier. At Michael's door, on my way out, she saw the hurt in my eyes.

'I love you so much, but I've changed,' she said. 'I don't want you to change, you must never do it. You're perfect as you are.'

Huh. It's not you it's me.

Still, maybe if she'd known me all the way from that moment to my demise she would have been satisfied. It was almost as if

I listened to her because I stayed as I was, I never *became*, never *grew*, never turned into a diamond, crazy or otherwise. The world didn't crush me into some palatable shape. To the end I was the lump of coal I always was, true to whatever dirty roots I had. I never knew my biological father. He was a man who beat my mother the few months they lived together. Once he knew she was pregnant, bang, he was gone. Never heard of again and thank God for small mercies. A one-time nightclub dancer in a life-size budgie cage, my poor ma managed to work her way down the ladder of success to end as a backroom brothel-worker with matchstick legs and arms of wire. She knew what she was, but she kept an image of what I could be. Sent me to that Catholic school believing Christian Brothers and God-fearing boys would keep me off her road of danger and discontent.

She tried hard but she came to an end somewhere between a balmy summer's night and a warm Saturday morning. She was supposed to be taking me to sport. Soccer, for which I had little skill and less interest. I went to see why she wasn't out of bed. Sea-weed hair straggled over one blood-filled eye – that was where she'd found a healthy vein to shoot into.

Years later, my new father, the man who joined in adopting me after he married my aunt, said, 'You must shoot straight or you do not shoot at all.' My first and only music teacher, I sometimes found his order strange, I never could quite divorce it from the style of my mother's demise – but what he meant had nothing to do with shooting drugs or louche living. If anything he was telling me the opposite. Shoot straight, be true – and in music that means keep things simple, keep out the bullshit, be true to the beat and let the beat be your truth. I tried to listen to him. I think I stayed true. Never took on airs, just stayed me, for better or worse.

My Maree gave me the same advice. So when she said goodbye, I didn't. My actions would speak. I closed my eyes, turned my back on her and started walking.

Didn't stumble or fall. Not for a long, long time.

V

But I know where and how I took my final fall.

Five nights ago while I was doing the sound for Dirtybeat. The boys were celebrating the news that they'd just got themselves a record deal, a great one, not a soul-eater. I left my post at the mixing desk to dance with a girl young enough to be my daughter. She told me her name was Ash. Final thoughts: how good Ash's tits feel pressed against my chest; how perfect miniskirts are for girls with good legs; how impossibly small her feet look. Was I dreaming, or was she really showing every sign of wanting to come home with me?

Then – the end.

The attack shouldn't have come as that much of a shock. My health went downhill after I got smashed up in my car just before my thirty-eighth birthday. It seems birthdays have been bad luck for me. After that I grew more sedentary; cooked and ate more; drank too much wine to go with my exotic culinary creations. I was always a drinker, but now I learned to end my nights with several big shots of vodka, best cure for the ongoing physical pain I lived with. Then eighteen months ago I had a balloon installed to expand the major cardiac artery just about choked tight with bad living.

A long time before that, and before the car accident, my body had had to contend with the excesses doled out by my ma's sister, Emma, when she took me in. They say you pay for the excesses of your twenties and thirties in your forties and fifties, but my excesses had started early, at nine years of age. Even before my ma was in the ground I started learning. Aunt Emma was not the world's greatest cook; she fed me shepherd's pie or spaghetti leftovers morning and night. Her idea of shepherd's pie was to fill it with the cheapest, fattiest meats in the supermarket; her spaghetti was boiled pasta mixed with a full bottle or two of Heinz tomato sauce, seasoned with two good fistfuls of salt. Mop up the dregs with white bread and clear your way to the tomb. She never had milk in the house, not even for coffee. She'd never taken to breakfast cereal. At the start of the day we ate what was left over from the night before.

She also didn't think a small boy shouldn't share at least a little of her nightly bottles of beer. I was the only kid I knew who was tipsy each of his pre-teen birthdays and falling over drunk on his thirteenth. No one saw; my ma was gone, I was living with my Aunt Emma, and the two of us we were an absolute island in a sea of beer and meat and tutti-frutti ice cream, just the way she liked it. It went like that until a little after my drunken first teen birthday. Things changed. A man with the unlikely yet mellifluous name of Concetto San Filippo, or 'Conny' as he liked to be called, came into her life. Into mine.

But back to the fall.

I was in a circle of sweaty dancers jumping up and down to a new original number by my boys. I call them 'my boys' even though I never was their manager or agent, only a sound man for hire. I didn't like my PA and sound gear to be monopolised by any band in particular – but these kids, well, I couldn't help loving them. They reminded me of everything my rock band hadn't been back in the seventies and early days of the eighties. These boys had ambition and talent to burn. My group had lacked the former and enough of the latter to ensure that we were never going to go far past being a loud booking for a Saturday dance.

Anyway, the members of Dirtybeat liked me too, liked me because I'd come up with the perfect name for their outfit and because I had a history, a history they could relate to: veteran of the days when music technology was all fat cables and valves. When sound was sound – the sound they wanted.

Maybe that night I should have stayed at my post at the mixing desk, but the attack could have hit me anywhere, I guess. I was dancing with the prettiest girl I've seen up close in years, and it was as if she was really thinking she'd let me take her home and zip her out of her little black skirt, and unclip her bustier, and let her beautiful young breasts come gliding out.

I think she was thinking, 'This guy's old, but not too old. He's still got something. All of his hair for one thing. No tragedy of a middle-aged man's ear stud. And at least he doesn't use black dye.'

She might have been wondering what it would be like to feel a forty-nine year old's pounding heartbeat against her sternum, but what I didn't know was why she should have been thinking these things, why she would contemplate letting something like this happen against the pristine white of her flesh. Yet I could read her readiness in the curl of her smile and the shine in her eyes.

I count myself lucky. My adult life was book-ended by beauty. Maree at the start, Ash at the end.

So, yes, it was going to happen and it was going to happen to me. Every sour-faced younger man in this place would have gladly traded places. Traded places, or dragged me outside for a beating in exchange for such good luck. I knew it too, knew how those faces glared with beery envy. I would have felt the same way, would have felt just as jealous of the fact that here was a kid maybe twenty-one or twenty-two, out with her friends for a sweaty night of loud, raw music, high from too much to drink and plenty of laughs, here was this stunner making up her mind to give herself to a man days shy of his half century.

Lo and behold that man was me.

Her perfume was sort of musky, sort of the scent of hair that's been washed and dried in sunlight, and she leaned in during the song's moody middle-eight and said exactly these words: 'My name's Ashley – Ash – and guess what, I know who you are. My dad's got an album, all scratched up, but he still plays it for me, and I know you by your picture, you haven't changed so much,' and when she said this last bit she was close, and sort of laughed, but in a nice way, sort of shy, and her left breast touched my shirt. Then she pressed all the way to me and I could feel a wave of heat surge up my neck. 'You played the drums. I love the violinist on that album too. What was her name – whatever happened to her?'

The violinist, Debbie Canova. The last person I wanted to remember while I felt Ash against my chest.

I shrugged as if to say, 'People disappear,' but Debbie Canova had never disappeared, not from this broken old heart. The strange thing was I'd seen her again, first time in two decades, just over a week back. I'd been in Sydney helping Dirtybeat get their contract and, out of nowhere, like a magician's puff of smoke, there she was.

Ash couldn't have known that, and she couldn't have imagined how seeing Debbie Canova after so long had broken me all over again.

There was a first shudder beneath my breastbone, like a needle going in. Ash leaned closer and whispered, 'You were a great musician,' and I was moved, no preening lucky guy any more, no too-fortunate old fart, and so I stopped dancing, stopped dancing to better feel this girl Ash lightly yet indelibly against me.

The pain went away and I smiled back at her.

I hope it was a smile full of awe because that's just what I felt, awe about her and awe about how extraordinary a world we can have when it's filled with solid three-quarter beats and electric guitars and a growly voiced singer. Not to mention stages and amplifiers and roadies, and mixed drinks, and people who would prefer to dance than to fuss and fight, and the Ashes of the world who make gold of the ashes in our lives, and just like that I dropped, not to my knees in thanks but straight to the ground with an electric pain inside. It was a long piercing flash, then it was gone, and the luxuriousness of sleep overcame me, sent me into the dream that all this seemed to be. While the good people of this world worked on my expiring body, my heart fibrillated as if there was a chance that I would come back, that I might be able to rise up and take Ash by the hand and to my car, and drive her to my home, where I could explain why an old man like me should feel such wonder in the presence of a girl like her.

It wasn't to be. My heart only jerked long enough for the ambulance officers who then arrived to want to slap their paddles onto me, one below my right collarbone and the other against the ribs just below my heart.

Don't know how many jolts they ended up giving me, but the twitching and vibrating inside grew weaker, not stronger. When the movement stopped altogether they put a tube down my throat and attached a bag to it so they could get on with their resuscitation work. They injected their drugs into the dead rock of my heart, trying to get some movement back so they could hit me with the paddles again.

Thing is, I was already sort of kneeling there with them, watching my own face turn blue, feeling sorry for the way their arms were getting tired and heavy from trying so hard to bring me back to life. Both officers took turns over me. Another ambulance was on the way. Heroic effort, but I wanted to tell them that it was okay: once the mechanics of going are done with, nothing is all that bad any more.

When they finally gave up they seemed immensely disappointed. They didn't really want to leave me to Heaven, Hell or in-between.

I guess I got in-between.

For I'm sealed inside my coffin, laid out comfortably, placed here to dream what people imagine is our communal dream of eternity. Instead I'm dreaming a little, but mostly I'm going back in time. If I had it in me to weep I think I would. Thing is, though, this is what I want. Father Death has smiled on me. Father Death has chosen that I should be aware. Good of Him.

I might be laid out nicely, but in a sense I'm up on one elbow looking at the crowd gathered in this non-denominational chapel, where the celebrant will refrain from using the words 'God', 'Jesus', or anything with too much of a religious notion. My mother's hopes for the Catholic school were in vain; not very much of its dogma permeated me.

Here, people are squeezed into the rows of pews and the rest have had to gather at the back. So many good folk, I'm surprised. Some are forced to politely jockey for space outside the entrance

25

doors. The predominant colour is grey. I would have preferred black, of course. Black is sleek, but grey is death's drabbest colour, the tone of an accountant's bad-news voice and the texture of the arithmetic ticking in his brain.

And enough time has passed since the moment I dropped to make it my birthday.

Happy fiftieth, old fellow.

VI

Ash is here and she's brought her dad.

They're a mixed generation of rock fans, and I like it when you get that, the parents leading their kids to the music they liked when they were kids, and those kids not putting their fingers down their throats at the sound of rock bands already three or four decades gone, but embracing it, really loving it, loving it enough to be twenty-one or twenty-two years old and want to go out to a dirty club to listen to some new band pound out a new song with a moody middle-eight, and then dance with a never-was of those golden days.

It's sort of a bitter pill to swallow, I tell myself, resting up on an elbow to watch the way her hair falls over her face as she puts her head down. The strains of *Crazy Diamond* wash over her in such a way as to make a tear run down from her eye, or maybe, just maybe, that music makes her need to bite down on the insides of her cheeks so that she won't laugh out loud at the absurd tragedy of her position here. The last to see me, feel me, touch me, out of these musically oriented, middle-aged, public servants, teachers, accountants, bus drivers and so on. They've gathered here at the

Holy Church of Pink Floyd to say goodbye to an old fart. I guess, more than that, most of them are mourning the passing of one crazy diamond shard of their own lives. That's the hardest part of all: the death of a friend that chips away at your own sense of immortality.

Ash gets to her feet after saying something to her father, who's about my age but is nothing like me.

I get a good whiff of the insides of him. He's a fifty-two year old with a decent hair-cut and a sharp – if conventional – suit, the type Bernie Taupin or Charlie Watts might wear to some Hall of Fame Award TV show. He looks broad in the shoulders, tall, sort of solid and rangy all at the same time, as if in a lifetime of loving rock bands and working hard he's also found the time for a lifetime of playing something healthy like tennis. I'd say he's a three to four times a week man, and he plays to win, and rushes the net, where he's no slouch, and forty years ago his dad or some semi-professional coach taught him how to punch away his volleys and he's never lost the knack. That's Ash's dad, a man who learned good things a long time ago and never let himself lose sight of them.

So what would a man like that have made of someone like me, a gone-to-seed remnant of his very generation, now after his daughter?

Say I was hale and hearty, and that night while the boys of Dirtybeat had a beer and cigarette break, what if I'd taken Ash to the bar and she didn't mind suffering the glowering stares of handsome, jealous boys? Say for whatever romantic notion in her head she really was interested in the piss and vinegar of, to her, an old, old man. And, even further, say she laughed at my jokes, and listened to two or three stories about what happened back in the day, the good day when someone like me could produce an album that would survive decades in her pa's record collection.

What if coming home with me was okay by Ash, and, even more fancifully, she woke in the morning wrapped in my meaty arms, her face against my beefy chest and didn't run for the hills screaming never – not ever, ever! – again to drink, but did in fact like being there, and found my morning coffee, toast and jam, and glass of orange juice, agreeable, and me even more agreeable, and we listened to old records and went at it again, and eventually decided, 'Hey, this is good,' so made the pact of togetherness beer garden strangers sometimes find themselves happily and inexplicably making in the headachy glow of the morning after.

Then, if more time passed and my pump still didn't blow, even with the eye-crossing exertion I was putting into Ash, *my* Ash, I might have become something of a fixture in her household, an old man able to meet on level terms with her old man.

What would he have thought, what would he have said, especially on the day I couldn't bottle things up any more and blurted out the fact of the love for his daughter in this crazy diamond of a diseased heart?

'You know, tonight I'm asking Ash to come live with me. Actually, what I really mean is that I want the kid (your kid!) to marry me.'

Would he have asked, 'Hmmm – have you been married before? Any previous children?' and to my 'Nope' then said, 'Well you're not starting now, arsehole.'

Or would he have stared and stared until that gaze became an unyielding glare, or, by contrast, maybe even a softening, an understanding, an acquiescence to the strange magic at the core of all human relationships, that self-same magic all we one-time rockers never believed in but always hoped for?

Yes, her pa to be my pa, his paternal love transformed into my physical love. Who can say; it could all have happened. It would have driven him crazy. I might have been happy.

Right now, sitting in his pew, he knows that and is thinking about it. He's not a bad man, but I can hear him saying inside himself, his words echoing over and over, 'Thank God, thank God the bastard's dead,' yet on the outside he's calm, sombre, a perfect member of this congregation. Well, who's to blame him his secret thoughts?

Ash is up out of her pew and moving down the aisle to the door, where the congealed crowd parts to let her through. She's on her way somewhere, I don't know, maybe the funeral of a complete stranger isn't enough to keep her in one place or from needing to go to the toilet. As she disappears into the sunlight her strapless dress reveals her shoulders and arms. She's like Bradbury's tattooed man, only not as completely of course, though her pictures are filled with stories almost as good and bad as his. I can't stop myself from getting up out of this thing that I will for a moment pretend is a soft day bed, and I can't stop myself from following her.

All of a sudden this sexy kid is as interesting to me as she was the night I died at her feet, and a whole lot more attractive than any funeral.

I let myself follow her into the warm summer breeze.

Ladies lavatory around the side, and there's a flush then she's out and straightening her dress and her hair. Washes her hands in the sink and when she's in the direct sunlight the decision in her eyes is clear, at least to me. She doesn't want to go back into the chapel and endure more psychedelia. Ash reaches into her bag and picks out a pack of cigarettes the brand of supermodels all over the world, and lights one up. Drags, exhales, and walks along into the cemetery proper. The sea of headstones is neat and orderly, like bleached skulls arranged in the sun.

I'm a friendly wraith in this glorious sunshine, tagging after her. A bead of sweat is forming at her temple and I'd like to lick it away with the tongue I had when I was alive. Ash continues down the little necropolis avenues and reads the names and the dates, and looks at the flowers that have dried and fallen over, or that remain neatly arranged from some recent visit. She can bring flowers and fruit and wine to my graveside if it amuses her; it would certainly amuse me. I'd like to see her from time to time, would like to watch the smooth skin of her legs as she sits by the stone that says my name. She can smoke a cigarette or two. I'll bask in her light.

I remember reading about a type of gravestone you can get that's shaped like a flute, and when the wind is up it whistles through the sound chamber and makes a ghostly ooh, ooh, ooh. I wish they would give me something like that. Ash, my only regular visitor maybe, could smoke and tell me the story of her days and nights or weeks and months since her last visit. In reply I'd make my lovely ooh, ooh, oohs, and in that way we'd talk more meaningfully than most people do their entire lives through. I'd terrorise kids and vandals too, and maybe I'd cry my lonely oohs to all the lonely others in this boneyard. We'll be together forever, or at least until this place is redeveloped into apartments, or a swimming pool and sports complex, or whatever future generations of City Fathers and fat business-types deem fit – but the only way any of us buried here will ever talk together is through the wind. God's got our voices now, and bastard that He is, I know he'll hold them silent.

Trees at the end of this avenue. Ash runs fingers down her long hair, pushes some straight strands away from her eyes, and looks back toward the chapel. She is thinking she can skip the eulogy and the well-intentioned music program, and will rejoin the crowd when they follow the hearse down here. She's got plenty of time.

There's a breeze rising through the leaves and branches of a thick knot of trees up the end of the way. Not another living soul along here, so Ash walks to a bench in a clearing beside those trees, but guess what, I'm already in there, and just before she sits down to light another cigarette and stretch out her legs, and cast her gaze over this ocean of stone and marble mementos of men, women and children no longer in this world, she senses me, and puts her packet of cigarettes and lighter back into her shoulder bag, and without a shred of fear comes into the trees to find me.

She isn't at all surprised that she does find me, and so smiles and drops her bag at her feet the way girls will do on a nightclub floor. Her hands touch my ghostly face and my hands reach in and push her heart. In a moment, in that sort of half-dreamy way that things like kissing and touching between two people can go, we find ourselves spread out on the grass, protected by the thick tree trunks. It's as if she knows that someone like me will need a little extra care, or maybe you could call it extra understanding, or just simple help, and she does do enough to help me, and more, and even more after that, and so in the freshest tattoo on her shoulder I come to see the story she's had inscribed there. It's about a man who fell down and who in her dreams she's raised up into consummation. It's something she's longed for without understanding, something that she hasn't been able to make head nor tail of, the fact that she should long to touch and make love to an old man who died at her feet.

The colour rises in her cheeks, becomes a raw redness spreading down the skin of her throat and chest, and when Ash cries out no one but me hears, and she's sitting by her father and no grass stains mark her skirt.

The lingering effects of so vivid a daydream make her bring a crumpled tissue to her eyes. Her father puts his arm around her heavily tattooed shoulder, holding his good-hearted daughter to him, and I'm back where I started, up on one elbow in my permanent bed, looking at these people, these friends, acquaintances and no blood-family. All of them will tell me their goodbyes, in their own way, just as Ash has done, and worse, much worse, I will have to say goodbye to them as well, and so the descent into the pit of God's eternal forgetting will really begin.

VII

Maybe there are some things even a pit of forgetting won't let you lose. Ash is just a kid, but Patti was forty-six when we first crossed paths. I turned nineteen, Maree Kilmister was long gone, and I wasn't playing in other people's bands any more. I had my own, a raw rock-and-roll three-piece.

Patti was on the large side and she was gruff, but you wouldn't have called her matronly. She was a free spirit in her way, more than enough for a young man to handle. It was my stacking-of-supermarket-shelves stage, which was probably more a decades-long lifestyle than a stage. This middle-aged woman looked at me over a mountain of baked bean cartons and said, 'You, kid, how old do you think I am?'

I liked the weird free-ranging conversations you had with people at one or two in the morning, the fluoros beaming down so that everyone looks like a cross between an angel and a zombie. Some of those work colleagues you'd know maybe two nights or two weeks, then they'd disappear never to be seen again. Some would be there forever, like fixtures.

So this question was no great shakes really, just an ice-breaker that might lead to a conversation or nothing. I thought about it, about the answer, me already old enough to know that if a woman asks you a question like that, you subtract five to seven to ten from what you guess is the truth. That makes you two things: a wise man and a potential playmate. By then I already liked women young, old and anywhere in the range. I never saw any reason to discriminate and would use flattery, charm or a simple forthright stare to let someone know what I was after. These were still innocent days in my hot city, when words like chauvinism had no teeth and political correctness hadn't even been dreamed up.

Still, fluorescent lights, pasty faces and echoey aisles make you do strange things, and one of those things is to tell the truth. So I weighed a can of baked beans in one hand and scratched the side of my nose with the other, looked her over and said, 'Forty-five, forty-six?'

She sort of blinked. 'Forty-six. As of yesterday.'

'Huh,' I replied.

She said, 'What are you? Twenty, twenty-one?' It was 1975 and two weeks to Christmas. I was nineteen by a month. 'Yeah?' she said. 'So what did you do for your nineteenth?' and I replied, 'Nothing,' which was God's truth.

'How about you?' I countered. 'How'd you spend the big one?'

She squinted with lots of lines around her eyes and the sort of stained, crooked teeth that a person with money would get fixed as their number one priority. Not her. She was a shelf-stacker like me and probably had a second job like me too. Waitress some-where maybe, or dishwasher, probably all to look after some no-good kids. Still, her teeth were stained and crooked in a way that wasn't really all that bad, and she was stocky and strong-looking without being dumpy or frumpy. I could easily imagine

35

her as the one-time lead singer of some all-girl rock band, now fifteen to twenty years post her career. Her voice was low and gravelly enough that it could have been true.

I'd come to like women like that, tough on the outside, but on the inside – if you give them enough thigh massages and back rubs – you discover they're like syrup. For the most part they're still the girls they were at eighteen, it's just that no bastard will take the time to find that kid any more.

Maree's gift was to teach me to not to be afraid of women or sex, not to treat it like some holy taboo or unmentionable offence. Sometimes women seemed to sense that in me, and like it too.

So this co-worker has considered my question long enough, and she decides to answer. 'I got myself a takeaway Mexican dinner and a bottle of tequila. The bottle shops have got a kind of margarita mix now, and I got some of that.'

'Salt and limes?' I ask.

'Yep. And then I sat in the dark and ate and watched TV, and drank until I could get to sleep. But you know what? At my age, sometimes the more you drink the less you can sleep, there's nothing you can do about it. I was up till dawn. Just drank the tequila straight while the sun rose. Isn't that the crappiest thing you ever heard?'

'No,' I told her, 'some people would kill to have a birthday like that. I liked my nineteenth – it was the best birthday I ever had.'

'Really?'

'You bet'

What I didn't tell her was the reason. I'd spent the first half of the year in a prison farm, put away after a week-long binge turned nasty. The best freedom now was to just be alone without gorillas and broken mummy's boys breathing down my neck.

'There was no one around,' I went on. 'I had some beer. Didn't

36

watch TV, but I played records and drummed with them. No one told me to shut up either. If they would've tried I would've told them where to stick it.'

'You're a real drummer?'

'Real enough. I just formed a new band and we're really good.'

'That's why you stack shelves?'

'That's why I stack shelves.'

'If you ever make a record I'll make sure to get it.'

'Just play it loud.'

For some reason that made the two of us laugh so hard the shift superintendent came and told us to get on with our work. A couple of minutes later, when he heard us laughing some more, he came and separated us. Patti got exiled to the laundry and kitchen products lane to help some dowdy girl with the longest, most depressed-looking horse face I've ever seen. I got some kid with knock-you-down bad breath, a hero-worship sort of gaze, and a tendency to pick his pimples so that the scabs stayed stuck under his chewed-up fingernails. I couldn't stop watching the way the blood and juice just oozed out of his face.

My forty-six-year-old friend wandered by at the end of the shift. 'Did I tell you my name's Patti?'

It was three-thirty in the morning. We went and stood on the footpath outside the supermarket, me to take my usual walk home, which I always liked at that time of day, her to get her Kingswood out of the car park and drive to wherever she lived.

'Want to come?' she asked.

I said, 'Why not?'

In the car, maybe just in case she wanted to make sure I was clear on what was going on, Patti turned the ignition and slipped her hand down around my legs. So, to let her know I was no ignoramus, I got up on my knees on the bench seat and leaned in and bit her neck a little, which tasted of perspiration and some fragrant soap. I cupped her ample breasts, feeling how fast her breath was coming.

She didn't want any oily small-talk or dancing around the subject. It was all just sort of plain and clear. So to what's plain and clear take plain and clear action. My stepfather always said, 'Shoot straight or you do not shoot at all, you understand this?'

Later, past midday, when I was ready to leave her flat, I slipped out of her bed and took a long shower. I thought it'd be good to get home and sleep a quiet four or five hours while the suckers of the world went on with their everyday jobs.

It was funny that Patti's flat was so small. My home was palatial by comparison, a nice house in a good street. It used to belong to my Aunt Emma's first husband's parents. Now there's a mouthful, but it's the truth. When they died, he inherited it. When he died, my aunt got it. Then she married Conny San Filippo and they became my step-parents. She passed away and the house went to Conny. Conny died and I got it. So shoot me for being lucky.

My place was all lazy and green and leafy, quiet except for the cacophony of my drumming, as safe as a girl's convent. Patti's flat was clean, but it was cheap. One bedroom, a sitting room that was half kitchen, and a bathroom you couldn't swing your arms in. It was an open invitation to anyone looking for an easy break and enter. When I came out of the shower, Patti was up and had poached some eggs and made some toast. Instant coffee, but hand-squeezed orange juice. 'You live alone, too?' she asked.

I was sitting at her table, munching on breakfast. It was good. Still wet from the shower, my long hair was in ringlets and I didn't have a stitch on. She took the towel off the back of a chair and started rubbing my shoulders with it, like polishing a mirror, gently buffing me up to a good shine for the world.

She wanted to know why I was alone and how I lived, but really I think she wanted to know why a decent-enough kid like me had no qualms about going home with a middle-aged woman, and even seemed to like it. That was something I couldn't really answer, so I told her the cut-down version of a story that would have run a hundred pages. My ma the God-fearing sex-worker; my aunt the dissolute drunk; and the sheer accident of Concetto San Filippo. I didn't tell her about the bitter tears I wept when he died and the mad drinking binge it sent me on, just said, 'So, I'm pretty lucky. Got a nice house of my own and all I need's enough money to pay the bills and feed myself.'

'Don't you want anything else?'

'Like what?'

'Maybe an education? A career? You know, a future.'

'The future's over-rated.'

She laughed, 'Come on.'

'No, I'm happy. I'm a drummer. And I like night-shifts in the supermarket, you never know what's going to happen.'

She grinned, but said, 'Maybe that all sounds good for now, but things change.'

'When they do, I'll be the first to know, right?'

'So at least answer this for me. Why live alone? Why not get someone in to help you pay the bills, get some company too?'

I shook my head. 'Hell is other people. I read that somewhere.' The way she was rubbing my back was as attentive as what the trained touch of a geisha must be like. And it was getting me pretty excited again. I said, 'Really, I don't want the company. I like it better when I'm alone,' and it was the plain truth.

My house seemed enough to me and, as it turned out, I ended

up staying there the rest of my life. Didn't need too much else except for the occasional company of women.

'So you don't remember your real mother and father?' she said. 'You poor boy.'

'Fuck my real father,' I replied, not being one to fish for sympathy or to enjoy it if it came my way. 'And I remember everything about my ma. She was good. I've got nothing to complain about.'

'You're nineteen, but you sound like you're forty or something.'

I thought that was a put-down. Now I knew I was going to get out of there and never come back – but she said something that changed my mind.

'I never had a baby,' Patti whispered, and that's when she wanted me to finish the breakfast. She led me back to her little bedroom and as she was coming she said, 'Just say my name, just say Patti.'

So I did, and spoke 'Patti' into her hair, two, three, four times, never asking her the obvious question of why she never had a baby. Some things don't need to be asked. Some people just get forgotten, and maybe sometimes you have to whisper their names in their ears so they can remember who they are, or who and what they might have become, if things had been a degree or two different.

The next weekend I took my toolbox and went back over, installing safety deadlocks and latches all through Patti's flat. I put a thick chain on her door, too, made those easy-access windows secure. She took me to her bed one last time, and when it was over her face was serious.

She said, 'That's my thank you, okay?'

'If that's what you say.'

I dressed, not really wanting to leave, but I knew that was it. For whatever reason she didn't want me back. When I left her flat it was like I was weighed down with bricks.

Patti quit the supermarket. I missed her. It was seven years before I saw her again.

VIII

Someone's coming down the centre aisle. A neat grey suit can't disguise spindly legs and gangly arms. In a way, he's a sail that's had the wind blown out of it, but in another way he's no out-and-out dud. Not many millionaires are.

Long before Tony Lester ever made a dollar I can remember him saying, 'Why don't you turn this group into something good, do originals?' He was slurring all over the place. 'Who needs covers? So you play Hendrix and Bad Company, so what? You need a real singer. You need songs. That's where the money is. Let me do it. Where's the microphone? Listen to this.'

It was more than a year after I'd formed the band and in that time we'd played parties and pubs and that was it. Our repertoire was the standard stuff for drinking beer and dancing without inhibitions. If you tried anything else you'd get booed off the stage. Tony Lester was a non-playing friend of mine who'd kept his talent in a sack where no one could see it. Then out of nowhere, full of bottle courage, he crashed one of our rehearsals and declared himself.

Tony grabbed a microphone and leaned hard into the stand for support. While we stood around he gave us an *a cappella* rendition of a couple of songs he'd dreamed up. His secret was revealed. When he was finished we shouted, 'Yeah!'.

Well, in our enthusiasm for Tony we also ensured our demise. It crushed him when we eventually bombed; it sort of cheered him up years later when he made his first property million – but the first dream always dies hardest and it's the one that stays with you for life.

Before Tony joined we used to split vocal spots, but now it was the start of 1977 and there were four of us: Tony Lester, old pal, new singer and hero; Peter Kelley on lead guitar; Joe White-head on bass; and me. Our communal decision was to declare ourselves a new group. We called ourselves Manoeuvres for the simple fact that none of us could get the spelling right. That included other people as well; if we were going to be so awkward and play only original material too, then our songs and sound had better be good. It took us too long to realise they weren't, and by then we were so burned out that even if success had come our way – which, with Debbie Canova joining, it nearly did – we wouldn't have been able to cope. Our biggest problem was ourselves. We infuriated anyone who wanted to listen to us by refusing to do the simple thing. Like have a catchy name; like write and perform music people wanted to hear.

So this rake in a $1500 suit was supposed to be our ticket to success. His shoes – look at them today, you could buy a small car for the price he must have paid for those Milanese works of art. Odd to think that for years this man was not only my band's vocalist, but also my soul-mate. Yes, sex does make you heartless, and Debbie Canova was entering our world.

Tony Lester's a rich man these days, on paper. His soul's a little less fertile. That boy always had a gift none of the rest of us in the band was ever blessed with. We used to think his gift was for song-writing but after the band ended our singer's real talent revealed itself: it was for the knack of reinvention, a scarce commodity, and important too, if you're going to give yourself any kind of life.

I liked Tony Lester better before he became a real estate prince. We used to howl, squelch and slam through his ever-increasing repertoire of original tunes. Every practice session he'd turn up with scribbled lyrics and brilliant ideas for new chord progressions and melody lines. These weren't little bits and pieces. All of his stuff was formed: beginning, middle and end. Untrained musically, he made abrupt key changes and awkward time signatures somehow come together. My drumming gelled with his weird approach and I could always find the perfect rhythms, beats and change-ups or downs to match his style. So then of course I'm to blame for our failure too. It wasn't that the songs didn't work, it was just that they didn't work *enough*.

We did what every band does to hide its deficiencies. We turned our amps up all the way. I played harder and louder, losing most of the fine technique and skill my stepfather had taught me. The bass player developed tinnitus. The lead guitarist wore ear plugs concealed beneath his greasy long hair. Still, even these things weren't what killed our dreams.

IX

Come the end, Tony lay in depressed silence for more than a year, then that was enough and he got his face up off the floor.

By now it was 1982 and he was twenty-six. He dusted himself off and put his notepads away, and burned – literally burned – his collection of over-tight cock-rock blue jeans and sleeve cut-off t-shirts. His heart sort of went up in smoke too. He went to an executive salon in the city and got himself three things: a trendy haircut, a blow dry and a manicure.

Newly coiffed after decades of greasy long hair, he fronted the reception desk of a huge real-estate firm. None of the principals would agree to see him today, tomorrow or ever. He smiled at the secretary and left. In the car park, behind the wheel of his ute, he wiped tears out of the corners of his eyes, consulted the list he'd made, and proceeded on a door-to-door mission until he got himself a job. By his list's number twelve, he had. The next day he traded his ute on a clean four-door sedan.

Tony sold houses. The market was good and it didn't take him long to learn the ropes and little tricks, like calling on the elderly owners of soon-to-be deceased estates and making friends with them. Or personally going in and scrubbing-to-gleaming said deceased estate once he had it in his listing. He was so focused on his new career he barely noticed a man named Bob Hawke come to power, or a boat race stop the country, or the nationwide drought finally breaking. He missed power-pop, Ronald Reagan, Rambo, New Romantics, goth-rock and Bananarama. Girls called him a yuppie and he took that as either a compliment or an invitation. It was both. By his thirtieth birthday he was moving toward becoming very rich off people's predilection for selling their homes to one another. We weren't on speaking terms any more, but I followed his career. You couldn't help it. Newspapers always love local success stories. Real estate gun, then mogul, then property developer, and, later, author of self-help finance books. I never read any, though I could never resist looking for the latest Anthony Lester title whenever I was in a book shop. They sold by the truckload; he was full of common sense.

He'd made himself a Beamer-driving reconfiguration of the lovely kid who used to keep one eye on me through each and every song. He wasn't yet twenty-one when he joined the band; Manoeuvres lasted four years and early on he developed that knack for using an uninterrupted sightline to keep the two of us in synch, voice to beat, so that all the other instruments breathed inside the glorious space we left in between.

I couldn't get enough of his songs. Some artists carry pain, but he owned whole worlds of torment. These ate at his heart even in his happiest moments. There were some that I knew about: for instance, I often noticed a moment's hesitation in his speech, his mind having to plan what his mouth was going to say, legacy of the stutter that had plagued him into his late teens. Then, some otherwise-kindly family friend molested him when he was nine – and, of course, there was the no-good father who kicked him out of home at age thirteen. Our stories weren't the same, but we had a commonality. I served those six months in stir, courtesy of a series of break and enters capped by a drunken misadventure in a closed-up bottle shop, where I stole nothing but did lie down on the floor at midnight and go to sleep. Tony was also behind bars as soon he could be legally incarcerated: eighteen months for the Porsche 911 he stole and tried to sell in a car yard three thousand kilometres away. It was his third car-theft offence. In stir, of course, he paid a price for the stutter that hadn't been completely tamed. On top of which the spectre of the molesting family friend was ever-present, now in the form of bigger men who were a whole lot less kindly about it.

Tony suffered all right, and the results were guitar riffs that could burn your skin. Sometimes when I listened to him sing and howl the hair on the back of my neck would rise and my arms would tingle. He had a primal energy and what he was able to make in his music was something I secretly shared. I would never have said it but I knew it deep down: we were adults who were hurt kids; we were sons with bad fathers and those songs contained the sound of it. Tony was the blood and I was the heart, and I loved him, the bastard, the treacherous little bastard, so reincarnated as an entrepreneur and businessman.

Funny thing is, last word he ever said to me was the same one: *Traitor.*

And here he comes into my funeral as if it hasn't been twenty-five years since I've seen his face, and twenty-five years since we wrestled and belted one another senseless over a girl, and he's stick-walking like he's got piles or something, or maybe that's the awkward swagger of successful businessmen. I preferred it when he was a swaggering rock-and-roll singer with an eye for the girls and a kind word for every pimple-faced kid who ever spent all their piggy-bank money on a first guitar or bargain-basement set of drums. And, guess what, he preferred it too, and that's what makes his heart such an arid no-man's land these days.

Tony sits next to a lanky guy I don't know, some grey-faced individual with a terrible paunch, receding hair and a face as craggy as a mountainside. They acknowledge one another. Icily. Wait, isn't that Pete Kelley? He's another one I haven't seen since the band broke up, but where you can still see the Tony in this Anthony Lester, you can't at all see the Pete in this Mr Peter Kelley. Not a bit remains of the kid he used to be. Not anything; he looks like a total stranger.

I try to get inside Pete but there's a wall, a veritable wall that he's built around himself. He needs it so that he can function as the middle-aged middle-management sort of guy he is today. Impenetrable. What must his wife make of him, his children, what must they feel living with a man so utterly well-defended? The two fat black moles over his left eyebrow give away his identity, but that's all. Those moles are the only part of him that hasn't really changed. Otherwise, he's a tired, different man. The Pete Kelley I knew used to do high kicks when he hit the high notes of his soloing.

Still, it's sort of a breath of fresh air to realise that the same sort of protecting wall isn't around Anthony Lester. Around Tony. I say Hi to him because I know that deep down he wants to say Hello too.

Tony smiles in recognition of my voice. He thinks to himself, I've missed you, you know, Max. You were my drummer, but more than that, you were the most like me. Weren't we sort of two of a kind?

That's it, Tony: two of a kind.

Funny thing is, Max, somewhere in the back of my mind I always wondered if one day we'd get together again. Me singing, you at the kit. Do some of those old songs of ours, but who'd want to listen, huh? Now it'll never happen, not unless we find some way to resurrect you. Which is kind of funny because I dreamed about you last night. You were back from the dead and we were still friends. The band was playing again, and you said to me, Where's a new song, you little prick, don't tell me you haven't written anything? You were teasing me for slacking off, for not being serious enough.

I tell him, Well, you used to be very serious.

Tony sighs. Peter Kelley next to him sighs too. One passes it on to the next. Someone further down the row also sighs.

In his heart or mind, whichever place it is that allows a living man to speak to a dead one, Tony Lester tells me, Goddamn you, Max, I hate sitting here because the whole thing seems useless to me now. Why did this have to happen? Why didn't you take more care of yourself? And why the hell did I come here?

He stops himself, now thinking better of trying to speak to the departed.

Instead, in his mind he turns over the way that he will go home tonight, and will have a few drinks on his own, and a bite to eat on his own, and maybe ring his daughter and his youngest boy and the kid in the middle too. Each of his offspring has a different mother and Tony looks after them all even though he lives with none of them, and his house is a pink mansion of quiet indifference that he shares with a parrot and two dogs. The only time the whole benighted place seems alive isn't when he throws another party, another gathering of the beautifully mummified and damned who are supposed to be his business colleagues and friends, CDs blaring the latest dance music as if anyone there knows anything about hip-hop, trip-hop, rap, MCs or new century pop. No, the only time that place is alive and Tony Lester a little alive with it, is when he throws out the dogs, locks the doors, shuts the little bridge-way to the kidney-shaped pool and pulls the windows tight.

These actions aren't meant to protect the ears of the neighbours, at least not in the typical sense, but to protect himself. To make sure no one hears the embarrassing music he really wants to play. And that music is so goddamned loud he might as well be on stage with a microphone stand in front of him and a stack of Marshals behind him, and me back there too.

And when all of this is happening, guess what but he's a tough, lost boy again, even though he's playing ancient, well-loved vinyl records on a professional DJ turntable that must have cost him five and a half grand if a cent.

In that noise that brings back to life the sadly lost but seldom-mourned dinosaurs, brontosauri and pterodactyls of rock-and-roll circa 1967 to 1975, Tony Lester can be himself again. The entrepreneur isn't born yet. Nor is the father in him, or the three times ex-husband, and this hour of abandon, or should I call it freedom, is good, I mean good, and he means really good, Tony knows it, clear and plain as day. That kid in him is still there somewhere and doesn't need buttoning down, at least not until the hour of remembering and dancing like this is over, and the grim day back again. Then the vinyl will be neatly restacked, re-alphabetised, all albums back in their proper place with the seven thousand eight hundred-odd of the rest of them.

Tonight, he tells himself, he'll do it in honour of his deceased drummer. On the way home from this funeral he might stop off at local vinyl revival store, treat himself to some new old records. Mint plus and mint plus and not a grade less. When you have money, nostalgia needn't come cheap. Pink Floyd through the chapel's speakers and Manoeuvres in his heart have put him in a mind for heavy stuff; he'll play it all night if he has to, and maybe not get to sleep at all, because it's not just me gone but the backbeat of Tony's life too. The thing is, he knows as he's always known, that he surrendered too early. There was no reason why he shouldn't have formed another band after ours fell apart, no reason for him to stop writing songs, but that's what he did, and soon enough he found that he'd lost his peculiar knack for writing so completely that the talent might as well have been removed like a blown gall bladder. Why couldn't he have used that dead time after the band to go to music school or something, and learn the real craft, and one day maybe have composed something *everyone* wanted to hear?

He returns to our conversation after all.

I thought we'd catch up one day, Tony tells me, and I tell him back, Me too. We're a dumb pair aren't we?

He nods. We could have made up, he says. All it would have taken was a phone call, Max, me to you or you to me.

Yep.

He sighs again. Three people in the row sigh with him. He says, I guess you remember her pretty well, don't you? and he might as well ask if I remember the last sunrise I ever saw.

X

It was a new decade and we'd been out in the country for two months already, on what you'd need rigorous self-deception to call a 'tour'.

The band was so broke that any money we earned barely put enough fuel in our tanks, vehicular or human. We were travelling in a big Bedford truck and Tony Lester's ute. In order to get us from town hall to town hall, watering hole to watering hole, to community group gatherings, or to whatever type of place was willing to pay us, we had to limit our food consumption to about one meal a day. Playing to country community groups was the best part of it; the locals were so starved for entertainment they welcomed us with open arms and often even fed us and donated jugs of beer to our cause. But, really, we were so unsuitable to be heard by families that we took it upon ourselves to tone our playing down. When we did, we sounded bad. When we played in our usual way, kids cried and grandmothers yelled at us.

Somewhere in the middle of this extended sojourn through the inner-continent we had a school fete coming up. Just the idea of it made us nervous, so nervous, in fact, we turned up a day early. Tony had been on the telephone for weeks, organising all of these gigs with a religious fervour. The thing was, the band had been together nearly four years now and nothing at all had happened. He said, and he was right, that a band that couldn't get out on the road and take the rough and tumble of the blue highways of this or any other country didn't deserve to get anywhere. We tried to be full of hope. With the start of the Eighties most of punk and new wave was already gone, moody synth-pop bands were all the rage, and if you made rock music at all you had to have big hair. We didn't. We still had our straggly Seventies look, but that was our badge of honour. No synthesizers for us, nothing but raw rock-and-roll the way God made it, and certainly no pre-fab image.

We might as well have shot ourselves.

For the upcoming kids' show we hoped there would be more adults than four-to-nine-year-olds, but we all shaved anyway, and pulled our long hair back with elastic bands so that each of us had pretty ponytails. In a laundromat, we used our drinking spare change to wash our clothes. By the time we arrived at the school – a big, government-run place that looked like it had been standing since Settlement – we were behaving so decently and with such respect toward the children, the families, the teachers and the principal, that they all could have been forgiven for mistaking us for some kind of Christian band.

It was a whole weekend's fete, and we got there on the Saturday and introduced ourselves, meaning to get ready to play on Sunday. There were going to be three forty-minute shows: at nine and ten in the morning, and one after lunch. We'd never had a booking like it, but the pay was good and we weren't about to complain. We pictured the entire town turning up; this place was called Thornberry and on our road map it was a half-speck of fly shit in a landscape of Martian red dust. Somehow, though, a river ran through it. Or so the map said.

Pete Kelley, so solemn and discontented now, was a livewire in those days. In a flash he befriended the maths teacher, seduced her so quickly and easily that they had sex in her car off from the school's secluded car park even as the principal was putting on 'meet and greet' orange cordial and school-made Anzac biscuits for us.

'Is there a lot of money in it?' the man asked, face as red as a beetroot and his big farmer's hands serving us our sticky drinks, 'Playing for the kids? There must be a lot of work in schools for the band, huh?'

'Well, it's not what we concentrate on,' Tony replied.

'No?'

'No, not really.'

'When do the girls arrive?'

'The girls?'

'The girls in the band.'

'There aren't any girls in the band.'

'Are you new to this?' the principal asked him, his scarlet moon-face still friendly and pleasant. 'The shows are going to be put on by the girls and their dancers.'

'Umm,' Tony replied, 'they're not.'

'What do you mean they're not?'

'We're playing.'

'Who? You?'

'Yes – us.'

'Aren't you the roadies or whatever you guys are supposed to be called? The set-up crew?'

'No.'

54

'You're the band?' Tony nodded. The principal looked at me and at Joe. 'You bunch of scruffs?' He sort of coughed, and I think I saw the redness draining from his face. 'What sort of a band are you supposed to be?'

'A rock band.'

'Old style? Elvis, Roy Orbison?'

'No.'

'But you'll be playing kiddie stuff here.'

'No. Rock music. We don't know anything for kids.'

That was the end of the orange juice and biscuits.

'Son, we've got about three hundred four-to-nine-year-olds being bussed in tonight from every mining town and regional school and back-of-beyond black stump in the territory. You better know kiddie music and plenty of it by morning, or things'll get pretty ugly pretty fast. You follow?'

How this misunderstanding came to be, no one was the wiser. Tony's protestations fell on deaf ears. He remembered speaking to someone at the school who asked if the band was prepared to put on a good show three times; when he'd said absolutely, that had been it, deal done.

Stuck in this situation, we sort of started shitting ourselves. Yes, we could haul out of there fast, but the sheer absurdity of the situation – being stuck in the middle of nowhere, about to be drowning in over-excited children – made us want to see what would happen next. We had a quick conference and decided to go ahead with whatever the school had planned. We were there, we needed the money, and none of us – good-hearted rock-and-roller's that we were – could even imagine disappointing such an abundance of kids.

Not our biggest audience ever.

After all, Tony reasoned, how hard could it really be? We were adept musicians, and could drag out all the poppiest tunes we remembered from when we played in our early bands: Elvis and Roy Orbison if need be. Plus the Beatles, the Bee Gees; even the Seekers or Frank Sinatra if we had to. He'd lead the kids in singalongs, get them up on their feet and show them easy dance steps, crack some jokes and get parents and teachers on stage to join in. It'd be a piece of cake, maybe even fun too. Tony almost had us believing we could do it; he said we'd spend the night boning up on the old tunes: for one day and one day only, Manoeuvres would be a cover band covering a whole misbegotten world of musical kitsch.

The most important order of business, then, was to set up.

In the meantime, Pete returned, a contented smile on his face and him constantly licking on his fingers as if he'd just made a cake. Just as he was about to help us put things together, his new paramour returned with buttered pumpkin scones. One each for the rest of us and about a dozen for him. The pair of lovebirds wandered off; we didn't see him again until nightfall.

Some dads had to help Tony, Joe and me rig up a stage. We cursed the fact that no one in the school had stopped to wonder where this band they'd hired would actually play, but we were also relieved we had a day's grace before we had to perform.

That was nothing; soon we discovered the real problem. No one had considered what power requirements this band might have, and after a few wasted hours looking for extension leads, and switch and junction boxes, as soon as we were able to plug in our instruments the school's main switchboard exploded, acrid smoke spiralling up into the forty degree heat, threatening to burn the hundred-year-old structure down. Kids whooped with the thrill of it all, but the volunteer fire brigade, already set up in the school grounds to display their proficiency, got an even better chance to do so. They had things under control long before any damage was done.

One of the teachers called his uncle, who'd been an electrician. Long retired, this old guy with a bulbous nose turned up, blind in one eye and mostly deaf too. Not to mention lame, so that his granddaughter had to come with him as he struggled along with his cane. She carried his dusty electricians' gunmetal kit and we stared at her as if we'd never seen a female before.

I noticed that every father stopped what he was doing. They knew her, but none had gotten used to her. Even the schoolboys in the field went a little crazy, and tried acrobatic and aerial gymnastic tricks and stunts that could only go wrong.

She was introduced to us as Debbie Canova. The young woman sat by her grandfather as he sweated and muttered and tried to remember little things he used to know about official electrical standards and which wire goes where and for what good reason. He set about rewiring the entire school switchboard. Whenever the old man wheezed for a particular tool, bit of tape, cable or certain-sized screwdriver, she dug in that metal box until she found something that approximated what he'd described, then would slap it down into his gnarled, impatiently trembling palm as if she was his nurse and he a great man of medicine conducting a delicate operation. She knew we boys of the band were thoroughly besotted, so she made the whole tool-slapping-down thing a game, always looking our way with a twinkle in her eye. Nothing would have torn us away.

If Debbie Canova hadn't looked quite so horny, hadn't exuded such a fever of sex from her very pores, we would have laughed at how comical the thing was becoming. The switchboard started to resemble an old pair of jeans covered in patches; Debbie Canova's grandfather looked like he needed some pills and shade. Instead, band members, fathers, some male teachers and not a few pre-pubescent boys, couldn't do enough to help the old man – and, by happy extension, his granddaughter – in their heroic quest to save the day.

She was twenty-two, roughly a year or two younger than the rest of us, and despite her age she looked like she had just enough experience of the world and its ways to know her worth and effect on the masculine tribe surrounding her. On the third finger of her left hand, however, were the killers: one diamond engagement ring plus one plain gold wedding band. The old guy turned out to be her grandfather-in-law and we kept looking around for a husband who never appeared.

Debbie Canova's hair was long and straight, dyed white-blonde. Dark roots were showing, but somehow this made her look sexier. Blue eyes and high cheekbones. Suede boots with tassels reached nearly to her knees. Her mini skirt – or maybe an item of apparel so small was called a micro-mini, I don't know – revealed an entire universe of exquisite legs. Her panties were pink; we kept getting glimpses, and these glimpses froze us in our places. We learned more about electricity in forty-five minutes than any of us had ever known in our lives. Debbie had a loose-fitting, no-sleeves sort of cheesecloth shirt on. About a half dozen strings of shiny, coloured beads hung around her neck, and she favoured bright red lipstick and heavy mascara. Pete might have been off with a homely, pot-bellied woman pushing forty, but this Debbie Canova, well, she was something else entirely. Your heart, mind and body ached simply to know you could never have her.

Finally, the old man was finished, and with a success that verged on the miraculous not only did the reconfigured switchboard work, but it accommodated the needs of the school, the fete, and our instruments, amps and mixing desk, without blowing up again. The weekend's acknowledged saviour, the school principal took the octogenarian to a tent especially set up for the adults and, over the next few hours, got him as drunk as a lord.

Debbie Canova had gone to talk to some of the young mothers and older ladies, but as soon as there was a break in the traffic Tony conveniently found himself beside her.

'What do you do for fun around here?' he asked.

'This is just about it.'

'But what about you?'

She smiled through long, darkened eyelashes that made butterflies in his belly. He wanted to simply stare past those lashes into her blue, blue eyes, and, if it made her happy, not utter another word.

'Well, I make my own clothes. This whole outfit, including the boots. Sometimes I sell stuff in town, but what I sew a lot of the ladies won't wear.' Her eyes travelled over a group of her local sisters clothed in tent dresses. A couple were in overalls. 'But I'm a musician too, sort of. Self-taught. Out of books but mostly by ear.'

'What's your instrument?'

'The violin. It got left to me by my aunt. I like composing too.'

If Tony had ever prayed for the one young woman in this universe whom he wanted to meet, not to mention marry instantaneously, he was beginning to understand that this was her.

'Did you learn properly?' she asked him. 'Get your music letters? I'm always jealous of people like that.'

'No, I'm self-taught too. In fact, in this band, I don't think there's been a proper lesson between us. Except maybe for Max. He had a stepfather who was a drummer.'

Her eyes travelled toward me. I was having a cup of black tea with Joe. We were standing in the shade of an elm watching Tony with this country girl who seemed designed for better circumstances than these. Somehow she knew I was the drummer Tony had referred to. She flicked a smile; I felt a hand reach down into my belly and squeeze hard.

Debbie Canova told Tony that she couldn't play anything she hadn't sat down and deciphered bit by bit from some classical record also left by her musical aunt – or that she hadn't made up herself. She showed him her left hand, how the nails were clipped down to the quick in order to help her play more smoothly, and her right, where in feminine contrast she had five very long and exquisitely manicured fingernails painted a startling pink. Tony wanted to know what exactly she could play on her violin. It turned out that Debbie Canova's song book was her own memory. What she composed and remembered were the things that must have been good. What she composed and forgot was all the better for evaporating into the ether. Her memory was the only arbiter of taste she trusted.

'It's your – quality – control,' he managed to say, already tongue-tied, already conscious of the way his stutter was returning, taking over his chest, throat and brain.

'Yes,' she agreed, and the happy lilt in her voice was an instant balm to his anxiety. 'And the best.'

'Let me – hear some,' he said.

He saw the momentary frown; now she was aware there was some faltering there, however, he liked the way she seemed to soften some more, as if she understood that he was suffering. She gave him the full effect of her wide, red-lipped smile.

'But my violin's not here.'

At that moment, an unexpected burst of afternoon fireworks in the football field by the school, followed by shouts, yells and scrambling activity, covered the details of the unlikely – unlikely, at least to Tony – agreement they made. Across the grass, the fire wagon raced like the wind. Most of the volunteers were, by now, as drunk as Debbie's grandfather and the principal, but this was yet another potential conflagration quickly brought to heel.

Debbie's husband, Phil Canova, a plumber whom she told Tony – for obvious reasons – stood six foot four in his socks, was going to be out tonight at the local progress association's future-vision presentation to the Thornberry community. It would take place here at the school and was the big annual event the weekend fete was planned around. Phil was treasurer and minute-taker, and when she mentioned that Debbie sort of giggled, and Tony pictured some behemoth with hands like hams, clutching a pencil in his paw and making indecipherable, scrawling marks that resembled the haphazard strokes of a three year old.

Once the formal meeting was over, Phil would also be official bartender. Tony couldn't come to the house, she wouldn't have that, but Debbie might be able to visit the camping grounds where the band's truck and Tony's ute were parked. Every year she was exempt from attending what was, to all intents and purposes, an all-night, mostly male piss-up. So – maybe – she'd come at about eight, with her violin.

We'd planned to camp for the logical reason that we could not have afforded food, drink and a hotel. Often we slept cramped inside our two vehicles. There was always a choice to be made between sustenance and comfort, and the latter never had the chance to win, young men living, above and beyond all things, on their bellies.

Pete rolled up as the sun went down, that satisfied smile still on his face. He didn't need dinner, having been fed all day long. So that night the rest of us got to dine on hamburgers and a bag of fresh carrots, plus a glass of beer per person, no other niceties required. We ate and drank our portions, and waited in the lengthening gloom of the world's red centre for Debbie Canova to arrive.

XI

She turned up before seven-thirty, which should have told Tony how she was as keen to see him as he was to see her. Being early, he hadn't even had much of a chance to become nervous, that rising stutter receiving no opportunity to grab control of him.

Debbie Canova drove into the camping ground in an overpowered Ford that she said her husband laboured over with unadulterated affection. She'd dropped him off at the fete and when he'd asked about the things she had with her — a casserole dish of pork chops and beans, a six pack of beer, an unopened carton of duty-free cigarettes she'd had stashed since some friend returned from an overseas trip, and three-quarters of a bottle of tequila, not to mention her violin — she told him that she and her girlfriends had planned to do the female equivalent of what he was setting out to do, that is, to eat too much and get blind drunk.

Phil made her promise not to drive back home; husband and wife would catch up over coffee and breakfast in the morning.

Now, upon seeing all those goodies of Debbie's, each member

of Manoeuvres was ready to swear eternal devotion on the spot. Maybe we did. Her face was like some renaissance artist's impression of a celestial being, that long, white-blonde hair tonight pulled back in a ponytail. She said that for one evening she wanted to play with the band, and so had adopted our ponytail look. We laughed and laughed that there was someone innocent enough to believe deadbeats like us would waste a second defining a band 'look'. Not only that but she'd changed into our 'uniform': black boots, jeans and a black t-shirt. Until the moment she said it, it hadn't crossed any of our minds that we all regularly dressed the same way. Funny thing was she really did look the part, a feminine flipside to this scruffy bunch of long hairs in matching clothes.

She showed us her violin, a Czechoslovakian model hand-made in the Thirties. Her aunt's mother had played it, then her aunt, now her. We were impressed by her left-hand nails and their absence but were even more transfixed by the red patch resembling a love bite that adorned the left side of her neck. She told us that you could tell just how serious a musician a violinist was simply by checking that part of the neck where their instrument pressed into; by this definition she was serious all right.

Despite our early dinner of hamburgers and carrots, and Pete's daytime gourmet-fest, we cleaned the casserole dish the way a pack of dogs would have done. Debbie Canova was gorgeous, sexy, she said she was musical, and now we knew that she could cook. We wondered if there were any more like her in Thornberry; if there were, maybe we'd settle here for life, men happy to have discovered their Paradise. We imagined ourselves like those mutineers on the *Bounty* who found their eternal reward amongst the sun-kissed, wild-haired beauties of Tahiti.

Dream on.

Soon came the evening's musical interlude. I had my doubts about how well an untrained violinist would be able to keep up with us. We tuned our acoustic instruments and there wasn't another soul in these spookily bare camping grounds to hear the music we were about to make. The caretaker had headed off to the school's activities for the night and there were no campers at all. We had light and power, cold water but not hot, and a toilet and shower block to ourselves.

Debbie Canova seemed without fear of being alone in a deserted place with a bunch of brutes she didn't know; instead she took off her boots and planted her feet in the dirt, her white toes curling as if to grip that dirt, and she started to saw delicately at the cat-gut strings. Within a few bars we knew exactly how good she was. The countryside of wild trees and shrubbery filled with the sort of strange magic you get in European art-house movies but not real life – certainly not your own real life, that's for sure. Instead of her keeping up with us it was going to be the other way around.

She said, 'Listen, this technique is called spiccato, I just love playing like this.' We listened and watched the way she bounced her bow over multiple strings at a time. 'This is a double-stop. This one a triple-stop. You like?'

We liked all right.

Tony played Pete's acoustic guitar and Pete went and dug out a half-broken mandolin we used in one of our repertoire's spacier tunes. Joe had a handmade cardboard box upright bass he used for practice. The neck was a piece of wood from an old kitchen floor, the strings were twine and the tuners were tap spigots. Truly a wonder of invention. I used my fingertips and the heels of my palms to create a shuffle on a snare drum. Without formal training, Debbie Canova's fingers were as nimble as those of any professional musician I'd ever known, and she wove melody after melody through our quite mundane notes and recycled rock-and-roll chords. The thing was, she was born to be a leader. When Tony had originally taken control of our three-piece we'd been happy to follow and make a new band. Now by virtue of her prowess and the way she assumed command of us, not to mention of the entire moonlit countryside, for one evening at least Debbie Canova created an entirely new musical enterprise. The look in Tony's face spoke volumes: he was usurped and didn't mind at all.

Gradually then, over twenty to thirty minutes, we learned to modulate ourselves and hold back, to not compete against Debbie's melodies but instead to play counterpoint and the sympathetic backing of them. We learned, really, not to lead – and as soon as she was freed from our rock machine restrictions, Debbie Canova let herself go.

It was extraordinary, easily the best – even as it seemed the most effortless – music of our careers. By the time we'd exhausted ourselves and Debbie stood dripping with perspiration, but smiling with a light that could have lit that entire camping ground, each of us knew with perfect, painful clarity what we lacked: Tony was good, but he was no genius. Neither were we. Here in Nowhere, though, here we'd stumbled on someone absolutely real.

Flushed with pleasure, Tony put the six-string aside and said, 'Let's go see if we can get some of this down,' even though he couldn't write music notation, and, from what she'd told us, neither could she.

'All right,' Debbie said, 'I'll show you our river.'

So there really was a river through this dirty landscape. That seemed miraculous in itself. Tony took his notepad and there was a blunt pencil behind his ear. Debbie carried what was left of the bottle of tequila. They went off into the night, leaving her violin and bow propped against a chair in the centre of our circle. The rest of us snuffled at the empty casserole dish. We didn't make any more music. With her gone it was as if our new soul and sound was already out of reach.

XII

In the chapel, a minute's passed, if that. Pink Floyd's crazy diamond tune is barely part way through. Millionaire developer and finance guru Anthony Lester, in his grey suit and expensive shoes, closes his eyes and nods as he sees himself in his heyday, Debbie Canova telling him, 'But if you don't think the band will work, why do you go on with it?'

Tony was too green to even stammer a worthwhile reply, however, the fifty year old tells her, What was the alternative, Debbie? You had a dream and so did I. Then that's what you do. The difference was that you had the talent I didn't. My writing didn't have the lightness of touch even the heaviest bands need. We had muscle but not sinew. We had heart but not soul. By the end of our tour we knew we were finished too. What's waiting for boys like us? Office buildings, prefab houses and interminable stories of gonna-be and never-was to tell your kids. The band was as good as it could be, but you, Debbie, couldn't you have gone on?

Tony can't remember it exactly, can't quite see how the first time with her came to be. The notepad was in the grass and the pencil lost somewhere, and only a few potential lyric-lines had been written down. He saw that the river skirted the camping ground and created moist green glades so unlikely in this wilderness. She led him to a quiet bank. The scent of moss and lichen was very welcome after weeks and weeks of choking in drylands' dust. In the crescent moon's gauzy light Tony watched as Debbie Canova took his Levi's down and started stroking his cock, her touch achingly feminine.

She didn't want him to lay a hand on her, not to caress her breasts inside her bra and black t-shirt, or her vulva sweating longingly inside her own pair of jeans. No, she was still too married for that, but she rubbed him smoothly then started to jerk at him with increasingly fierce determination. His prick grew darker and darker in that small fist and her other hand pressed back against his hard lower belly as if she wanted to separate organ from body. And she wouldn't get any closer, not with her lips, mouth or tongue.

Tony doesn't remember the exact sequence of events, though to this day he can still see the intensity of purpose that grew in her blue eyes, and then he was coming, and his shriek was some animal's that had its heart pierced with an arrow. He spurted again and again into the long grass, great lumps of fear, hurt and pain coming out of him like cancers excised by a surgeon's knife.

He managed to gasp these words as his breath returned, Come with me, Debbie, just say to hell with everything and come with me, and she, still at heart a young girl, with enough broken hopes of her own to contend with, answered, Do you mean it? Are you serious?

Yes. Yes, yes.

But you don't know what it's like to have responsibilities. To be married. How can you ask me something like that?

They lay back, bodies comfortable in the soft grass even if

their souls weren't. Tony clearly remembers this: he shut his eyes briefly, or so he thought, and when he opened them again she was gone. Alone by a river; a quarter of a moon's light in his eyes. He trudged back to the campsite, where the rest of us paced disconsolately, unable to sleep. The reason: Debbie Canova had returned long before him. Without a word she'd gathered up her things and driven that hotted-up Ford away at speed. Pete, Joe and I imagined the worst – that somehow Tony had lost control of himself and done something terrible, and we waited, nervous as fish, for him to return from wherever they'd been in the surrounding darkness.

We saw him coming.

At first his shape was silhouetted by the crescent moon. He looked like some lumbering monster, then, with a heart-stopping abruptness, he stood out in clear relief. The entire countryside lit up. Headlights flashed, glared and swooped, bringing day to the night of the campsite. I must admit my blood turned cold; the town was arriving to lynch us – what had Tony done to that girl?

Instead, the brilliant lights came from convoys of buses: it was the audience of four-to-nine-year-olds that the principal had warned us to be musically prepared for. They'd finally arrived from their distant places and they were going to camp in the grounds for the night. Bus after bus after bus; and more buses and more buses and more buses. As they pulled up doors rattled open and children were liberated into the grounds. Over their shrieks and cries were the futile, barked commands of teachers trying to get them into order.

We hadn't practised a thing; in the face of these hordes, as one, Pete, Joe and I lost heart. Any misdirected confidence we'd had disappeared in a flash. We turned to our leader.

In the artificial glaring day, there was a new crease in Tony's brow. He had his notebook and he stopped in the dirt and tore out the pages, shredding them like a madman. Pieces scattered in the breeze. The pages were almost completely blank anyway. What was left of the book went arcing off into the trees. He had nothing to say; we didn't even wait till morning. We packed up the truck and the ute and drove out of the camping grounds in our own convoy. Without any of us discussing it, or needing to agree to it, we headed off in the direction of home, more than two thousand kilometres away.

XIII

In those days I became haunted by fears I could barely put a finger on. Waking in the dead of night, I'd stumble from room to room asking out loud if anyone was there. Mostly I'd pour myself a drink, sit at the big open picture window and look at the stars floating above the treetops behind my home. Strange things played on my mind, such as, What if my real father suddenly turned up out of the blue and wanted to know me? and, What if this place caught fire in the middle of the night?

For most of my life, every time some new turn came along that threatened to kick me in the teeth, I moved sideways and simply avoided the blow. I'd never really thought much about that jerk, my progenitor. The idea that there was a man out there, somewhere, who with his prick inside my mother had helped to create me, was an odd but abstract concept. Like knowing there are rings around Saturn, or that the tail of a comet is either Type One or Type Two, and if it's the former it looks blue and if it's the latter it's white or just about pink. If someone told me, Guess what? They made a mistake, there are no rings around Saturn and comets have no tail at all, I would have shrugged and left it at that. If someone said, No, your mother had a divine conception and you have no father other than the Father we all share, I wouldn't have been too cut.

So why these small anxieties started to play on me, I never quite put a finger on. I felt it had something to do with the band being on its last legs, the fact that once it was over I'd be useless to anyone, a drummer on his own having to find someone else's dud band to join. I didn't have a clue how to write songs or put lyrics together, so I'd be at the behest of others for the rest of my days – and it looked like it was going to be the covers band circuit for me again, plugging into jobs that were as regular and pointless as any nine-to-five grind.

It wasn't so much the idea of needing to strike out in a new direction that bothered me, but the fact that failure sat immoveable as a mountain at the end of my road. Years back that co-worker Patti had asked me about my future and I'd shrugged the question off, but now I saw it, the mirage we all start with: everything is limitless and full of potential.

Loneliness crept inside me. I started fantasising about who my real father was and what he might have been. I started to think about my mother again. I remembered prematurely grey hair that she seldom brushed. It always looked straggly, like dry seaweed. She must rarely have coloured it either because all the grown-up pictures of her in my aunt's house showed her looking older than her years, which of course she was. Old, stick-thin, grey hair. Hard to imagine anyone willing to pay money to sleep with her, but whenever she hugged me she'd been a woman, a mother, real and dear to me as any ma to any kid.

Then there were the other photographs.

In her younger days she was like any child, sort of freckly around the nose, a bit of a gap between the teeth. Big eyes let you know that she believed the world was a good and solid place, full of reliability and achievable dreams. Around the corner there would always be a new glass of lemonade and slice of cake, another nice frock and more days of clean-smelling rain.

Little kids are so creamy; I looked at mildewed photographs of my mother as a young girl and wondered if I'd ever have children. The signs weren't good. For all my anxieties about aloneness, for all the little affairs and discreet little fucks I had, most mornings I was in my bed without anyone beside me. Then, more and more, I found myself inviting some of these strangers to stay a little longer, to have coffee and breakfast with me, to talk.

All that did was make them nervous. So I tried to tell myself that aloneness was what I wanted anyway. It's something to love, that sort of aloneness – but first you have to love yourself, right?

Way back, after ma died, on a hot morning maybe a hundred Fahrenheit in the shade, a police car drove me to my aunt's house. I was an orphan and it was 1965.

Aunt Emma was waiting at the front door and not too happy about it either. You don't need to be much more than eight to be able to read the emotions in people's faces. I barely knew the woman and sort of felt sorry for the way she was getting lumbered with me. Clearly, she would have preferred getting lumbered with a snake, maybe, or a rabid chimpanzee, but I was full of relief. There'd been terrible thoughts in my head, of being sent to a prison or something for not having parents, or to a boys' home where you slaved on your raw knees scrubbing miles and miles of polished timber floors; then there'd been the more romantic deliberations, such as the possibility of living in the streets like a new super-hero and helping to eradicate all the city's wild crime even though there wasn't much around, or escaping to the jungle and living like an animal-boy.

Instead, there was this safe but mundane option. My auntie. There'd been sixteen years between her and my mother so they'd never been particularly close. That was history now because I was on her doorstep and the thump of a cheap little suitcase said I was ready to stay.

She showed me a sewing room made into an artificial version of a young boy's bedroom. Sporting pendants for teams I'd never heard of and would never care for were stuck up on one wall. A leather football that hadn't been inflated since her own father was a boy sat in a chair. Strangely, a volume about the two great boxing matches between Joe Louis and Max Schmeling was the only book in the small set of white-painted shelves. In my first three months of living there I must have read about the battle between the black man and the Aryan, the American and the German, America versus Germany, fifteen times.

I didn't watch much television because auntie didn't like company spoiling her appreciation of the game shows and laugh-track comedies she consumed liked grapes and cherries. 'The Lucy Show' and 'Theatre Royal' were her favourites, but Sundays were always for midday's 'World Championship Wrestling', which she watched after coming home from church, her excited frame literally bobbing up and down on the couch as she drank beer and exhorted those muscle-men to kill one another.

The only times I did get to watch television were when she went out to her local singles club dances, organised by her church and a bunch of spinsters hell-bent on finding suitable husbands for their over-the-hill selves and likewise sisters.

One night she came home with a Greek named Elias, and I returned to my room, reading yet again about the Nazi being floored by Smokin' Joe in the very first round, the sweetest revenge any capitalist society ever had over some totalitarian state. In the living room Aunt Emma let herself be wrestled, pawed, man-handled and generally rendered *deshabillé* by an individual twice her size. He had legs like tree trunks and arms like girders, a head fatter than my now-inflated football and shoulders as square as a concrete wall. I caught her slurping in his lap when I went out for a glass of water, curious, unable to bear the sounds of sighing and groaning any longer.

Elias looked at me with lazy, dark eyes. Aunt Emma didn't raise her head; I doubt she even knew I was there. On the coffee table there was a colony of empty bottles of beer. The nights went on like this for three weeks, then he simply was never there again.

Loneliness followed her the next few years until the night she came home with an Italian, a man whose acquaintance I made over breakfast. He told me his name was 'Conny'. He gave the rest of it, which I couldn't catch because of the thickness of his tongue and the strange lilt he had to his accent. She'd dragged him home sometime after midnight and he sat at the kitchen table nursing what I could see was a massive headache. By then I'd experienced quite a few hangovers myself; only three and a half months earlier my thirteenth birthday passed in a blur of froth-headed drinks taken with my aunt.

She seemed terribly old, but was a woman only in her mid-forties. Conny was close to twenty years her senior so seemed thoroughly ancient to me. It was 1970 and he moved in just as autumn's brown leaves were beginning to fall, bringing with him two ratty suitcases, a broken-down EJ Holden Premier that none-theless had very swish leather seats, and a drum kit that he put together in the bare open space under the house, by the laundry tubs.

XIV

Where Elias the Greek — the only other man I'd seen my aunt with — had been stout as a gnarled hoop pine, Concetto 'Conny' San Filippo was slender and elegant, like a lovely sapling. His voice could be so quiet, a whisper that sometimes you had to strain to hear, and often even then you had to think hard in order to decipher his accent and strange word usage. Other times that voice became a real baritone, when he either sang in the bathroom as he shaved and showered or when he raised his voice at Emma or me for transgressions real or imagined. When he shouted his voice didn't go high, it went deep. In many ways he was a gentleman, a *gentle man* in an old-world sense, but he had a temper that could make me go hide and Aunt Emma make herself very scarce. He was no visitor in that house either; he took it over like a benevolent lord. She adored having him there.

Conny had been some kind of salesman by day and musician by night, but at his advanced years he'd given up all of the former and most of the latter. Before he moved in I'd had a freedom few other of the boys at my school ever experienced. My fellow students could only dream about the so-called good fortune of an orphan with an uninterested guardian. I was free to do whatever came into my head almost without limits. I'd disappear for entire weekends; stay out as late as I wanted doing whatever I wanted. It was easy to take a day here or there off from school, absconding sometimes into the city and the malls, or as far away as some sandy beach. Aunt Emma had plenty of money, so there was no need to take me out of that mercilessly rundown old Christian Brothers school and move me into the state system, but she had no talent at all for discipline or any other niceties of child-rearing. For these things you had to care and most of the time she didn't.

Conny, however, was a different kettle of fish. The first time Emma poured me a glass of beer at the dinner table, a new template came into existence. He watched the glass get filled, my hand go around it, and the practised way I raised the drink to my lips. He reached out and stopped me before I could take a sip.

'Little boys, they no do drink alcohol.'

And that was it. Emma nodded. I was thirteen and didn't complain, not even for a second. I found it curious that this man should tell me to do what was so obviously correct. For a moment I sat back in my chair and considered him. Conny had already resumed eating his meal and didn't look back at me. He'd made his rule without fuss or fervour and we were going to follow it. All I could see was wispy hair that only just covered a monk's pate. Who was he, really? It took me years to find out.

As part of my free-wheeling ways, I'd been breaking into houses. Mostly it was just for pocket money and the fun of it. Never got caught. One night past eleven I raised a half-brick to smash the back window of a darkened house in the neighbour-hood, one I knew was empty because the family had headed to the beach for the holiday season.

A spirit-voice rose behind me: 'Max.' He always pronounced it 'Muxx' and my heart skipped a beat.

I put the half-brick down. Climbed off the trestle I'd been balancing on. Conny put out his hand for me to take. It wasn't as soft as I'd expected it to be. His drumsticks had created lifelong calluses in the skin. We walked away hand in hand, a pinkish moon overhead. I hadn't walked like that with anyone since the last time I went shopping with my mother, must have been five or six years past. He didn't say anything at all, not a word. *Muxx*, and then his hand for me to take. When we arrived home Emma was in bed asleep and he went to the living room to kick off his shoes and drink a small glass of Cynar in front of some late-night television show. I don't know why or how he succeeded in doing it, but I simply stopped every single one of my larcenous activities. I stopped skipping school. All of this was a relief. A relief to have someone in the home who expected a little better of me.

They were married in a ceremony attended only by Aunt Emma's church friends and me. No one came from Conny's side. There might not have been a side. He seemed a perpetual loner; a solitary man who for some reason had decided to make this house his home. What attracted him – my aunt Emma? It was hard to believe. The only way they were suited was in their respective loneliness. She was content with her church, television and beer. He liked the quiet inside our home's walls and the sound of his jazz music playing softly from the record player.

I know that what came next came from him: it took time to get through, but they adopted me, became my legal parents. I overheard him once saying, 'Emma, *mi tesora*, this boy he need help, yes? Is for us to do the help – who else can?' I think I was shocked to hear someone say something like that, to be so ready to be concerned about me. Still, I never stopped calling her auntie and him Conny. I kept my mother's surname. Nothing was going to change that.

As time passed and he became more of a fixture in the house, gradually I learned more about Concetto San Filippo. What he'd sold had been men's apparel in department stores: suits, ties and the shirts you needed to go with them. My new step-father was also an ex-swing orchestra drummer and across four decades he'd played shows at church halls, small and large jazz clubs, the city hall and the Cloudland Ballroom. His main gig had been with an outfit called Jimmy 'Knockout' Jones and His Incredible Sixteen-Piece Orchestra. Band leader Jimmy Jones had his entourage together for nearly twenty years and Conny said that in their time they'd entertained everyone from debutantes, desperate bachelors and discouraged spinsters, country women's associations and Masons, to political leaders, visiting dignitaries and royalty – but, to Knockout's eternal consternation, never the Queen of England.

'He from the great London. To him, the Queen she is the Virgin Mary come back to life. To me she is *cafone* – twit – but there you go, huh?'

I checked his old, out-of-date passport. Born in 1908, Conny had arrived in Australia after the Depression, a young man with only minimal understanding of the English language. *Hello; good-bye; nice country; nice sky.* He had musical training and distant relatives here who'd helped ease his passage to the new country. Where these people were now, I didn't know. He never spoke about any family or his old community of Italian friends. What I did know was that somewhere along the way there'd been a schism in his life; something had happened and maybe it had ended up isolat-ing him.

As I learned about retired musicians, their old instruments

tended to stay close to them. Only the most bitter people, usually those who've tasted success only to see it melt into a fiasco,
will sell their guitars, pianos, saxophones, drums, what have you,
all in a fit of pique – then spend their lives wishing they hadn't.
Conny kept his drum kit under my aunt's house, covered with a
sheet, but when the mood was in him, usually on Sunday mornings, he'd whip it off and clean and polish his set-up within an inch
of its life. The stool, the snare, the bass drum, the foot pedal, the
high hat, the tom toms, the crash and ride cymbals, all of them
kept ready for the next sixteen-piece orchestra extravaganza, the
one that never came.

It was nearly a year before he actually started playing. Sunday
middays were no longer for the wrestling on TV – he'd put a stop
to that, saying barbarity should never be allowed into people's
homes – and the house was as quiet as it now was every Sabbath.
This particular Sunday he went down for his usual dusting and
polishing, then an hour later it started. The previously languid
air vibrated to a beat. The day was no longer owned by birdsong
or the mild croaking of cicadas. Conny played for an hour, then
two, finally stopping after three hours – and once the dam was
broken his percussive concerto became a weekly occurrence.

The neighbours put up with this for a half-dozen sessions
then went crazy. It was a miracle they took it for so long. There
were no walls under our house, there was nothing to cushion
the relentless, all-permeating sound he made. The neighbours came and, when called, so did the police. Two officers
explained to him what the words 'public nuisance' meant.
Conny explained to them that no worthwhile music was ever
made in silence. He asked them if they danced, which they had
to admit, they did.

'And who makes the beat so you know when to move your

feet and your girl to shake her rump? Me! Then how this can be a problem?'

He had them laughing. Tempers cooled. Conny struck a deal – he'd only practise his art for one hour, one day of the week. Sunday. He'd start at eleven in the morning and end at midday. That way everyone would know it was coming. They could go out to church, or take a walk, and be confident in the knowledge that they wouldn't be disturbed for another week or at any other time of day or night. This compact was to be inviolable, and while it stood there'd be no more trouble.

My poor Aunt Emma suffered the weekly thrashings on his set with the grace of a middle-aged woman getting her teeth drilled. She adored him, but not the racket he made. He'd go for the allotted hour, our house above him rattling as if made of cardboard. In his heart and in his head he must have been rehearsing – or maybe reliving – some brilliant dance brackets. At the time I didn't recognise them for what they were, but he was playing syncopated rhythms peculiar to swing and to jazz, all at varying, hip-swinging tempos. Sometimes the music was feathery – something to make you want to hold your girl close while she caressed your face and put her full lips next to your soap-scrubbed neck – then the tempo would increase, the bite of the beat sharper and actually cracking in the air. The lucky dancers in Conny's mind would sway and shake their hips, whipping their hair to the jubilant rhythm of another fabulous ballroom night.

When it was time to come upstairs for auntie's waiting roast he'd be in a steaming lather of sweat and in fine spirits too. His brown eyes would be shining and there would be a smile on his face, a smile so impish that it belied his almost-seventy years. Emma would be wearing her best floral apron and her tight, pained smile. He was good at his craft, even a kid like me could hear that, but there was seldom a word of appreciation or encouragement from his new wife. I was quietly proud of this man who wasn't my father but who acted as good as one, yet Emma never had a question or comment about technique, never any wifely interest in what songs and tunes made up his mental set list. There was only her weary relief that it was over for another week.

Still, for his reward there was roast beef and cold beer. He'd have a single glass while Emma downed four or five. I'd have to do all the cleaning and washing up while they retired to their regular Sunday afternoon siesta. After about twenty minutes the house would start rhythmically moving on its tall timber stumps. In the kitchen I'd turn up the radio so I wouldn't have to listen to the sounds that came next.

Life wasn't always so harmonious in this place. Little things could set Conny off and when they did I'd have to run for cover. I wrecked his razor by using it to sharpen my pencil. When he went to shave he opened his chin. Bleeding profusely he shouted that I would have to stay in my room two days and nights, his eyes as wide and wild as though I'd tried to use that razor to cut his throat and kill him. At least he relented by evening and I was allowed out for my meal. One day I did kill something: the pumpkin patch he was attempting to establish. I was digging in the garden for worms I could use when I went fishing off Redcliffe pier, me with no idea there was anything trying to grow there anyway. The next day he came at me, for some reason screaming the pumpkin's Latin genus: '*Cucurbita pepo! Cucurbita pepo!*' I thought he was going to strangle me, veins standing out in his forearms, temples and neck. I ran for my life and Emma locked herself in the bedroom.

One weekend my stepfather attempted to help me with an English assignment, which was to write a review of a book called

Brighton Rock. Knowing I was useless at something like this he had sat and slept with that book for a week, reading it painful page by painful page. The English language, so hard for him to speak, so tricky for him to interpret when written down.

He composed the review for me, him dictating and me obediently writing it out. Even I could see what a bad idea this was. He used pompous phrases and naïve clichés that might have sounded good in his native Italian, but which were comical in this language, especially when badly translated: 'The most beautiful story ever written about this evil boy gangster who don't know the church is there to save him'; 'A mystery of razors slashing blood out of delinquent youthfuls before the war in the great England before she went bad'; 'Perfect story that is maybe a bit hard to understand because the language it is superlative'.

When the assignment came back with a big fat 'F' on the front, and the tight, pained handwriting of a Christian Brother providing a critique that included the use of the word 'childish' seven times, Conny spun out of control. Tears of rage and hurt sprang from his eyes. In English and Italian he cursed the church, the brothers and all Christians of all denominations. He tore up the assignment, but he wouldn't go face the teacher in question. He was humiliated, utterly emasculated, in his mind proven to be a fool. Cut to the quick, he took his hat and left the house. Neither Emma nor I had the slightest clue where he went. When he turned up the next morning there was no explanation. Emma gave him the cold shoulder for days; he gave it back to her. Then he succumbed and brought her chocolates and a fresh leg of lamb wrapped in butcher's paper. The following Sunday his hour of drumming was followed by beer, lamb roast and twenty minutes of house-swaying. I turned the radio loud. Life resumed as before.

The angriest I ever saw Conny was the day the neighbours came to see him, in a pack. They told him something they thought he ought to know: the increasingly cacophonous and chaotic sounds that had been smashing and crashing from under the house on most of the occasions when he drove his Premier out of the driveway and was away for any substantial period of time.

I arrived home from school. Fourteen years of age, I was still quite short, still a couple of inches shorter than Conny – who was by no means a tall man. There was an oppressive mood to the house. It was dark inside though a hot sunny afternoon outside. Windows were shut and curtains were drawn. No one seemed to be home, then I noticed Conny, stiff as a statue in the couch by the black-and-white television. The TV was switched off. My stepfather's arms were folded and his chin was buried down into his chest. At first I thought he was asleep or dead, then he moved. He stood. Something about his manner made me back out of the lounge room, but he confronted me in the corridor. His eyes blazed and I noticed there was something white and gummy dried at the corners of his mouth.

'The neighbours they come. They tell me what you do.'

'I haven't done anything. I've been at school.' I tried to get around him but without even touching me I felt pushed with my back against the wall. 'What are you doing, you crazy old man?'

His voice came low and deep. 'You never touch my drums, *figlio di putane che sei.*'

'What does that mean? What did you say – what did you call me?'

'Son of a whore!'

I tried to push past him. He slammed me so hard against the wall that the back of my head hit the timber. My jaw snapped shut, almost cutting off my tongue. I still tried to get away, but he pinned my arms with his hands. His grip was like steel, far stronger than I could have imagined. I was stuck there.

'You do never touch my drums, they is mine!'

'Learn to speak English!'

'Is not toy for stupid boy!'

'Grammar! Verbs! You dumb wog, you sound like a moron!'

He looked with horror into my hate-filled face. It was the worst of the insults I could have flung at him. He let go of me and with great deliberation raised one hand so high that I couldn't help it, I cowered. Flinched.

That stopped him, the way I drew back from the coming blow. He lowered his hand, but steel remained in his voice. Each word extracted its own pound of flesh. 'This word you want to use when you do look at me. You must never. Never. To call a man this is to say him he is stranger in this country and will always be. You learn what I tell you right now. *Right now.*'

So I couldn't call him a wog, but he could call me the son of a whore. In my mind's eye I could see my ma, thin, grey and dead. I ran into my room and slammed the door. Locked it. Had no idea where Emma was or when she'd be home – as if I could expect any sympathy or help from that drunken old bitch anyway, I told myself. Light footsteps stopped outside my door. There was silence. I held my breath.

Then came his voice. It wasn't angry but gentle. 'Muxx.' He waited. 'Muxximillion.'

I didn't answer him. I would never answer him. Either he would have to leave this house forever or I would. One of us had to go.

For the present it was him. Conny stayed there another minute, then I heard him walk away. The front door opened and closed. Outside, the EJ Holden's engine started up. He's off, I thought, I'll never see the dumb dago again, and I threw myself down on my bed and covered my head with my hands. Good! I don't want you in my house! — and I started to cry.

He didn't return that night, nor the one after.

XV

Three nights he was gone. From there we lived in deathly silence for days on end. A week passed, then two. Conny was like a corpse and my aunt Emma stayed deeply, silently angry. Conny was never in any room that I went into. He avoided me and at dinner time he ate alone outside by the vines. Each night he slept in the spare room.

The house was no better than a morgue and no one could seem to face anyone else and make up. Then one morning I heard Emma speaking to Conny as he shaved in the bathroom. I was in the hall, sleepy and not all there yet. I couldn't quite make out the entire conversation, but it was clear she was quietly grilling him. She ended with something like, 'Don't lie to me, you've gone back to it, haven't you?' or maybe it was, 'Don't lie to me, you've gone back for more, haven't you?' but, either way, I could tell he wasn't going to answer.

I moved closer to the bathroom and could see him over her shoulder. His face was half-frothed, half-shaved. He was silent — but in that studiously vacant, brown-eyed gaze I thought I saw the unconscious assent all men betray when their wives have got the whiff of some secret truth in their nostrils. She turned and pushed past me. He resumed shaving without acknowledging my presence. For the hell of it I went into that bathroom, lifted the lid of the toilet and urinated copiously into the bowl, making as much noise as possible. He didn't flinch.

We entered the third week of familial misery and I kept working that new information over and over in my mind: You've gone back to it or You've gone back for more.

A woman? I doubted it. An old man's not going to have a paramour hidden away somewhere. Then maybe it was gambling, but that seemed just as unlikely. Drinking was out because other than a Sunday glass of beer or a nightly shot of Cynar he was the most moderate person in the house. The only thing I could come up with was the obvious answer: after all, Concetto San Filippo had been a musician all those decades, had played in so many bands and with so many other musicians, he must have come across plenty of drugs and addicts in his life. Maybe he had a habit. Something as simple as smoking spliffs or something as hopeless as the hard dead end of heroin. I wished I could warn him off, wished I could let this old guy know some of the wisdom in this teenage boy. It would have been useless, of course – why listen to me? He'd probably seen and experienced more human misfortune than I could even imagine.

Then, just as I was thinking of packing my bags and disappearing forever, things changed.

It was a Friday afternoon and I came home from school to find the front yard full of building equipment. Emma and Conny were standing there looking at it. They were shoulder to shoulder and whispering together; it might have been the most intimate moment I ever saw between them. Their storm was over. I stopped. They hadn't heard me come through the gate and it was the first time I thought I saw something real between them, some shared complicity. In the way their shoulders touched, in those quiet words I couldn't hear, there existed the key to the mystery of how two people so utterly different could be together, could be married, and could forgive whatever transgressions drove them crazy. The answer was that they needed one another, but more than that, each knew he or she needed the other. The rest didn't mean much at all – and that was their contract.

I looked away, embarrassed to be observing something so private, so tender between them. Instead I stared, baffled, at what was in the yard. There was a petrol-operated mixer, bags of concrete, piles of sand, loam and gravel, and pallets of bricks and blocks. A lot of them. There were tools as well: two long-handled shovels with round lips, two short-handled shovels with square lips, a pair of picks and mattocks, and other things that I understood had to do with the business of mixing cement, applying concrete and making something. Someone was going to be *constructing*, and it was going to be substantial.

Emma turned to me with a sort of kindness in her eyes and some small sense of pride. Not for herself, but for her man.

'Your stepfather hired all this stuff, Max.'

Concetto San Filippo, my nemesis for three weeks now, turned to me. This was just about the first thing he'd said to me in all that time: 'Make sure you go bed at good hour. Tomorrow you are up with the sparrows.'

Well, things might have turned sweet for them, but the hell I was going to do something like that. Instead, I went out to a party that ended in a half-hearted, half-drunken beach fight somewhere down the south coast. By the time someone dropped me back home we'd covered several hundred kilometres and it was three in the morning. I had a split lip and a throbbing arm from being throttled by some surfer twice my age.

Sure enough, despite injuries and wretchedness, I was to be up with the sparrows. Conny shook me awake in the gloom before dawn. Through half-closed lids I saw him flinch from the rotten stench of me.

'Come on, Muxx, is best time to start.'

Five a.m. Saturday. Bleary-eyed, cloudy-headed and still half-asleep, I found myself under the house with him. Conny got straight to work, starting to take mysterious measurements here, there and everywhere. He had me hold the tape for him while he committed some figures to paper, but most others to memory. He staked out the area with twine. That was about as easy as the day got. It turned out we had foundations to dig; then we had to fill them with steel-mesh and concrete for strength and support; of course, Conny explained, after that we had walls to build, starting with twelve-metre high walls here where the house stood tallest on its stilts and overlooked our large jungle of trees. My aunt's house was on level ground at the front but the land it was on fell away at an almost perfect forty-five degree angle so that it was held up at the back by tall steel struts.

So it came to me: this mad bastard Conny had decided to brick-in the underneath of the house. For the time being I had no idea why he'd gotten it into his head to do this. Maybe it had something to do with appeasing my aunt. Whatever the reason, we simply started the process of labouring hard; or should I say, he laboured and I followed. Stripped to the waist, he had the physique of someone half his age. He was a sapling, but was firm and toned. Whenever I thought he was busy with something else I looked for tell-tale signs of marks near his veins. There were none. It was ridiculous. He didn't look like a drug-taker and he certainly had a far younger man's energy, much more than I did. It didn't even seem so extraordinary to me that he knew exactly what he was doing, could figure things out so quickly, and could work so swiftly and with such assurance — even with such happiness. You could call it joy. This work of ours gave him, if anything, even more pleasure than his drumming.

It took all of the weekend simply to dig the foundations for the walls. By Sunday night my hands were blistered and my body ached. I slept like the dead. Monday morning I was due to go to school. I set my alarm early, but I still missed him; by the time I was into my stinking work clothes and had fixed myself a bite to eat, it was five-thirty. I went downstairs and Conny was preparing to get the mixer going.

'What you do? Get dressed. You have school today.'

Picking up the shovel that was now mine, I said, 'What do you want me to dig?'

I didn't go to school, not for another month. Emma called the principal, a crotchety old fool with a violent streak by the name of Brother Langford, and explained I had chicken pox, a really terrible case. Brother Langford said he was happy not to see me till I was recovered and then some. I worked with Conny. That's what I wanted without knowing why I wanted to do it. Labouring by his side and under his tutelage gave me a feeling I couldn't remember experiencing before. I felt safe; I felt needed. It was good to actually *make* something. We painstakingly built in the underside of that wooden, colonial-style house, gave it no windows, simply bricked it all up like some terrible mausoleum and had a high time doing it.

We finished our handiwork on a Wednesday. The hire company came and cleared away all of its things as the afternoon fell into a gathering gloom.

The next Saturday morning, just when I thought everything in Conny's scheming of things was over and done, I woke to see the man sitting in the chair by my bed. The expression in his face said there was something new to add to the mystery of his plan.

'Awake?' he asked.

I nodded. He took me into the kitchen and fried bacon for me, scrambled some eggs with horseradish and salmon, and gave me buttered wholemeal toast. When I was finished, he sent me to get out of my pyjamas. He washed up. Aunt Emma was still asleep.

When I emerged he said, 'Okay, you come downstairs.'

We went outside, walked around and down the side of the house, opened the new door into the cavernous gloom of the walled-in area beneath our home, and there a new drum-kit stood beside his much older set. Its chrome was shining and smelled of fresh polish. The labels said it was a Rogers.

'Is no one hundred percent soundproof down here yet, I have more to do, but I think will be okay.' He went and touched the shiny kit with a love that was palpable. 'Look here, Muxx, the fittings. Really do look at them. See what holds this into this? This piece here, how it fits with this one there? This is quality.' I walked around this thing, barely believing what had been planned in this man's head. He'd been insanely angry at me for touching and playing his own drum kit, now here he was saying, 'Take driver's seat.'

I sat in the stool. He handed me a pair of drumsticks. He didn't beam with pleasure at the enormity of his surprise. Instead, he was very serious.

'Okay. You have to say. You, Muxx. Now you decide how it must be. Is you choice, because is choice for life.' He looked at me, posing his question as carefully as he knew how: 'You want to be boy who go boom-boom-boom – or you want to be musician the finest?'

I swallowed hard. 'I want to play really good.'

'Yes?' he said, then took my hands, folding the drumsticks into them. 'Hold like this. Don't be scare. Feels wrong but I tell you, is right way. Is called the traditional grip, proper way to play all jazz-styles. Then if you want you learn to flick you fingers around like this and you change the way you hold sticks so you can play meat-head rock. This now is called the match grip. But is for later. For now we start with one way only, the traditional. From today into the future you do things the right way. You shoot straight or you do no shoot at all, this is the rule. Okay?'

I nodded.

He moved to his own kit and I thought he was going to start showing me what and how to play. Instead, I hadn't noticed that beside it there was an old, wind-up style metronome. He picked it up and turned the key as far as it would go, then set it down by my side.

'This is the click. This click must go in here.' Conny gently tapped my skull. 'Once this click it is in here, it will never go out. Nearly every musician you will play with will start at wrong tempo, lose beat somewhere, but not you. You will always bring everyone back to the click.' His hand on my head became a caress of my hair. His fingers lingered in the waves and curls. He smiled and flicked the switch on the metronome. I'd soon come to recognise the insistent click of a basic four-four beat, and yes it would go into my skull and never disappear. Conny said, '*Figlio mio*, now is start.'

XVI

Despite all the new love that was being heaped on her, Aunt Emma began to wither before Conny's eyes. He knew what was going on long before a teenager like me did, what with the band I was playing in and all my other extracurricular activities. Even so, her decline was so quick that neither we men of the house had all that much time to absorb the fact she was actually dying.

The diagnosis was colon cancer, which had spread through the abdomen. Then, when headaches became unbearable, tests revealed tumours inside her skull. The surgeons performed a craniotomy, the tumour resection cutting out most of a beast the size of a small orange or mandarin. They hoped to treat the rest of it with radiotherapy. Head shaved, eyesight all but gone, Emma came home after a surprisingly short stay in hospital, but she was frail as a moth and her heart gave out a day later. Maybe weak hearts have been a familial thing, but bad living can be a familial trait too. Even at the start the consulting surgeon had told Conny and me, 'It's going to be difficult to be too optimistic. It appears that her liver's not in very good shape either.'

Conny had her buried in her best Sunday church dress. He purchased an expensive gold crucifix and chain to thread through her fingers and hands, but he also had wit enough to place her favourite beer stein in the coffin beside her. With his glasses on, he sewed black cloth stripes to every one of his shirts, at the bicep of the right arm. He was in mourning and he took it seriously. At the funeral he wept without reservation and seeing him like that made tears run down my face too. I didn't quite know how to feel or think; I'd been in this position when my mother passed away, but this time I was thinking, So what's it gonna be like, just me and this man Conny from now on?

With time, the quiet of the house seemed very little changed from when Aunt Emma was alive. Sometimes it was as if she'd never been there in the first place. How many days and nights had she spent in her dressing robe, smelling like a cat, drinking beer and watching every piece of junk that turned up on the television? Now she was like a shadow that had passed through the house and left no residue.

I was playing in my first band, effortlessly switching from the match grip for their tumbling style of surf music to the traditional grip for Conny's jazz-influenced tuition. The click in a vast array of forms had gone into my head all right, so what he taught me now was more technique and refinement. These were the heady days of Concetto San Filippo and Maree Kilmister, my dynamic duo of tutors. From him I learned that playing drums should be an endless process of finding and acquiring new ways, and from my little hippie-chick I learned just about the same thing, only applied to her.

As time wore on Conny became less interested in his official mourning – which involved offering thanks to Emma before the evening meal as if she'd cooked it herself, and praying for her soul before sleep each night even though he never darkened the door of a church on Sundays or any other days, and modulating the sound of the television and stereo as if not to disturb a slumbering spirit. He started to come home with more and more esoteric jazz-fusion style records. From week to week he played them a little more loudly and frequently. He wanted to hear new things, then he would trek downstairs to try them out for himself, me following if I wasn't occupied with Maree. The work of artists such as Sun Ra, Ornette Coleman and even the Art Ensemble of Chicago soon filled our minds, and whenever those tricky, spaced-out rhythms started to drive us a little crazy we always went back to the touchstones of swing music and the jazz of Miles Davis and John Coltrane. From time to time Conny could even take something as left of his field as the first three or four Carlos Santana albums, but I knew he never really listened to the guitars or voices, but was instead decoding the pulse inside those Latin-infected beats. The time for tranquillity and sombre reflection was passing. Our practice room became an endless cacophony of experimentation, but with those brick and block walls at least no neighbours or slumbering spirits needed suffer.

However, despite all of this, the truth is that Concetto San Filippo found himself sharing a house with a teenage boy who had plenty of outside interests, and while I was always a willing pupil for his drum lessons, loneliness started to eat at him. After the anniversary of Emma's death came and went he seemed to decide his official mourning was over. No more dinner thanks and no more evening prayer. Conny unpicked the black stripes from his shirts and joined a quintet of aging musicians. These men played mostly weddings and had been after him for years. Now at a loose end and freer than he'd been, he gave in.

They wore tuxedos wherever they played and called themselves

I Pinguini – Italian for 'The Penguins'. The band would practise in our big room downstairs and often I sat in to watch and maybe learn a few tricks. Sometimes I helped them set up in the small places they played. It was the usual stuff. They did traditional wedding music numbers: slow waltzes, a bit of old-time rock-and-roll, and well-known ethnic songs like 'Volare' and 'O Sole Mio' just for fun. Of course, they always had to end with Tom Jones' 'Delilah' and Johnny Preston's 'Running Bear', these were what people expected and paid for. There was no jazz or experimentation in the least. The old guys were all Italian and one of them had a decent voice, but their sound was crowd-pleasing and cheesy. It didn't seem to bother Conny but it did me, seeing someone with his skill slumming it with lesser musicians in these types of venues. Well, it didn't matter. He was finally enjoying himself and for the last years of his life he had a good reason to get out of bed.

The real problem was that all the good times and new friendships had an unforeseen effect: he drank more and took up smoking again, having given up, he told me, on the ninth day of August 1945. That was when 'Fat Man' was dropped on Nagasaki, three days after 'Little Boy' destroyed Hiroshima, and 'The human race, Muxx, he loses his heart.' The nights he didn't have a job to play he sat alone in front of the television after cooking some lovely Italian meal. He would light a cigarette and drink wine or Cynar and stay there, often falling asleep on the couch, so that if I came in late I'd have to get him up and put him to bed, cleaning up his ash and butts, putting away a half-empty bottle.

Funny what ends up killing a person.

For you, Conny, it was those stupid cigarettes. Early 1975 and you were driving your EJ home from the wedding of some ethnic princess to the heir of a local hairdressing chain. It was a big night, a happy one. Your quintet played its heart out and for the entire final hour its repertoire was at their request nothing but Thirties' and Forties' swing. The new husband and wife had met while taking ballroom dancing lessons, hadn't they, and so you led the band through a set-list of as many Count Basie, Artie Shaw and Benny Goodman standards as they could find it in their fusty old memories to remember. You even threw in some lesser-known numbers, including some that Gene Krupa made his own, just so you could show off a little in that flamboyant Krupa style.

Did you keep to shooting straight or did you let yourself go a little wild? For this, your last performance ever, I hope it was the latter. Just a bit. I remember one day you demonstrated to me how Krupa had influenced rock drummers such as Ian Paice, Keith Moon and John Bonham, and I'd been staggered that you knew the names of rock musicians like them and could even ape their styles.

Driving home from the wedding you lit a cigarette and smoked in contentment. The window was open. You had your hat on and the AM radio station was playing an old Dean Martin tune. You flicked out the butt. Five minutes from home the hunger for tobacco, that craving that never really goes away, was still gnawing at your lungs. You thought you could have another smoke before getting in. You plugged in the car's dashboard lighter, waiting for it to pop while Martin sang something dreamy about a lazy ocean hugging the shore. You remembered how your old band leader Jimmy Jones used to croon tunes just like that, and with almost as much verve as men like Martin, Al Martino or Tony Bennett.

The lighter clicked. You put a cigarette into the corner of your mouth, a practised move you learned from the movies years ago. You pulled the lighter out and held the glowing grill to the tip of the cigarette. The paper and tobacco started to send up tendrils of smoke. The car turned a corner and a strong breeze off a bend of our river blew diagonally into your window, sending an ember of the cigarette's glowing tip into your left eye. It hurt like a needle-jab, didn't it? You dropped the lighter, which fell into your lap, where it burned through the soft cotton of your trousers. In sudden, ridiculous agony, and momentarily blinded, you swerved off the road into a giant fig tree. Your neck snapped.

You heard Dino ask his love to thrill him as only she knew how, to make his longing body sway right now, then it was goodbye.

I know all this because you're sitting in this chapel, aren't you, Concetto San Filippo, sitting in the third row amongst these mourners. I'm so happy to see you again, and, but for the music of Pink Floyd, I know you're just as happy to be here too.

Salvi, old friend. That's what you taught me to say. *Ciao, bel'amico*, it's so good to see you.

XVII

We hadn't forgotten her, but we never expected to see Debbie Canova again. Despite this, she re-entered our lives before 1980 was out, nearly ten months after we'd abandoned our tour.

Christmas was coming and things were going downhill. Pete Kelley had re-enrolled at university to finish a science degree and wasn't inclined to practise or turn up to gigs that didn't pay good money. No one paid good money. Our bass player, Joe Whitehead, shaved his head and went to live in a small Baha'i commune on the New South Wales coast. We barely played outside the practice room any more and sometimes Manoeuvres was just Tony and me under my house, him now on electric guitar as we tried out his new songs.

Do you remember all this? I ask as he sits waiting like everyone else for the music to fade down. Any moment the celebrant will tell them what a good man has been lost, but if we will hold him in our hearts, and remember him and his times, he will never really be gone.

Tony shifts in his seat. My question pricks at him. At that time, we were in a pit of despair all right, but one day Tony opened the front door of his little rented workers' cottage and who should be there but Debbie Canova, violin and bow in hand.

'Have you got fifty dollars?' she murmured, her head lost in another world. 'If you've got fifty dollars you can treat me like a whore, I'll let you do anything you want to me.'

Then she fainted.

XVIII

I've been inside two brothels in my time. The first visit occurred when I was eighteen and with Tony Lester, the next time I was alone.

My aunt was gone, but Conny was still alive. Tony hadn't joined the band yet. I don't know why the eighteen-year-old me got it into his head to go out and pay for sex. The good year before had mostly been about Maree Kilmister and after she dumped me I wasn't heartbroken enough to avoid a few very nice dalliances with other girls. Everything should have been okay, but it wasn't. This night was a bad night and I was out with Tony, and the two of us were in a mood, the sort of half-foul, half-confused mood that afflicts boys when they're on the town and don't know what to do or who to do it with. My three-piece band was playing heavy rock standards in pubs, but by day we'd started dallying with the idea of going progressive – and we tried out tunes by The Nice, Tangerine Dream and, yes, Pink Floyd, all in the hope of discovering some real spark in ourselves, some absolute direction forward. I couldn't have imagined that direction was standing right next to me.

Tony and I blew what little cash we had on drinks in a big club where three live bands a night played. No one danced to any of them. Between their sets a DJ spun the sort of sugary tunes that were featuring on the 'Countdown' TV show and in pop magazines: here John Paul Young, Sherbert and ABBA reigned supreme. Whenever any of them or their ilk came through the PA the crowd went wild. It must have driven those poor musicians nuts to see their audience sticking to the bar or their tables until some over-produced gloss had every-one up and dancing.

The place was a pseudo-trendy hole and its patrons a bunch of jerks, and to piss people off and get ourselves drunk we whisked away the expensive mixed drinks left at tables while people danced. A big group of guys cottoned on to what we were doing and wanted to smash our faces. Tony always had a gift for sooth-ing tempers. We got away, but didn't have a single dollar left in our pockets. Even if ATM machines had been invented then, there wouldn't have been any money in either of our accounts. There was nowhere to go that didn't involve a cover charge, then, just like that, as we were walking through a darkened car park I spot-ted a crumpled note lying next to a crumpled handkerchief.

Fifty dollars.

Someone's too drunk, sneezes, reaches into his pocket for a handkerchief, but his nerveless hands won't work. The result; a loss becomes a gift. The pseudo-trendy bar had put us in foul spir-its. A red light across the way flashed everything we needed to know. The woman who opened the door was short and dumpy, but had a pretty face and a cute lisp. She managed to make the Bill of Fare sound more attractive than it was. Something like fif-teen dollars for topless hand relief, eighteen dollars for topless oral relief, and twenty-five dollars for a bit of both plus a ride in the missionary position. Other positions escalated in price but we told her to stop there.

Tony picked her. I don't recall choosing, but a tall woman in a wrap-around skirt soon entered the cubicle I was waiting in and pulled off her blouse. She finished smoking a cigarette as I got out of my clothes.

'Bad night about to get better, Honey?' she asked.

I felt like she was talking to the wall. She would have spoken that line a thousand times. When I asked her how her evening was, she didn't answer. When I told her she had nice breasts, she was opening a bottle of baby oil and didn't do much more than nod.

'Are your hands cold?' she asked. I told her I didn't think they were, and she said, 'All right, you can touch my tits while I jerk you a bit. If you come straightaway, you don't get any money back.'

She poured some oil onto me and got to work. Her labour was as automatic as her speech. She wanted me to come fast, so she could have the full amount of pay without having to do the rest. That woman tugged away as if my prick was a root in the ground that needed to be torn out of the earth. I wouldn't let myself come; I watched the way she worked with increasingly grim determination. Her breasts swayed to the firm movement of her arm. I think I started to feel sorry for her.

'Do you mind your job?' I asked. She was surprised that I'd ask something like that, instead of the more usual, Use your mouth, or, Open your legs now.

She eased off a little, started to caress me with a gentleness that years of work had not completely extinguished. 'I like some of the older men who come in,' she said, thinking it over. 'They always smell a bit funny, like something wet and musty, but with them I guess I feel like I'm doing something sort of worthwhile. That makes me feel good.'

I wondered if my mother had ever felt that way. That she was doing good for others. I almost wanted to ask this woman if she'd known her.

She was careful now, using the tips of her fingers, running them up and down like a flower opening and closing. She wasn't resorting to brute force any more. The oil was okay. That was when I really did feel sorry for her, felt like I wanted to save her a little trouble.

'I'm going to come now,' I said.

She nodded. 'Sure you want to?'

'Yes.'

I could hear voices in the adjoining room. A bunch of guys waiting after about as bad a night as Tony and I had had. Ready to switch their night from fucked to doing some fucking. Their leering bravado seeped into the cubicle.

'All right,' she said. 'But when you blow don't make too much noise.'

I said, 'Do old men make much noise?'

She sort of laughed, but was half-serious when she whispered, 'They do, especially if they're a little deaf. Then it's like you're killing them.'

I did as she asked, was silent as a dying sparrow. She said, 'You're a nice kid,' and left me with tissues, a towel and a key to the shower room at the back.

Later, Tony caught up with me in the street. We both smelled of rose-scented soap. He'd done just about the same: paid for the full treatment but in the end had been happy to spurt into his woman's fist. Waste of money, we agreed, both surprised at our lack of enthusiasm for getting our money's worth. Well, it was someone else's money anyway. I felt okay. I thought, One day when I'm old and I smell like wet rugs and blankets, maybe there'll be a woman somewhere who'll feel good to make my life easier too.

I hoped I'd be deaf by then. It'd be good to be like a grizzled lion, still roaring.

XIX

So, I don't know what came over Debbie Canova to make her stand at Tony's door and tell him something like that.

Tony can see her now just as she was that day. He's staring at my coffin and in the wood-panelled gloss there's the full picture of her: Debbie in a cheesecloth shirt she should have changed three days ago, and a dirty gypsy skirt frayed around the edges, and her feet bare and black with broken toenails, remnants of pink polish on them. He remembers Debbie's small weight as he caught her in just the way some Thirties movie hero might have caught a fainting starlet. No real hero this boy, he looked up and down the street, not to see if the neighbours were sizing the situation up, but to see whether the husband was ten paces behind. Because if Debbie Canova had been Tony's escaping wife, ten paces behind would be exactly where you'd find him.

He carries her inside and he places her onto his couch. She opens her eyes.

'Do you remember me?'

'Sure,' he tells her. 'Nice of you to drop by.'

'Good to see you again too.'

'How did you find me?

'Telephone book.'

'And how did you get here?' Trucks, she tells him. Despite the warnings police gave, it was still the days of easy hitch-hiking, when you could get wherever you wanted to go by power of your thumb alone. 'So what's this about some money I'm supposed to give you?'

'I don't know,' she answers, and though he looks for it there's no subterfuge that Tony can detect.

Debbie Canova is filthy and pallid. She looks like a road rat, a truckie's wet dream, a biker's moll or a rock band groupie thrown out of some travelling van to make her own way home. What worries Tony is how vague she seems, how starved. Should he give her a bite to eat or call a doctor? What also bothers him is the husband, because despite the fact that so much time has passed since he first met her, who would forget hearing about a very large plumber with two giant hands? Ten paces behind, or ten thousand kilometres, sooner or later Phil Canova could be at the door – and the one thing Tony learned in stir to fear most is the personal violence of other men.

'When did you last eat?' In reply she shakes her head as if there's no such thing as food, nutrition or consumption. 'Water maybe?' He gets her a small glass half-filled, thinking of the word 'thimble'. When lost sailors were dragged out of the sea, crazy with heat, hunger and above all else thirst, didn't the captain or the ship's doctor always only allow a thimble-full of water? What *Boy's Own* volume had he read that in – and who carries a thimble with them anyway?

Debbie sits up, drinks and wants more. He brings her another. She wants more again so he brings her a carafe, unsure if he's killing her. So then something to eat is what she wants and he makes her a white bread ham-and-cheese sandwich. When he gives it to her on a cracked plate handed down from his late grandmother's English crockery collection, she turns up her nose and pushes it away. One, she would not eat white bread on pain of death, and, two, she will never again consume something that has *known* the pain of death. In her new incarnation as a free woman she can finally be who she's always wanted to be. Now, first and foremost, she is an animal lover, so naturally enough, she's a herbivore, a vegetarian.

She stretches out on the couch and closes her eyes. Tony goes to make her something more palatable. He thinks of mung beans and green tea, and in his mind mixes up alfalfa sprouts with brussels sprouts, legumes he knows only tangentially. When he returns with crackers, cheese and milk – cow's milk – he wonders if she will have a reason to find these offensive. She's asleep anyway. He carefully closes the curtains. It's ten in the morning and the sun is already eating up the lawns, applying a blow torch to the tin roof and the sides of the house. He sets up the electric fan from his bedroom and turns it low so that its breeze travels very lightly over Debbie Canova's face and torso. Her clothes ripple; he would love to get her out of them.

Now at least he can relax a little and get a good look at her. Stretched out on his couch, he sees she's as he remembers her, slender but strong, and not exactly a stick figure because there's some good meat on her bones – even for the new non-carnivore she says she is. In repose her hands rest lightly on her belly, the fingers sinewy. Her violin has attended to that. He can't help looking at the fingernails of her hands; the one with the nails cut back to the quick and the other with nails as strong and elegant as a courtesan's. Then there's that pinkish love-bite on her throat, courtesy of her violin. More than anything he would love to press his lips to that spot.

Debbie's face is relaxed, but is as dirty as a potato. So are her arms, not to mention her feet, which really don't reveal any white skin. Her neck is sticky with grime and perspiration. Tony eases closer to inspect the smoothness of her cheeks and the fullness of her breasts under her filthy peasant blouse. Her lips are parted, as sensual and red as the first time he met her. He thinks that even asleep, in exhaustion, she exudes the same fever of sex that aroused every male in Thornberry. Tony would like to slide his hand up between her thighs, feel the coolness of her skin before what he imagines will be the warm pulsing of her pussy. His prick is becoming very hard. He'd like to wash her clean all over, would like to do it with the application of soap, a cloth and his tongue.

If you've got fifty dollars you can treat me like a whore, I'll let you do anything you want to me.

How does a girl come up with a line like that? Tony has to go lock himself into the toilet. He jerks himself hard and fast, coming into wadded toilet paper while thinking of Debbie's sleeping face. He leans with his forehead against the wall, catching his breath, barely able to clean himself up.

He's got no answer for why she's here. He assumes she's run away from Phil the plumber, has left her home in Thornberry, but why did she decide to come to him? They had a few hours together, an interlude on a mossy bank by a river, and now ten months have passed and here she is. Debbie must have realised that she could have found him at home with a girlfriend or a wife by now, even a kid on the way. So what's this about? Is this a side-track along the route of some longer journey or does she think his home is her actual destination? Tony shakes his head and can't figure it out. That night he did ask her to leave everything behind and come with him. But it took her this *long* to decide she would? The fact is she's dirty, broke and alone. Tony wonders if maybe she just needs money. Fifty dollars could only be the start. If so, he knows he'll give her every cent she wants.

Shit, to be such a sucker, he tells himself.

He checks on her. Her slumber is so heavy he can see it would take something like an earthquake to wake her. So after twenty minutes of staring he drags himself away. He sits at the kitchen table and composes three short poems that he knows would be badly written for a fifteen year old; he searches for one or two lines that might be worth using in a song. Nothing. There's even a moon–June rhyme. Since returning from our country trip it's been exactly like this; he knows he's as empty as a witch's teats.

He flushes the toilet and checks on his guest, willing her to wake up. She doesn't so he goes and sits in the shade of the back step, where he tunes his guitar and tries to create something that might be the romantic musical equivalent of Debbie Canova. There's no rush, she's out like a light and it's probably better that she gets some sleep. The hot day shimmers and the inflated Santas and reindeer on the roofs of his neighbours' houses all look wilted and tired. What a fucking summer, he thinks, but within an hour he's forgotten the heat that keeps de-tuning his strings and has found a chord progression he likes. Against a doorstep his foot taps the beat. There are seven chords that he intermixes, sometimes reconfiguring them into a backward progression. A nice little bit of linking lead guitar here and here, not bad. There's an obvious melody line so he hums it, then starts pushing and stretching it, looking for the really unique melody inside this music, something that will make it memorable. He likes what he's doing so much he doesn't hear Debbie Canova behind him.

She listens, then returns to the living room for her violin.

With several expert plucks she checks its tuning, makes adjustments and returns.

The violin's scratchy tones catch Tony by surprise. Debbie has picked up the melody he's been half-humming, half-whistling and she's sticking with her instrument's deep, thick strings, giving the music real resonance; Tony could almost call it profundity. She accompanies his playing for a while then takes over.

'Drop that chord there, I don't know what it's called. And that one. Add something like it here, but sweeter. Then this nice turn-around here, can you do that?'

Tony tries and soon gets the hang of it.

'Good, now keep this rhythm,' she says, marking the new beat with her bare, black foot. 'No, like this.' Her foot stamps more urgently. Tony gives it his best and even warbles a few of those bad couplets he composed at the kitchen table, but what Debbie Canova wants for the part and expects out of him is more than he can handle. His compositions might be idiosyncratic, but when he meets someone musically his better he just doesn't know how to follow. His guitar playing falls apart and he feels like he's a three-legged dog trying to keep up with a greyhound.

Tony gives up while Debbie Canova's bow flies on its own wings. The bassy notes pour out, more Shostakovich than Tony Lester. It's nothing like what he'd started out with. Debbie Canova brings it all to a peak, but the magic's gone and that's it. She smiles at him anyway. It'll be better next time around, huh?

XX

He's kneeling beside the bath and while he soaps her back and takes in how good she looks naked and wet, she tells him she hitched for three days, maybe four. In fact, it could even have been five or six. The route to here hadn't been particularly direct. Bruno, the long-distance truck driver who took her most of the way, gave her two blue pills a few hours after he picked her up. They made her lose count of more than just days. He took a few every time he ate. She started joining in, also every time she ate. Or maybe it was more often than that. The world, she says, went funny from there.

'Poor, poor Phil,' Debbie mutters with a resentment that seems directed at herself. 'Abandoned in Thornberry, betrayed one hundred percent.'

'Did you leave him a note?'

'At first I was writing it just to say goodbye, but then I couldn't stop. I wrote pages and pages. Everything I think's wrong with him. From the way he smells to the noise he makes when he eats to the way he uses his cock. Maybe he still wants to come find me, I am his wife after all, but I don't know, after he reads what I had to say.'

Tony can't even imagine what pages and pages of personal critique would do to his own psyche. He imagines curling up into a ball. 'You told him where you were going?'

'We never lied to one another. Not really.'

It's not the news he wants to hear. Apprehension crawls through his gut. 'You mean, *exactly* where you were going?'

'Well, not the address, but yes, to see you,' she nods. 'One night while he was having sex with me I said your name. It wasn't too hard for even him to work out that I fell in love with you.'

Fell in love. Tony's part-thrilled, part-horrified. What will he do when Big Phil the plumber turns up at his door? He's already thinking that maybe they can move, take an extended vacation in the mountains or at some beach, somewhere a long way away. And go there fast.

'Poor Phil, he's gonna be so lost.' Her voice is still sort of spacey and Tony has the impression she's still somewhere between this world and the next – the one that exists at the end of a long trail of blue pills. 'Faithful to him since the day we met, then as soon as I'm out of his clutches I do it with just about the first man who comes along.'

'Me, you mean?'

'Huh – oh, by the river? No. I just wanked you off, didn't I? I wasn't thinking about that. It's Bruno.'

'Bruno?'

'Bruno and his drugs. God I wonder what they were? He picked me up at a bus stop a couple of hundred kilometres west of town. Two truckies already gave me lifts but neither of them was coming this way. I was just sitting there thinking how to get where I wanted to go and an eighteen-wheeler pulled up down the way a bit and I saw a man hurrying into the toilet block. When he came back and climbed in, there I was in the front compartment. Nearly scared him to death. His eyes were already all sort of big. Really, he must live on those pills. You look like a ghost, he said. I said, Flesh and blood and I need a ride. He was heading south-east. South-east is more or less heading here, but he had to take the coast roads to do his pick-ups. So it took a long time, lots of stops.

'He's one of those kinds of guys who drives in a hurry and rides every radio station along the way. Sometimes I'd give him company with my violin. We talked a lot and were quiet a lot. He told me he had two girls and a boy and he was a widower. I didn't really believe that. Funny how many divorced men and widowers I meet. But he was okay, he was fun, and when all of the riding in the truck started making me sick he pulled over to let me spew, and sat it out for an hour. Then he gave me some white powder in a plastic cup of water. That made me feel better. I lay down in the sleeping compartment behind the seats. When I woke up he told me he liked me and asked if I'd consider giving him something in return for this free trip. I played him two sonatas on the violin. That made him happy, but it wasn't exactly what he had in mind.

'By then he was crunching more pills, I mean really crunching them between his teeth, and I felt like my eyes were dropping out of my head. My arms and legs wanted to fall off. Day three I think it was and those pills had me seeing skeletons dancing in the highway and giant red dogs running beside the truck. He said, These are blue too, but they're a little different. They should sort you out.

'I tried one. After ten minutes I felt like my legs were melting. I was tingly and warm all over. My toes were curling up like someone was kissing my neck and my nipples felt like they were going long and hard as bullets. I was sure there was a blush going all the way up my throat and through my face. Bruno said, Wow,

I've never seen anyone react like this, and so fast. Are you okay? I told him I was. He asked me again if maybe I wanted to give him some sort of repayment. I remember it was the middle of the night. The moon was up there somewhere. No clouds. I told him to pull over. We went around the side of the truck away from the road and I leaned him back and told him to open his pants. I took out his dick and rubbed it so that he came standing right there. Three seconds and three great spurts of a load that landed in the dirt. That was all he needed. Then we were on our way again and he was happy as a lamb.'

Tony soaps Debbie's shoulders and watches beads of water slide down the ridged curve of her spine. He knows that if she were to take out his dick for him and rub it right now, he'd spurt in all of three seconds too.

'So you didn't do any worse than that?'

'Well, that's the thing. Not until about an hour later. I took another of his little blue pills. It made what I was feeling worse. Or better. We were driving again and the thought of him exploding in my hand sort of stayed with me. There's something about that. Bruno was forty-five or so and not really completely unattractive, though his body odour was getting a bit rank. But I couldn't stop thinking. While the truck hummed and vibrated down the highway, I just wanted to come in my seat. Then I asked him to pull over again.'

'And he could do it?'

'Poor Phil. If he knew. After the first time, I let Bruno have sex with me whenever he wanted to. It was kind of dirty and fantastic. We did it all the way here. Well, not right to your street. He dropped me off at a train station about twenty klicks away. Gave me the fare too. I was sort of relieved and sort of sorry to say goodbye to him. I told Bruno I was heading on to Switzerland.

It was the first place that came into my head. Don't really want Bruno the Truckie coming after me. And he thinks my name is Virginia Bach. I don't know, that was the first name that came into my head too.'

Tony lets out a long, pent-up sigh. He wants to have sex with Debbie Canova, but a bigger and better part of him wishes that glazed, distant look wasn't in her eye. He thinks this is the reason she's prattling on so, telling him things he'd much rather not hear. She's not quite with it and he'd like her to be a bit sharper – and maybe for a little more time to pass since her dalliances with Bruno. He asks the main question that's on his mind.

'Debbie, why are you here?'

She doesn't have to think about it. She's been thinking of the answer such a long time.

'When I met you and your friends, it just seemed like the perfect way to be. Minstrels travelling in their truck, you in your ute, bringing music with you wherever you went. And I liked you and what we did in the grass by the river. You were so gentle with me. After you let out that shout, that *howl*, you said, Come with me Debbie, just say to hell with everything and come with me. Most guys, well, you know, they'd say that before they ejaculated, not after. Even Phil when he's nice to me, after we do it he just clams up. I'm not so pretty any more, not so alluring. I'm just there and I think he'd prefer it if I wasn't. My mother used to say, When the balls are full the brain is empty. I've added a corollary. When the balls are empty the brain moves onto something else.'

Tony nods in sympathy but asks, 'What's a corollary?'

'Doesn't matter,' Debbie sighs. 'I think I'm feeling sick again.'

He helps her up. She emerges dripping from the bath and just makes it to the toilet bowl. Sliding wetly down onto her knees she hangs on as if for dear life and heaves and heaves again. Mostly it's just juice and dry-retching. Tony holds her hair away from her face. The smell is bad, but not as awful as some of the things he's experienced in the dumps we played, or within the confines of travelling in close quarters with dirty rock-pig musicians. He's happy to be lending a hand, it makes him feel strong and protective of her. Okay, let Phil turn up here, he thinks, just let him.

After she's done, Debbie Canova sits on the floor of the bathroom with her wet messy hair hanging over her eyes and cheeks. He wraps a towel around her shoulders. She presses another into her lap.

'That was so disgusting. You must be wondering what you ever did to get someone like me arriving at your door.'

'No, it's cool.'

'I had a bag of things, but I lost it somewhere. Change of clothes, underwear, lipstick, notebook with I don't know what ideas written in it. My purse, my bankbook, everything's gone. All I managed to hang on to is my violin and bow.'

'Well,' he says, 'how long do you want to stay?'

That worrying vagueness is still in her eyes and now that she's conducted a symphony of spewing, her face is beyond white, it's translucent. He can see the tiny veins beneath her skin. She gazes up at him. Debbie Canova had said that she'd fallen in love with him, but even twenty-two year olds can be predisposed to adolescent crushes, can't they?

'How long can I stay?'

'It's up to you. It's really just up to you.'

'Really? You don't mind?'

She must think he lives the big rock star life of parties, travel and women on tap like water. Inside himself, Tony promises: Fuck it, stay forever if it's up to me, Debbie. Just forever.

XXI

ut it wasn't up to him and roughly three or four weeks set
him straight. He was right about the crush thing; infatuation
has a short shelf life and forever's what they're doing to me. My
corporeal experience was that love and forever were two words
that should only go together when applied to romance novels
or close-knit families, and even those would have to be the lucky
ones.

From the front of the chapel I can see this whole flash-second
of memory inside Tony. Poor guy, it's like an entire reliving. Debbie wanted to have sex with him as soon as they were out of the
bathroom, but when he took her to bed she wriggled in his arms
and opened herself wide and was comatose within about thirty
seconds. This is okay, he told himself calmly. Better she sleep that
vagueness away.

The next morning she wasn't vague at all, only ravenous. She
went into the kitchen and with trembling hands cooked up everything that was edible and had never possessed a face or an anus.
Only when her stomach was sated and his was full to bursting,
did they get it on. Unfortunately, it was no Barry White moment.

Things were anti-climactic; Debbie was so excited she came almost as soon as he penetrated her, and his belly was so distended that he thrusted like an obese pensioner and somehow managed to ejaculate into her navel, which she didn't appreciate. No matter, they told one another, there's always tomorrow. Or tonight. Or this afternoon.

I came into the story a couple of evenings later when I stopped by. I had to look twice. I couldn't believe Debbie Canova from Thornberry was in the kitchen doing Tony's washing up or that an appetising aroma was in the air. Tony's house usually reeked of sweaty socks and fried meat or sausages. He told me Debbie had cooked an elegant mess of rice and steamed vegetables. I ought to try some. Even though it sounds basic as dirt, he said, it was the best dinner he'd had in a long time.

'But what she's doing here?' I asked, and she emerged from the kitchen into the cottage's pokey living room with a bowl of her dinner for me. She wore one of Tony's shirts, her legs long and white, her feet small and graceful as a dancer's. White-blonde hair fell across her shoulders. Those blue eyes, well, it would be hard for even the Pope to stop gazing into them.

When she stepped, there was a slight pop to her walk; it was the walk of someone with a zest for life. She's happy, I thought, I can see it a mile away, and there was no need for Tony to tell me that they'd spent yesterday and today copulating like rabbits. While Debbie returned to rattling the pots and pans in the kitchen, Tony did it anyway, his voice an exultant whisper.

'The first few times, not so good, Max, but we kept at it. Then, wow, you wouldn't believe it, things just sort of clicked. She comes and comes. And she's fascinated by – you know – she just loves to see the stuff coming out of my dick. I've never known a girl like this.'

I ate slowly, having a hard time enjoying a meal made by someone whose hands had been so thoroughly coated in my singer's
sperm. Debbie joined us while I was idly pushing the food around
my plate.

'So what are you going to do?' I asked her.

'Well,' she looked at Tony, 'this young man and I are going to
compose together. We're going to make some new music for the
band.'

So that was the second half of what went wrong between Tony
Lester and Debbie Canova, and any bad feelings I might have had
about my band being colonised by a stranger were immaterial. It
was no Ono–Lennon thing and didn't come into the equation.
The problems were what happened between them. The music
part came second because the main thing was that despite what
Tony had told me, after the first few weeks Debbie realised she
and her new man were simply not very physically compatible.
She liked him and gave it her all, but it was never as good as she
thought it ought to be. Soon enough her ardour cooled. The
more it cooled the more he wanted her.

She tried to make music with him and that didn't work either.
Tony wasn't the genius she'd taken him for. Why had she thought
that way? She couldn't even remember. Her expectations had
been fuelled by not one shred of reality; he was a crush all right, a
means to escape suffocating in Thornberry, suffocating with Phil,
suffocating in an environment that valued a violinist less than it
might value the worth, say, of the NASA space program.

Still, at first they spent their nights staying awake, talking.
Tony knows that was the best of the short time they had together.
She nuzzled his neck and his ear, he lapped at her nipples and her
sex. He put a love bite onto the right side of her neck in order
to balance her violin's proprietorial kiss with his own mark of

ownership. They told each other secrets and hopes, those nights stretching into the sorts of gold-rimmed dawns that made them finally close their eyes with satisfaction and happiness. No wonder it was *she* who put her mark on Tony forever; they had a week or two of fire followed by an interminable slide into ashes. Those days were the most important of his life; nothing would seem so sweet for him again: not the birth of his children, the making of his first million, or the annual good news from his doctor, who tells him he's healthy as a horse and will likely live to see his one hundredth birthday.

In the chapel with my dead body a few arm-spans away from him, Anthony Lester, millionaire, wonders what it is he really misses the most about Debbie Canova. He knows how ridiculous it is to fetishise the memory of a girl, but it's been the inescapable story of his life. She had a sensual smile, but so have plenty of others. Her lips begged to be kissed, but so do those of professionals and amateurs alike on porn websites. It was exciting the way she planted her feet and created melodies with her violin, yet certainly not as exciting as seeing the crowns of his children appear at their births. They had heady sex in his bed, but in the many years since then he's had a ton of that too, and some of it a lot better. So what was it that put the hook into him? The way Debbie watched with concentrated fascination when she jerked and sucked him onto her breasts? No. Tony knows what it is: she came into his life at the point of his deepest low, when everything seemed finished and his future as empty as a politician's promise. He was at his most open and most vulnerable, then suddenly here was someone who promised a life for him – a Life – and he'd believed her. She was redemption from failure. She hadn't been a girl, she'd been Hope.

Right?

Tony puts his hands to his eyes and bows his head. No, fuck it, he's lying. He's rationalising and knows it. The hook was this and this alone: during those good nights in each other's arms her quiet voice would whisper in his ear, and with those whispers she would effortlessly reveal her soul. That was the thrill. He'd never, ever, had a sense of touching such a thing before.

Never did again either, he thinks now. Not even in himself.

XXII

They tuned their instruments, guitar and violin, and set out to play and compose. In the playing Debbie Canova was such a natural virtuoso that Tony had to endlessly yield. Not only that, but one day when she gave him some lyric to sing beside her violin's melody lines she stopped, head cocked.

'What?'

'I thought I noticed that before. But you're singing too much on your throat. Don't you know to project from your diaphragm? You won't have a voice left in five years.'

She was right. He went to the primary school down the road and asked the music teacher to teach him how to sing.

That summer's heat was building daily and by Christmas all the roads would either melt or crack open. Tony sang his heart out; at least the music teacher showed him how not to sing his vocal chords out. Still, he hadn't quite got the hang of it and the sounds he made were a little more strangulated than usual. We persevered, inveigling Pete Kelley to give the band his best, last shot. It was university holidays anyway – and we brought in a new bass player, a nice hippie sort of guy who kept quiet except to ask every now and then, 'Is this the riff or the chorus?' His name was Stavros and his beard reached to his chest. His fingers were nimble and he had a good ear. Listening to Debbie play, he would nod to himself, 'Cool. Cool.'

She'd taken over. In the practice room we all simply waited for Debbie to tell us what to do. We wanted her to tell us. Things weren't so bad; whenever she was amongst us the band seemed to cohere, seemed to have a point, and the point to which we cohered was her left hand moving spider-like over the frets of her violin. To her existing repertoire, in a few short weeks she added new pieces of infinite lightness and we filled in the background like a behemoth of a machine, an iron giant pursuing a butter-fly. After a handful of particularly fruitful sessions we all nearly came to believe we could make a breakthrough, get famous, have a career. Just make the whole thing work.

Then we nearly did.

Without the band knowing about it, not even Tony, not even hearing about it in their conjugal bed, Debbie Canova tracked down a record producer by the name of 'Iron' John Tempest. Over more than twenty years this man had broken a half-dozen acts in a variety of music forms, including country, rockabilly, be-bop and Mersey-soundalike pop. His main claim to fame, however, was that he'd produced one rock album that for the first part of the Seventies was the prototype for all that followed, at least till punk and disco came along and kicked everyone in the teeth.

She went to see Iron John with a cassette tape of four songs she'd composed and that we played on. How she'd bluffed her way through his door and persuaded him to listen to this music, I don't know, but he hadn't had a hit in years and was probably always on the lookout for that magic new sound. Her smile and cheesecloth shirt probably hadn't hurt. The first we knew about

Debbie Canova's doings was when she organised us to be ready in my home practice room on Christmas Eve.

Sweating like hogs and waiting for who knew what, this man with iron grey hair and an iron grey beard and iron grey bushy eyebrows swept up in a swirl of terror walked in. He wordlessly sat himself in a corner beside our electric jug and coffee cups. Debbie said, 'John's going to listen to one or two songs.' All of us, including Tony, assumed he must be either a newly discovered uncle or maybe the proprietor of some venue Debbie hoped for us to play in.

Our tunes, or should I say Debbie Canova's, had no titles. Few had lyrics, giving Tony not very much to do. We learned the songs and gave them their names in the order she'd presented them. There was DC#1, DC#2, DC#3 and so on, all the way now to DC#11. Admittedly, everything over the number seven was pretty haphazard and only part-formed, but we'd created a lot of music in a very short space of time, and some of it was good.

Our audience sat in the corner and didn't move except to occasionally rub a hairy brow.

Tony sang when required and when not required tried to look involved. A tambourine shake, a go at a pair of marakas, even a few strikes of a cowbell. Debbie's violin leavened the thunder-wall of the band behind her. It was a sort of light and shade. She called it her *chiaroscuro* and was always doing this, quietening us down no matter how dark her melody, and we came to see that her instincts were good. The more quietly we played the more menacing it sounded and the songs became *music*.

After several numbers I saw that Debbie meant us to finish our small performance, or audition, or whatever it was, with our longest piece. We thought it our finest. When it hammered to its conclusion, she looked toward this still-life of a man. We all did. He lifted his chin; that meant he wanted more.

Tony said, 'Okay, great. Let's do a couple of our old ones,' meaning his own compositions.

Debbie stepped forward and pivoted the violin into its place, tucked in hard under her chin. 'This one isn't finished yet, so I'll just get Max to accompany me, but I'd like you to hear the melody.'

Debbie Canova gave me a nod and I understood what she wanted me to do: I was to follow her cues. What's the beat? With three fingers on my shoulder she gives it to me. She raises her bow and an arpeggio becomes a melody line. It's a simple twelve bars, and at the end of the twelve comes another twelve then another. Then she starts varying things dramatically, playing with the mathematics of her music's structure. Debbie's quick glance holds me back; she doesn't want me to come in yet. What is she, crazy? My palms are itchy. I want to start, but no, her melody is spreading out. It has tributaries that move away from the main theme, then wash back in again. She's like a woman bringing herself to a sexual peak and not letting her man thrust inside her until she's good and ready. My heart actually thumps with anticipation. This music is deeper and more resonant than anything she's played before, and the rest of our DC-numbered compositions sound like nursery rhymes by comparison.

Yet nothing is written down and it sounds note-perfect exactly the way it is. To my ears there are no glitches she has to cover up with clever playing. This is pouring out of her like the radiant heat of a fever, then I get it, the fever is a flame and soon it will be a fire, and Bang! there's her glance.

In I come. Her face is pink with exertion and something that looks like the start of a tremendous orgasm. The sheer satisfaction of joining her makes fresh perspiration break out on my already sweaty brow. I haven't felt this connected to music since the first time I was able to hold a beat beside a scratchy piece of vinyl that Concetto San Filippo played for me. The good thing too is that I'm barely there. I'm inside of this and outside of it as well. Debbie Canova is the same. The music is making itself. She looks at me straight now, no more sharp glances, just a strong and steady stare as she stands right in front of the kit. It's like the gaze between Tony and me in the best of our times, singer to drummer and the world in between, but this is even better, even more intense. We lock eyes, lock music, we shoot straight and true and then there is the heart and the final note pierces it like an arrow.

The room hums into silence. I stop the ringing of my crash cymbals with my hands. I'm bathed in sweat and full of awe. So is Debbie Canova. Things like this don't happen every day. I can see the way her bow trembles in her hand. For what's just happened, this is why we try to make music.

Our audience gets up and straightens a sore back. He goes outside and smokes a cigarette. Tony goes and puts the kettle on. Breathing deep, Debbie Canova takes a wooden chair and sits almost facing the wall. Tony gives her a glance as if to say, What's this all about? He gets nothing in return.

I take off my t-shirt and wipe my face, under my arms, the back of my neck. No one looks at me, except Debbie, who gives a quick look and a small smile. Something makes me feel like I've betrayed my compadres. I have to make my own cup of instant coffee. As I'm adding sugar, our audience re-enters. He makes nothing of this unhappy silence. He speaks as if continuing a conversation, his voice growly as a talking dog's.

'So we'll do this one fast. We've got no background and no profile, but the material's good. I say we hit it running. Let the record do the talking. You—' he says to Tony, 'you I'd replace if I had time, but I don't. You—' he says to Pete, 'we'll have to mix down. One day you'll learn there's more to life than distortion. What's the electric guitar bought to music? Amplification. And that's all you've got. You—' he says to me, 'you're good, you're okay. Christmas tomorrow, so we're lucky, we can get in straight away. Next studio booking I've got starts New Year's Eve so that's all we get to make you guys right.'

'Hang on,' Tony says. 'Right for what? What are you talking about?'

'Who's the clown?' this grey stranger asks Debbie, then before she can answer he tells Tony: 'To record the album. I'll do the mix. I'll add some instrumental bits and pieces if none of you guys is a multi-instrumentalist. That gives us three days to get the tracks down and three days for me to do the engineering.'

Only Debbie was clear about what he was saying. The rest of us must have been thinking we were imagining it. Someone is actually going to let us make a record, a full long-player? And in three days?

'Who are you?' I ask him. 'And what makes you think we can record all of this so fast?'

He tells us his name. That shuts us up. 'As for speed, ten years ago Black Sabbath did their debut in three days and how long do you think it took Led Zeppelin to record their first album? Thirty hours. Thirty fucking hours. What, you can't keep up with that?'

'But Christmas Day?' Pete asks.

'Unless you're too sentimental,' Iron John replies, and with that he strides out of the airless fug of the practice room.

'What time tomorrow?' Debbie calls after him.

His disembodied voice: 'What time do you fucking think?'

XXIII

Sparrow-fart, dawn. Christmas Day dawn, that's what time. Dumbfounded to find ourselves in a recording studio, we bashed around in those unfamiliar surroundings and conditions for three days and three nights, emerging bleary-eyed into some other dawn. For all our labours, time seemed to have frozen, except that Christmas was over and a new year was nearly here.

We'd done take after take of every song we had, and by that I mean the ones by Debbie Canova. Iron John was as interested in Tony's music as he was in gonorrhoea. He twiddled those multi-track buttons and levers in a control room that looked like it should have housed a half dozen engineers like him. Yet, even so, he'd been perfectly in control and full of energy. We did very few overdubs and even some of those were done by John himself. He knew Tony was a limited singer; he didn't like Pete's guitar sound at all; and as for Stavros, he simply pretended our Greek hippie didn't exist. Whenever we stopped for toilet, drink or lunch breaks, Iron John picked up one of our instruments and recorded the part the way he wanted it. For two songs he even took it upon himself to downturn Pete's guitar from the key of

E to C#, and made the bass player follow suit. It was a trick he'd picked up from Black Sabbath records and he did it so that there would be a deeper tone to offset Debbie's violin. Pete wouldn't touch his Gibson that way; Iron John played it himself.

We didn't have time to rebel, but Pete called him a cunt anyway. Stavros told Iron John it wasn't cool to take away a musician's own outpourings. Iron John could have told them to disappear, but he didn't. I knew that when he had our stuff to himself he would rearrange it, re-record it, re-anything he wanted to do with it. Pete and Stavros would cease to exist, if need be. Maybe I would too. None of us mattered in the slightest.

So, we'd been relegated to being not a band, but a bunch of not very desirable session players. The artist was Debbie. The heart was Debbie. On our first day there he presented her with an electric violin to try to use. It was sleek black and must have cost a few thousand. I saw her legs practically go weak, but she couldn't master such a new way of making sounds so quickly, so she had to stick with using her aunt's old Czech stalwart and promised to learn how to play her new violin as soon as the sessions were over. Then she'd front up to his office and play it, just for him.

Iron John nodded, that would be good, because, of course, he was in love with Debbie Canova. He didn't give her puppy-dog eyes or follow her around or even try to talk to her all that much. His love showed itself in the exquisite care he took with everything that had to do with the sounds she made out of her violin. She'd discovered, really, that second part of her own equation – the complementary particle that would allow her work to blossom into its fullest creation. Iron John was what she'd hoped Tony Lester would be. Even more than that, because John could make her music into a product, which meant he could liberate both it and her into the world. No more suffocation. She was on the verge of absolute freedom.

He told us he'd probably only end up using about twenty percent of what we'd recorded. Even then he'd be splicing good bits of takes together and getting rid of the rest, crafting the music 'Like an artisan', he said. It seemed he didn't think very much of us as our own craftsmen.

'But why so little?'

'The forty-minute rule. Best vinyl fidelity is under that length. Any more and you sacrifice sound quality – and that's what we won't be doing. I'm aiming this album at about thirty-three to thirty-five minutes.'

So we had no idea what he would use and what he wouldn't; no idea of the running order of the tracks, except for this: the one we'd improvised in the practice room, just Debbie's violin and my drums, that would be the final, epic number. A full instrumental, no Tony. The others wondered if they would end up appearing on this record at all.

Christmas dawn we'd signed contracts over instant coffee and dry biscuits. Iron John made us do it before he allowed us to step through into the soundproof recording rooms of his studio. None of us much thought about those pieces of paper again, at least not until there was nothing we could do about what we'd given away. John Tempest, we later discovered, owned everything we made; the music; the acetates, the eventual album, and all musical copyrights in perpetuity; he was even proprietor of the Manoeuvres name. First thing he did was to change that name to Xodus. He even paid us a breadline wage in lieu of a percentage of sales, that is, he only paid us for three days' work, no holiday penalty or overtime included. The only one who would get anything extra was Debbie Canova, because she was the listed songwriter.

There never was anything extra. Not for us, for Debbie, or even for Iron John. He had paid for the recording and the manufacture and distribution of our 'product' – and saw just about no return for his investment. Not the worst washout of his career, but bad enough to signal that the Eighties would not herald a return to his glory days.

When I think of it now, a few things did come out of this project, and they were these: it well and truly ended the band; it brought Debbie Canova to me; and twenty-five years later it gave me the chance to die at the feet of a young girl named Ash.

Maybe there are worse things, right?

XXIV

Tony shifts in the pew. No wonder he came to hate that record.
Would never speak about it, even when it had a minor resur-
gence fifteen years after its aborted first release. A low budget
Australian horror film in the mid-Nineties used segments of that
haunting last track over a number of sequences featuring young
women being sliced and diced by a psychopathic half-man, half-
beast creature with no face. Every time *No-Face*'s vengeance hit
the screen Debbie's violin soared and my drums pounded. When
I saw the film I felt sick. Even though Debbie was long gone by
then I knew she would have felt as brutalised as those characters.
Violence was the one thing she found utterly unforgivable. For
his part, Iron John wouldn't have worried about what any of us
thought: in his mind it was probably all a happy miracle that the
worthless music rights he owned finally brought in a dribble of
cash.

For a year or two after the film, in vinyl revival stores, people
sought out copies of the album by Xodus (featuring Ms Deborah Canova). Iron John had entitled it *DC* and the front cover
was a gauzy close-up shot of Debbie's face and beautifully naked

shoulders all the way down to the tops of her breasts. Just a little behind her was my grainy face, then the others, but the focus was so intentionally blurred there was little sense of their individual features or whether these musicians were eighteen or eighty. All of us were superimposed upon a grainier stock picture of a ragged multitude travelling an endless road through some burned out, war-ravaged countryside. *Exodus*. The back cover was a straight black-and-white band photograph, us standing behind the featured artist in a white peasant blouse and gypsy skirt, a violin bow in her hand. It made us look like the sort of cheesy polka outfit that plays beer-barrel singalong versions of popular songs. There was no insert. In his misdirected confidence Iron John had ten thousand copies printed. Three weeks after its release it was in every record store's markdown bin. Within six months you could buy it for ninety-nine cents. A year, fifty cents – if you could find it. Oblivion for two decades, then film and/or music buffs were paying up to forty or fifty dollars for an old copy.

One person who didn't purchase a copy either new or old was Tony Lester. He'd never had the album in his collection and never would. He'd read a tiny article in some magazine where Iron John spoke about the possibility of a CD re-release with extra tracks, but it never happened. The only thing that ever did happen was that an abridged version of that tune made it onto the film's soundtrack album; cutting it down like that leeched most of the life out of the music anyway. The *No-Face* soundtrack compact disc was going for ninety-nine cents last time he looked, then it disappeared. Good, Tony thought then and still does. The whole thing is better wiped out of existence.

Once the recording sessions were over, Tony finally understood that Debbie Canova didn't care for him. She'd found his presence stultifying, as suffocating as Phil's and maybe even more so. He'd been sulky and angry every minute of every one of the three days; after all, he was finally in a recording studio, but for all the involvement he got to make he might as well have been the tea lady. Together they caught a bus home in the sweltering mid-morning of the day we were released from that studio jail-cell. Her exhausted body rocked beside his, they were shoulder to shoulder, and when he took her hand it was limp. Tony turned her face to his and saw that he wasn't inside those blue eyes. He knew who was.

As soon as they arrived in his lounge room, both of them putrid with three days' confinement, he stripped her half-naked, pushed her face-first over the back of his couch, and made brutal, forty-five second love to her from behind. Like the fifty dollar prostitute she originally asked to be. He ejaculated with vehemence, slapping her ass and her limp, long hair around. Then he cried. Debbie barely uttered a word, moan or sigh.

We'd had our three days of recording. It was December 28th. She escaped from him a few nights later, New Year's Eve.

It was six-thirty in the evening after nearly two full days asleep. There was some kind of New Year's party I was supposed to go to, but my head was fusty and when I heard the soft rap on my front door I knew I wouldn't be going anywhere anyway. Since that experience with her in the practice room downstairs, when we'd played for Iron John, the gaze between Debbie Canova and me had remained constant. Those days in the studio everyone had seen it; Tony included.

I opened the door. When I'm lucky someone will turn up with a bottle of something strong to drink or good to eat, but Debbie Canova stood half-lit under the naked porch bulb and she was carrying her violin and bow. Her eyes took me in. Her hair wasn't white any more, but a sort of new, messy honey-blonde. She looked great. Nothing could stop the smile that spread like relief across my face; it was mirrored in hers.

She said, 'I thought you might feel like drumming into the New—'

Her voice cut off as I pulled her to me. I held her by the waist and kissed her. She gripped her violin and bow as her hands went behind my neck and her heel locked my leg to hers. I felt her violin pressing against my back; Debbie rubbed against my prick. I can't remember saying anything. I don't think she did either. My heart thumped but the whole thing was easy because I didn't love her, not yet, only desired her.

We went into the most open room of the house. The night was hot, airless and still. The dining room had a long, sliding wooden window that opened to a patio twelve metres high. My back yard stretched away and down for a good half acre and all of it was full of shrubbery and trees. Above us, the stars were out and the moon was porcelain. I sat in a hard-backed wooden chair. Debbie sat in my lap facing me. Behind her was the universe of the night sky. Whenever she kissed me I closed my eyes and saw another dark universe, the one her lips and tongue created. At first she was sort of feverish, but I calmed her down, slowed her down, caressed her shoulders and ran my hands across her back. She took one of my hands and rubbed it into her breasts, and that was nice, but she was too eager.

I lifted her off me and she sat looking at the view while I got us some drinks. I said, 'Does Tony know you're here?'

She replied, 'Tony knows I'm gone.'

I nodded. Didn't need to ask much more. This was the place it was right for her to be. She looked at me and I felt my legs all warm and weak. I wasn't so much in control after all. The curve of her cheek, the slender line of her throat, her long hair and blue eyes — I took a sip of red wine then threw the glass out the window. It thudded into the grass far below. Debbie sort of laughed and did the same thing. She bit my bottom lip, shook her hair into my face. I picked her up and fucked her there, against the window sill, on the dining table, on the hard tiles of the patio where my aunt and Conny used to sometimes arrange their chairs and watch the Milky Way, drinks and crackers at hand.

Later, when we were in my bed, the ceiling fan was turning slowly. She pulled me over her. We locked eyes again. Her fingers dug into my arms, urging me further and harder. This time she bit her own bottom lip. I was falling. Debbie Canova. My Debbie.

In the morning her head was on my chest. We were damp with the heat of maybe thirty-eight degrees. What woke me was the banging on the front door. I knew it was Tony. At least he'd waited till morning. I eased Debbie's head onto the pillow and shut the bedroom door behind me.

The first thing to hit me was the stench of stale booze. The second was a hunk of branch he'd found somewhere in the street. It was heavy and split open a line down from my forehead, across my nose and through my upper and lower lips. He swung again and missed, drunk, almost knocking himself out in the process. I backed up, bleeding, eyes watering, holding my face while Tony howled like an angel thrown back into Hell. When he couldn't hit me again he hit the walls with that branch, and when he hit a wall too hard and the branch reverberated out of his grip, I grabbed him by the shoulders and pushed him ahead of me down the corridor. He tried to punch and kick and bite me, called me every name under the sun. He fell down. I picked him up. He kicked me in the shin and spat at me.

I wouldn't hit him. I'd hurt him enough already. In his drunken abandon, plates smashed, glasses, the front of a cabinet, and a kitchen window shattered to a hurled can of baked beans. A muesli packet erupted against a wall. A bunch of bananas hit me in the face. The whole place was a mess and he wasn't about to stop.

I tried to shout above his shouting, trying to get him to calm down. No use. He overturned the dining table and chairs. When he was satisfied with that he turned on me again and tore at my face. I only just managed to keep out of his grip. Warm blood was in my eyes anyway and the clammy morning ensured that it ran like soup and didn't congeal.

'Come on, Tony, stop this. Get yourself together.'

He wasn't listening. If anything, he was just warming up. When he picked up one of those heavy dining table chairs and tried to smash it over my head, just as he must have seen done in a hundred westerns, well, that was enough. I wrestled it out of his grip. In the process he fell over again. I had a stroke of genius and used that chair to trap him under it. I sat down. He wriggled and kicked but couldn't get out, and so howled some more.

Debbie Canova crept out of the bedroom and into this farce. What a sight it was that met her. If ever a picture was needed of what a rock band's break-up might look like, well, this was probably it.

XXV

Finally on his way out of my house, Tony said, 'How could you do this to me? You of all people. My friend.' He glared at me and added '*Traitor*' with just enough inflection that I'd know he would never have done something like this to me or anyone else. A knife went into my spleen, but I wasn't about to back down. From that moment to this I never saw him again, except when his picture was in the paper or on the back of his self-help books.

Iron John couldn't have cared less about Manoeuvres or Xodus or whatever-we-were breaking up. In the new year he spoke to Debbie about putting a backing band together and going on tour to try and save the disaster that was the record. Of course she liked the idea. Her as leader, me on drums and a team of hand-picked musicians with us. Iron John even volunteered to be a guitarist in the band, or a sound mixer-cum-engineer-cum-anything that would keep him close to her. For he would soon break the news to Debbie, news she hadn't quite been aware of. It came many months after the break-up, many months after she'd moved in with me, many months into the tour rehearsals with our crack new musicians.

All that time we were like one person, together almost every minute of every day. On the nights I went to my shelf-stacking so that we had a little money to feed ourselves, she'd be practising with her new electric violin, discovering the sounds it was capable of making. When I came home she was always waiting, didn't matter what crazy hour of the morning: freshly showered, hair like silk, her smile welcoming and warm. Supper would be ready and the bed made up with fresh sheets. In those days, nights and early mornings Debbie Canova's love fell as easily as rain.

I was happy; I still believe we both were.

Eventually, she thought her new electric violin skills were good enough to demonstrate, and she'd even composed a new piece called 'DC-E', for Electric. She arranged to go to Iron John's office and play it for him through a small practice amp. I stayed home with the fellows of our refashioned Xodus and hoped she wouldn't be gone long. We boys sweated through several difficult portions of the DC repertoire as Debbie Canova set up the amp in Iron John's office and checked her tuning. Feet planted, she started to play.

Distracted and pensive, he stopped her after two or three minutes.

Debbie thought he must have been worrying over tour dates, venues, and wanted to talk things through. His bookings had been going well enough despite the absolute bomb that was the album; we could thank the power of who he was – or used to be – for that. Disappointed he wasn't interested in her proficiency with an instrument he himself had given her, she waited to hear what he had to say. Instead of dates and ideas came the confession he'd bottled up for too long.

'We should be a team, Deborah. Imagine what we could do. Your talent and my smarts. Your looks and my contacts. The way you compose married to the way I arrange. From the day you came in to see me, I knew. We could make this big. We could make a fortune. It's us, Deborah. Us. You don't need to be in a band, you just need musicians to back you. We can pick that up anywhere.'

He had more to tell her of course, the grey nightmare of his eyebrows jumping as, for the first time in his life, that iron in his heart was peeled away. What did he say? Things I knew myself. That when she planted her feet, lifted her violin and tucked it under her chin, and when her bow swooped and the music soared – so did the tired spirits of men. For Iron John specifically, when she smiled at him, well, he just felt his old blood roar. She was young, he was middle-aged, but together they'd get things that were timeless: success, money, influence. They'd be that new kind of royalty the world adored: rich celebrities.

Poor Iron John, just like the rest of us, but with nothing but glass beads to attract Debbie Canova.

'What about Max?' she asked. He stared at her. 'Max' barely rated a comment. 'But I love him,' she said. More staring.

Then: 'DC, I love you. That's all that counts.'

She wanted to make music and be successful, but in the process she hardly wanted to give herself to a man she didn't want to be with. She'd had more than enough of that in her marriage. Even if she hadn't been with me, he didn't have a chance. She found him physically repulsive, emotionally stunted, and she baulked at the bad, old-man sort of smell about him. No amount of money or success could make her want him; no amount of money or success was going to make her leave the man she already thought she loved.

Gamely, she did as she'd done with Phil the plumber in her ridiculously long farewell letter. She told all of this to Iron John – all of the truth. Gamely, but gently too and very, very kindly. She thought the worst that could come of it was that he'd put an end to this personal angle to their professional relationship and insulate his feelings. He'd forget about it and from here on in he'd treat her the same way he treated everyone else: slightly contemptuously, but as one professional to another. He'd look to the business. After all, she had a contract with him, and wasn't there an album to salvage? Then of course there'd be the next one and the one after that. The music wasn't going to dry up and the story of their brilliant partnership wasn't going to end just because she didn't feel the same way he did.

Well, she'd misjudged what sort of a new world she was in and to whom she was telling the truth.

Iron John's office was in an alley off another alley that housed his recording studio. The back of Brisbane's Fortitude Valley; a dump inside a bigger dump. Above his office, a sweatshop clothing factory using Italian and Greek migrant women to stitch shirts together. The vibrations of the machines sometimes drowned out his very telephone conversations. On his floor, some sort of coffee and tea importing firm that never seemed open. Below him, a rat- and cockroach-infested warehouse for second-hand goods like musty pillows and broken bedding. So Debbie and he were, to all intents, alone. Even Iron John's secretary only worked two days a week, and this day wasn't one of them.

She'd put the violin down and had switched off the amp. Now she was sitting in an easy chair, uncomfortable with the situation, but certain the problem would pass. He was behind his desk. Debbie had listened to what he had to say and he'd listened to her reply. His eyebrows had stopped working and his face was – naturally – quite, quite grey. Iron John made a series of non-committal grunts. He stood up and nodded sagely, as if, yes, this was understandable. Debbie, what am I but a stupid old man lovesick as a schoolboy? So now let's get back to work.

He came around the desk and before she could even understand the torment raging inside him, he literally threw himself
upon her. The sheer shock and bulk of his immense weight
knocked the breath out of her. They fell to the floor. Like a
drowner, she gasped for breath, but she couldn't get air into her
lungs. As she struggled, voiceless, he ripped away her skirt. It
inflamed him even more to see she wasn't wearing underwear.
He sent his raging face deep between her legs, Debbie clawing at
his hair. Then she was breathing and almost able to scream, but
he pushed her down and punched her in the stomach. She felt as
if her body would explode. She kicked out with her legs and his
fist ploughed into her again. And one more time. That stopped
her. She'd never experienced such pain, had never been struck in
the belly by anyone, even as a little girl playing too-rough games
with boys in the schoolyard. She knew that to avoid it again she'd
do just about anything.

Eyes squeezed tight, she felt his cock push inside her, then he
was ramming hard, and he was muttering too, muttering the
same word over and over. What was the word?

'Debbie – Debbie – Debbie.'

This wasn't enough. He didn't possess her enough. He pulled
himself out and rolled her onto her stomach. Phil had begged her
for this part of herself, but she'd never let him. Now Iron John
forced his way in, using his own saliva to make her take him. He
ripped inside her and as he ejaculated his head reared up and a
long gasp tore itself out of his chest and throat. His face was
a rictus of agony. Looking over her shoulder, Debbie had only a
glimpse of him; still, the merest glimpse of that tortured face was
enough. She'd never seen anything like it. She thought he was
dying, actually dying. Unfortunately, there was no such luck. Iron
John's body shivered and then his great weight went limp and

fell onto her, pinning her face-first to the floor. She was suffocating again. She beat the palms of her hands against the threadbare material of the office rug, but she was a sparrow trapped beneath a boulder. Finally, however, he pushed himself away. Sat on the floor beside her flattened body, gasping. She was gasping too, and afraid, almost too afraid to move.

He reached for his coat draped over a chair. Found a pack of cigarettes and a steel-plated lighter.

'Have a smoke.'

She pushed herself onto her side, curled herself up into the foetal position. All her hair curtained her face. 'Don't smoke.'

'Have one with me, Deborah.'

The tone of his voice said he might not be finished yet. She straightened herself. Forced her body into a sitting position. Every part of her seemed to either sting, throb or cry out. Added to that, her hands weren't just trembling, each finger individually quivered. She'd never felt so scared, so terrified. What a word – terror. She wanted to vomit, but made herself take a cigarette, to play along. It was time to placate the monster in him, not aggravate it. This was how she'd get out in one piece. Time to be clever. She'd smoked sometimes with Phil, especially when he rolled joints. All right then, anything to keep Iron John calm. She forced herself to be calm too. The worst was over.

He gallantly lit her cigarette for her and they smoked, both still sitting on his office floor. To protect his rug, he used the cupped palm of his left hand as an ashtray. He encouraged Debbie to tap her ash into it, too. She did, but never looked at him. She wondered why there were no tears in her eyes – but there was that awful swelling pain in her belly, and down below her belly, and in her back passage too. She wondered if she was bleeding, and if so, from how many parts. She wondered how she would make her way home to me in this condition. Above all else, she wanted to lock herself in a room and be quiet and alone.

'Want to go now.'

'Stay a while. Just stay a while with me. I'm sorry. I'm sorry about what I did. Too much. Got too much.' He lit himself another cigarette. This time, when he offered her one and she didn't want it, he didn't push her. 'Just sit there a second. I want to get something from my desk. Promise me you won't move, won't try to run out. You can go in a minute. I just want to talk to you about something. Okay?'

She nodded. 'But then, I have to go. Max is wait—'

'Shut the fuck up with Max waiting.'

A tremor ran all the way down her back. She cringed from that voice, feeling how it made her bowels want to go loose. Debbie didn't think she could get to the door before he'd catch her anyway. She didn't think that if she screamed anyone would hear. Now she watched Iron John get to his feet. He pulled up his trousers, but she noticed he forgot to zip the fly. She put a hand on her belly. If she breathed shallow, not too fast, the pain looked after itself. She was feeling stronger. What could she hit him with? There didn't seem to be anything at hand.

Debbie looked up at Iron John. All these months of working together, making plans, arranging music, and he was a stranger. Nothing like the man she thought he was. As unknown and unknowable as the nightmare monster you can't quite picture when you open your eyes.

Oh, but she'd picture him all right, all the way to the end of her days. That was something she was certain of.

At his desk he opened a drawer. What — a knife or a gun and a bullet to finish her off? He fished out a bottle. She saw the label. Brandy. He returned with two small, dirty glasses. Poured the brandy and leaned down, offering her one. She knew she had to take it: the man loomed over her, heavy as a bear, fly undone, but that awful prick of his tucked away inside.

'So drink up.'

She took a sip and it burned all the way down, but when the brandy hit her stomach it actually soothed the pain.

'DC,' he said, reaching out to caress the hair that fell over her face. 'You've been teasing me since the first, since the day you came in here with your cassette. The shy little looks, the little flirts, they work on a man. Gets to him sooner or later. You've been doing this since you were a kid, right? Back home in the bush, with all those dumb little boys who fall over every time a sweet girl like you bats her lashes. Gets you things, correct? Gets you what you want. Girls learn, I know that, I don't blame you. On the one hand you act like sugar wouldn't melt in your mouth. On the other hand, well, you give out the opposite and poor salivating mutts like me follow at heel. It'll be brilliant on stage and with the media, but in daily life—' He shook his head. 'So let's be real. Let's work with what we've got here.' He took a deep sigh, then another. Swallowed his brandy. Poured again. 'Drink up, Deborah,' he said.

Debbie took another sip. She knew how this was softening everything that had happened to her. Rape? But, miss, you did have a post-coital cigarette with the accused, didn't you? Even a shot-glass of brandy. Brandy? Now that's a sophisticated drink for a common rapist, isn't it?

How much longer? How much longer before she could get out of this hell-hole? This was the end and she knew it; this made everything over; the next move had to be a train, bus or eighteen-wheeler to somewhere else. Somewhere a long way away and her with a new name that no one would ever know. Max would come. Max wouldn't. She already wasn't sure she cared – because escape is escape, running is running, and she wanted to run now. She stopped the fantasy that she could pick something up and smash him down and save herself.

'Why do I have to stay?' Debbie bit the inside of her cheek hard. Now the tears wanted to come; now she wanted to cry like a frightened four year old. Please, let me out, she wanted to plead. Please set me free. Instead: 'What more do you want to say to me?'

He hadn't left his fly unzipped by accident. He reached in and tenderly pulled out his lump of cock.

'Well, the other thing left to tell you is that just by looking at you, I'm getting hard again.'

XXVI

What sins did I commit when I was alive? I did plenty of bad things and if I did anything good there should have been more. The worst bad thing – this. I listened to Debbie Canova and didn't call the police.

I knew something had happened. The Xodus inductees had gone and Debbie was dropped off by a taxi, something we couldn't afford. She came in shaking. Her mascara had run and though it looked like she'd tried to clean it up some was still smeared across a white cheek. She didn't fall into my arms, but went straight for the shower. Soon, steam filled the bathroom. That water must have been about as hot as a human body could take it. I watched her through the steam, washing endlessly, scrubbing hard as if to censure her own skin. She emerged pale and shaky. It took a lot to get the story out of her, but as she made herself do it she stopped trembling. Colour returned to her flesh. Coldly and dispassionately, she explained what Iron John did to her. Her words were like slow footsteps that you had to follow: we start here and we end there, and it's a place like Hell. There was nothing cold and dispassionate in me. My eyes, my skin were on fire.

She took me in. 'Max, I don't need another animal in my face.'

Her voice was quiet, but her gaze pierced me. I pulled myself together, though I wanted to hurl things across the room. She huddled in on herself, but even so she kept talking, thinking it through – and the reasoning in what she had to say was clinical in its analysis and as cruel as a needle in a vein.

How was it a rape? she asked. After the smoke and drink, she'd let him do it to her again, in the normal place. She'd made him withdraw just as he came; he shot into her wispy pubic hair. Finally that was enough even for Iron John's long-withheld passion. He was done; he gave her the taxi fare home.

I was listening hard, but despite my act I hadn't calmed down. I hid the fact of my burning blood. I wanted to look after her and make her better, but most of all I wanted to see Iron John suffering agonies that I made for him. The robotic cool of Debbie Canova's voice, the way she told me the thing was finished and over, and I'd better make myself forget about it, well these were things that just shredded my insides.

She said, 'Don't try to make it worse, Max. I'm begging, please. Let it be through. Just hold me. What will make me feel better is to go to sleep, then one day soon we'll talk about where we're going to go and what we're going to do, because I'm not staying here, and there is no more band and maybe no more music, okay, do you understand that?'

Then that icy resolve was cut by a single hot tear that ran down from her right eye.

'This isn't going to haunt me. There's always a new life waiting when the old one's over. And this one's over and everything about it is done. All right, Max? All right?'

I nodded, but it wasn't. Nothing was over, nothing was done.

I was listening to her, but only heard the voice in my heart that wanted hate and more hate. We drank some whisky and she fell asleep. That was the moment a sensible man would have rung the police. Let the law handle such matters. No. I drank another shot, then drained the bottle while Debbie Canova's body trembled against me. I'd seen three circles of bruising in her abdomen. Iron John's fist. Thanks to the bottle sometime later I lost conscious-ness too, but my last thought was, I'm gonna get Iron John, that bastard – you bastard.

Because here you are.

The speechifying and the eulogising haven't started yet, so he's not late, not technically, but who would blame him if he was a little tardy, because he moves slow as a snail, gasping, stutter-ing along with a walking frame and his eldest son to help him. So many years later and he's remembered me, of course he has, who wouldn't remember the one who put you into premature old age? His pastime these days is checking newspaper obituary columns. How nice for him to have finally found my name there, ahead of his.

I stayed with Debbie Canova, John. I stayed with her day-in, day-out for two weeks. No doctor, no medicines, no outside help at all. She went into a rage whenever I suggested any of these things. Quiet was what she wanted. To be left alone. I imagined sexual disease and her insides ruined. I watched those bruises grow darker as if they were getting black all the way through her. I wiped blood from her anus, not sleeping at night for worry-ing about what you tore inside her and how would she ever be the same? When she wanted to be held I held her and when she couldn't stand human contact I sat in the next room, in case I was called back again.

One day she was a little less inclined to keep staring into the dark corners of the house. That was good. That was the day I could make an excuse. Told Debbie a half-truth: I needed to go out and rehearse with a band I was soon meant to play a few dates with. It was strictly fill-in work, a chance for some cash in the hand. The band's drummer was in hospital getting bone spurs taken off his knees, and I hated their style of bullshit synth-pop-rock anyway. 1981, that's what it was all about. The rehearsal would take a few hours, but I told her I'd need to be away most of the day.

With plenty of time to think about it, I'd already found what I was going to bring with me. Amongst the dusty tools and garden paraphernalia left under the house there was a mattock with a broken head. Just right for you, Iron John. I used a hammer to separate the tool head from the handle, which was a little splintered in the middle, but still good enough. The swing of it was true, close to what the swing of a baseball bat must be like.

Debbie didn't see me drive away. She was at the kitchen table looking at road maps, planning by which route her new life would start. Maybe it would be our new life, but I wasn't so sure; a distance had grown between us as vast as a desert. Whenever I tried to speak with her she seemed even more absent. It was as if she was withdrawing into her own world where she was safe. On the outside she was almost totally inert, but on the inside the rape, violence and fear ate at her; I know that. If I'd understood the first thing about matters people take for granted today, like support groups, say, or therapy, I would have gone looking for them — but in those days I knew just about nothing about anything. I was a drummer. A useless drummer. You were a man of the world, Mr Iron John, but the wider world outside of my life was a mystery to me.

What wasn't a mystery was this: what you inflicted on Debbie tore her apart, but what made the emotional wound so deep was the way she'd been betrayed by her twin. Or her hope of a twin. That was you, you old fool. You were the person she'd been looking for all her life, not me, not Tony, not Phil or any other man. *You* were the perfect other side of her coin, the one who could free both her and her music. Didn't you understand that? Couldn't you have lived with that? Why wasn't it enough?

Let me watch you suffer a little, old man.

Iron John comes down the centre aisle with the heavy clump and thump of a new septuagenarian who has already endured three hip operations, each of variable success. His son, Tom, a fortysomething who couldn't care less about music in any form, wishes his father hadn't chosen to come to another old fart's funeral. There have been plenty he's had to escort his dad to, each occasion more mind-numbing than the last. Tom helps him get to an available pew. It's Tony Lester who slides over and makes room. Neither man so much as glances at the other; even if they had, there wouldn't have been much opportunity for recognition. Iron John doesn't look anything like Iron John, and the inconsequential singer of Manoeuvres is less than a memory in the old man's head; added to which, of course, Tony never even had the chance to know about what this ancient and legendary figure from rock music's antediluvian times did to Debbie Canova.

Once Thomas Tempest has Iron John's brittle and bony backside down, he parks the walking frame beside the pew and goes to stand at the back of the chapel. There, he sighs at the thought of having to endure Pink Floyd all over again.

Meanwhile, Iron John stares at my coffin with eyes made hard and small by age. His face is deeply lined, it's a worsted leather, and there's no sign anywhere of the untamed grey hair that used to be his trademark. Even his eyebrows are gone. He is wizened and full of hate, as if he has eaten himself up from the inside. He can't look at anything, but the polished finish of my coffin.

He sees that day one more time and as I tighten my grip on his odious thoughts so do I.

It went like this: yet again, Sammy, this seventeen-year-old, lead-fingered guitarist out of a band Iron John was recording, called Devil's Tail or something like it, had fluffed the lead guitar break of the last track they were working on. Iron John's temper exploded and he threw the band into the alleyway where they could smoke their joints and be out of his plentiful hair. While they were gone he told the engineer to roll the master tape. Iron John sealed himself behind the sound-proof doors of the studio, plugged little Sammy's hand-me-down Gibson into the bass player's amp so the SG could get a little more throaty bottom, perched himself in a stool by the microphones, and, on cue, nailed the wailing, growling, twenty-three-second lead break that had been driving Sammy and everyone else crazy.

Through the glass, the engineer gave him a grin and a double thumb's-up. Perfectly done. Iron John unsealed the door, returned to the desk, and mixed volumes, mixed instrument positions, then sent Jimmy into the alley to call the boys in.

'We managed to splice three of Sam's solos,' he lied. 'I think I might have got the effect you've been wanting.'

The engineer rolled the new master of the song while Iron John went into the alley to smoke.

I shut the door behind me, he thinks now. I didn't want to hear that fucking song one more time. That was my mistake.

Iron John brings a trembling hand to his hard little eyes. In his hand is a white handkerchief, the type he always has to carry. He has to carry it because, just as his lower plumbing is not what it used to be, his eyes leak incessantly. There's nothing any doctor can do to help him. While what's left of Iron John curses my corpse – 'I hope the worms eat your eyes first, your hateful fucking eyes' – others in the chapel are tremendously moved to see this old man openly grieving the loss of someone who must have been a great friend.

Fuck it, he remembers, I shut that door. Stupid me. I leaned outside and wondered if I really wanted to ever record another miserable little band like this again. One more bad group of so-called musicians blowing one more otherwise good recording session would just drive me nuts. So long since I made a hit. Time to sell the business, the studio, that's what I was thinking. Since the girl, Debbie Canova, nothing had much taste left, anyway. Nothing had any sizzle or spice. My life went cold the moment I let her leave my office. And in my office, when I was on the rug with her and saw that soft pussy, and rammed into it with my iron cock, I wonder, did she come? Then the other way. Did she? She must have. DC, I must have made you come. You remember that little fact, wherever you are now.

Then, in the polish of mahogany, the old man Iron John sees how the younger Iron John lit his cigarette, took a drag, looked up to the corner of the alley where it met with the next, and saw his avenging angel coming.

He was on me in a flash. I fell under the blows. What was it, an axe handle or something? I don't exactly remember the pain, but I'll never forget the crunching and cracking sounds my own bones made. He worked on my arms and my legs, but the worst of it was on my hips, both of them. He attacked them like a madman. With those big arms he really did some damage. Fucking drummer.

I remember I asked for mercy. His mercy, if he had any, was that he didn't bring that thing he was swinging down on my head. That would have killed me, but what he did to me, mostly that killed me anyway.

Then, fast as the cunt arrived he was gone, and the band fell into the alley grinning like loons because they loved the magic I made in their recording, and so they loved me, Iron John, yet another rock band's hero and guru. Little Sammy was grinning to split his spleen: he thought he'd actually made the leap from bum to rock-God guitarist – but the kid looked up the alley and he saw a crumpled heap of a man and that broken thing was me.

They all rushed over. What happened? Who did this to you?

I don't know, I told them, pain whistling through my teeth. Some crazy, never saw him before. Black like the ace of spades. A boong after my money. What else could I have said? That drummer, boyfriend of Debbie's, he would have told the police exactly why he decided to do this. So I stuck to my story. I went away to recover, but I never really did.

Now Iron John addresses himself directly to my coffin: 'I never really did recover, Max, except for one thing. I'm still here on Earth and there you are in Hell.'

Then Iron John stops himself as the Pink Floyd music fades and a bearded man I've never seen before emerges from the back room. This man makes a small production of coming reverentially to the side of my coffin, where he bows his head over the lid. I look up at him. He closes his green eyes in what everyone will think is silent prayer, but is really the well-practised move of a thorough professional. The eulogy he's prepared for me, a complete stranger, is folded in his coat.

I turn my attention back to Iron John. Seeing nothing of the present but everything of the past, bent and frail in his pew, he says inwardly, I raped her.

It's the first time these words have ever coalesced and meant something. For a moment he's as injured as if he stepped on a nail. A moment of clarity. But, but why am I thinking like this, he wonders. Another fucking funeral and this one for the cunt who half-killed me, and instead of feeling good I feel like the eye of God is looking into me. The eye of God, or the eye of—

No, no, no. I'm crazy. The eye of nothing. There's fuck-all out there. You die and you're dust and everything you were stops like a dog dead in a ditch. The only eye is my eye. Max is gone. That drummer is dead.

But why do I feel like he's still watching me?

XXVII

My celebrant's name is Buddy. His eyes remain closed in impersonation of prayer, but what this man is thinking is what will he say in ninety minutes or so when he faces the head-mistress of his teenager daughter's Christian-values school? The headmistress will ask him to explain why Kelley has been selling marijuana to her fellow students. He knows he will bow his head as reverentially as he is doing now, but he also knows that, inside, he will be fuming.

I say to him, Come on, tell that headmistress the reason your sixteen-year-old daughter has been selling MJ is because she's ferociously alive and utterly bored by the tight-assed aesthetic of your tight-assed school. And add, if it feels good, You stupid bitch.

A flicker of a smile crosses Buddy's lips and he has to try hard to suppress it. This thought that just crossed his mind, courtesy of me, is deeply rewarding. He'd love to say all of it. Indeed, why not? The divorce agreement might have established that he doesn't have a voice in what school Kelley attends, but nowhere does it say he can't tell that school what he thinks of it.

If we lived in a free and loving society, he rehearses, you wouldn't get your knickers all sweaty because of something every kid does. And anyway, it's my fault. The girl found my stash and decided to make some money.

He doesn't quite know why, but this does happen sometimes; sometimes he leans over the coffin of a stranger, as he's doing now, in preparation for delivering the eulogy, and a warm wave of love grows inside him for this person about to be buried.

They're talking to you, that's why, Buddy.

He waits another moment so that the congregation will see that he's not rushing. Buddy Bettridge has been in this burying game a long time. Even his ex-wife now works for a rival firm. Ah well. He gives a nod over the coffin lid, nose close to the flowers, and as he walks to the podium he reaches into his coat for his notes. However, always a true professional, he's memorised what to say to the bereaved about me. In front of a mirror at home, for an hour before bed, that's his way. To not be prepared would be to not care, and he does care, this burying business keeps his debts paid.

Buddy has a neat, full beard. I hate neat full beards, but he seems a decent-enough guy. He turns his head away from the microphone, politely clears his throat, and leans in.

Buddy speaks, but I hear Debbie Canova's voice as she says, 'I know it was you, Max. What is it with men? To destroy, only to destroy. Did you think I'd thank you? Did you think I'd be proud of you?'

XXVIII

Debbie Canova found out about what happened to Iron John two days later when it made the six p.m. news.

She was waiting for me on the couch, curled in on herself. I'd been stacking shelves in the supermarket, starting at eleven p.m. It was now four-fifteen a.m. No suppers prepared any more, no fresh sheets on the bed and the coverlet turned back, no love falling like rain. I expected her to be fast asleep, but there she was in the living room. An ominous weight settled on my shoulders as soon as I entered the house. That day all those years back when he'd been in his worst rage at me, Conny San Filippo had been waiting in just the same way.

Her hair was no longer white, no longer honey-blonde, no longer even the mousy brown it became when her colouring started fading. It was dyed inky black, like fake raven's feathers. The texture of a night sky when there's no moon to see. I crouched in front of her, took her hand and with the other brushed away lank strands of that unfamiliar hair. It was like looking at someone who wasn't quite Debbie Canova. Her face was pasty and her breath was sour. The blue seemed to have washed out of her eyes.

'Made a change, baby?'

'I know it was you, Max. What is it with men? To destroy, only to destroy. Did you think I'd thank you? Did you think I'd be proud of you?'

I tried to touch her face. She jerked away and slapped my hand. Her bottom lip quivered with anger.

'I said it had to be over. I said I couldn't take any more, that I didn't want things to be worse. I begged you, really begged you.'

I couldn't hold back any more. 'Why would I let him do that to you? Why wouldn't I make him pay? What sort of a man sits around and does nothing after that?'

'Stop shouting! Max!'

'I'll shout! I should have killed him! He's lucky!'

Then the room reverberated into silence. Tears ran down her face. She took a ragged breath.

'Listen. I will be going. Alone. I can't live with you. You disgust me. John went mad, but you, you had time to think about it. You planned it and you enjoyed it. Tell me it isn't true. Tell me you didn't *like* doing it.' She gritted her teeth and I saw the hard muscle in her jaw working.

'Don't act so quickly,' I told her. 'Just wait.'

'Men are – insufferable.' Debbie closed her eyes. 'Thank you for letting me stay in this house.'

'Please.'

'Please what? No. No "please", no nothing. I thought I loved you, Max. I really did and I really tried. But after what you've done. Never.' She kept shaking her head then looked at me, one hard final stare that was as brutal as what I'd done to Iron John. 'Don't you see? The man I loved couldn't do this, so I couldn't have loved you.'

I backed away from her. The words repeated in my head. I left the house. The words came with me. I drove away and tried to sleep in my car under a tree in a park, but instead I got out and watched a lousy new day break over this city's muddy river.

The next night I had my fill-in job with that synth-pop-rock band. When I went home to prepare, Debbie was well prepared for leaving. There were just a few bags, nothing heavy at all. We exchanged no words that I can remember. I left the house, the front door ajar after me.

At the show I went through the motions, played everything by rote. By now she was going. Had gone. No movie-moment goodbye, no last minute change of heart while strings swelled.

Everything was wrong about the gig. The singer was a dickhead in a foul mood. The crowd, no better. For some reason, partway through, he wanted us to do an extended jazz version of 'Smoke on the Water'. It must have been the band's little bit of fun; at least it was one part of the night I might have enjoyed. Concetto San Filippo was by my side for the seven-minutes-ten it lasted. He was laughing. I wasn't. Even improvising my way through the song, I should have played better. It shocked me to learn exactly how much technique I'd lost since concentrating solely on the hard-driving boom-boom of rock music.

The singer drank about a bottle of vodka, switched from singing to screaming to shrieking, then he tried to do a Jim Morrison and asked who wanted to see his prick. He got pelted with paper cups and warm beer, and so did the band. I was soaked. The singer couldn't take a hint. He pulled out his slug. It was a worm, a veritable worm, and he danced around like a marionette. The audience howled its derision. He threw up and the show fell apart somewhere three-quarters of the way through. I packed up my things, swearing at anyone who came near me.

Didn't quite make it away. In the car park, someone was waiting for me. It crossed my mind that this was a police officer, or maybe a detective or something, and the road to jail was about to begin. Iron John must have finally disclosed who'd attacked him. What do you get for extreme assault and battery these days?

Not to be. Instead, it was a neatly dressed guy a lot younger than me.

'Hi,' he said. 'You're Max.'

He was a scrawny stick of nothing with bad acne and a tendency to stoop. Very pasty white skin and floppy, unkempt hair. He looked like the type to sing enthusiastically in Christian revivalist meetings. I opened the car and was shoving bits and pieces of my kit in. It would take me four trips to get everything, one of the main disadvantages of being a drummer. Hard to make a running exit, but there was no pleasure in knowing I'd be heading to a ghost-shell of a home.

'I've heard you're a good drummer, so I came to see the show.'

'I hope you enjoyed it.'

'It was, quite possibly, the worst performance I've ever seen. But you did do that jazz thing.'

'Another shocker.'

'The band put that on for me.'

'Why? Who are you?'

'Jamie Lazaroff. My grandfather played with your father, with Conny.'

'Bullshit. I knew who he played with and there definitely was no "Lazaroff".'

'No, not *I Pinguini*. Long time before that, when he started in this country. The first outfit with James Jones. Jimmy "Knock-out" Jones and His Incredible Sixteen-Piece Orchestra, right? My grandfather and your father were great friends.'

164

'He was my stepfather.'

'Well, I never knew the details. Anyway, I wanted to hear you play. We need a drummer.'

'Who's "we"?'

'A bunch of us. It's up to about twenty now. We're all studying at university, but every one of us is a jazz enthusiast and wants to keep playing. So we've got this little collective going. We do gigs all over the south-east, under different names when we need to, because we create little pick-up bands as required. With whoever's available when the gig comes up. That way we all get to work, but only when we want to or need the cash. Want to join?'

'How old are you?'

'Nineteen.'

'Nineteen? What's a nineteen-year-old know about anything?'

'I know enough.'

'Do you? Well, Jamie Lazer-what, here's something you should know. I'm twenty-five and I'm not at university and I don't play jazz.'

'We're short of drummers who can really swing.'

'What *the fuck* makes you think I can?'

'Your father – I mean your stepfather – used to tell my grandad about how good you were. And now I've seen it for myself.'

I shook my head. 'Thanks, but whatever you saw, I think you can call it the end. This life is the pits. I've had enough. Over. You can make an offer on my kit, if you like.'

'Don't be ridiculous,' he said. He had a notepad and pencil in hand now, and scribbled his name and phone number. I read neither. He tore off the strip of paper and wedged it into my top pocket.

'Max, you call me.'

I slammed my car door. 'I won't.'

'Well, what do you want to do?'

The car park's security lights all went out, leaving my pasty-skinned companion and me in darkness. I trudged across the gravel for the next load of my equipment.

'Supermarket shelf-stacking, a specialty.'

PART 2
SOUL CAKES

I

Contented bees drank the nectar of summer and I curled up in my house drinking whatever came to hand. I spent entire days flicking through the absurd television channels of the early Eighties. At night I'd walk through the house like a drunken ghost, looking from room to room to see if anyone was there. Conny? Aunt Emma? Ma? Mostly I hoped it was Debbie Canova. Well, hope all you want.

It hardly seemed possible that I could miss someone so much or that the thoughts in my head could make me so physically ill. All the anxieties building inside had finally come to a peak. At the supermarket I worked just enough to cover bills and buy alcohol. To keep costs down, I ate less and tore the telephone out of the wall. Hardly used the electric lights; hardly bothered the gas stove. I filled out a newspaper classified form and put the Rogers kit up for sale. On good days, sometimes I'd sit in the garden my step-parents had taken so much care with and wonder why I'd let it turn into such a lousy jungle. I didn't care. Let the whole house go back to nature.

I was losing weight. In my mind, I always saw Iron John

writhing under my blows, could always hear his bones cracking. Debbie Canova was right to hate me for doing that to him; it was the action of a coward. Now I hated myself; at least Debbie and I could share that in common. The television news seemed full of bad things happening, but none of it bothered me, only what I'd done to that man. I was in hell while Iron John was probably off recovering in some luxury resort attended to by beautiful prostitutes and Swedish masseurs. At least that's what I tried to tell myself, but I knew it was a lie; nothing was going to diminish my actions. I understood why Debbie Canova left; it made sense. Who could blame the girl?

We'd had a good thing and there was no one to blame for losing her. Yet she was with me more than if she was with me. Memory became everything. Like this:

One early morning in the dead of winter I came home from stacking shelves, my body shaking and my eyes wet and sore with the cold. The house looked dark and quiet; she used to always stay up for me, but for once my Debbie must have been asleep. I didn't mind. It went beyond the call of duty to keep a supper on hand at such a ridiculous hour. I'd just crawl into the bed with her and get warm in a flash.

When I went inside I saw an orange glow beneath the living room's door. The house, the corridor, everything creaked with the wintry chill, but I could also sense a warmth emanating from somewhere. I walked down the hall and the timber boards groaned beneath me. Opened the living room door. There were three candles lit. One on each of the stereo's speakers and one on the low coffee table. Also on the coffee table was a spread of dips and unleavened bread, stuffed vine leaves and smoked cheese. A bottle of red wine, open. Two glasses with long stems. A record of Mahalia Jackson singing gospel. Debbie was on the couch covered in a soft wool rug. It was red. She didn't really need it because a kerosene heater was lit and its radiant heat made the room warm as toast. We didn't own a kerosene heater. We never could afford treats like this.

'Phil sent me my portion of the house sale. Not much after the bills got paid off, but enough to celebrate.'

'Hmm,' I said. 'And you waiting there.'

She slowly drew the blanket down from her chin, revealing her breasts, her white arms, her flat stomach. Then she pulled it aside and opened her legs slightly.

'And me waiting here.'

It was just after four.

She said, 'Why don't you sit down and let me look after you? I think such a hard-working man deserves a little TLC, right?'

More than a little. Everything Debbie Canova had to give. I was happy. I believe she was happy too.

Afterward she held tight to me. We lay on the couch under the blanket, sated, a grey chill dawn outside. I nodded off into a dream of oceans and iridescent creatures but she gently shook me awake, her mouth on my chest and her tongue licking and flicking at my nipple.

She stopped and pulled her head up to face me. Word for word, I hear her.

II

Don't go to sleep yet, Max, there's something I want to tell you. Let me look at you while I talk. Comfortable?

Guess where I was born. Yep. A town just like Thornberry. Well, at first, a long way outside of a town just like Thornberry. Country girl through and through. Learned to ride horses while other girls where getting on tricycles. Used to start my days feeding chickens, pigs and goats. And foals, whenever our horses delivered them. The good days were when the mornings started at daybreak, the sun starting to shine. The bad, when we had to be up in the dark mist and wet fog of our winter. I didn't mind, at least not when I look back on it like this. I was lucky. It was the going to school I didn't care for. Keep me in the fields of sorghum and I'm happy. The whole thing was beautiful until it went sour. Money, of course. Not enough rain. My father lost the farm and we had to move into town so he could work in the only place that had a job for him, the local produce store. Lucky he knew a thing or two about animal husbandry, even if he wasn't so smart at managing his income. He started in the store tending their birds and livestock. Mum got a job in the local bakery. They used to joke that now they didn't have the farm they were million-aires. They probably were, relatively speaking.

Still not so bad, really, but that's not everything about what went sour. We could have all lived with that sort of life, me too, but Dad had a friend in town and this friend started having sex with me just before I was fifteen. No one knew and I didn't fight it, not even the first time. I was curious. I liked it well enough, so maybe I should say *we* started having sex, not just him to me. That's the truth of the way it was.

I knew him from about when I was five or six. He was unemployed and at first used to come work on our property a little, but then he said he hurt his back and he didn't work there any more. His wife supported the family as a country solicitor and his home was free most days. When Dad moved us into town they became reacquainted; we only lived three streets away. Sundays we had barbecues together. When big games were on we had to huddle around one or the other family's television.

I never thought he was an unkind man. I even used to think I loved him. Way back he'd been a banker or something and did something bad with their money. He didn't go to jail. Instead, he couldn't work in finance any more. They moved from the city to our town and he stayed home all day and listened to classical records and read thrillers. He told me once he was an escapee. To remember it now, I think he was a prisoner, a prisoner because he just couldn't make himself move back to a city, any city, and deep down he didn't like our town at all.

When we got over being shy, those first few weeks of just going at it hard, quiet and blind, the way I used to see our animals doing it, he started to show me the way to do more interesting things to him. He'd do the same to me, and more. And he always said, Don't you for a second imagine I think about my

Roxie this way, because he had a daughter a little older than me. I hated Roxanne. She was a stuck-up, netball-playing little bitch, but she didn't even know I was alive. She had boyfriends galore and when she wasn't at school she was always off in some boy's car. Mostly I went over on sports afternoons; they were the easiest to get out of. Roxie was never there because other than being boy-crazy she was completely sports crazy too, and his wife, well, she was a workaholic. I knew why. There wasn't much love in that home. Added to which, she hated cooking and housework and left it all to him. So we didn't have to worry about her, just had to remember to straighten up, make sure there were no tell-tale signs of something going on, and make sure to wash things. Sex is a messy business. At least the way he wanted us to do it.

Mainly it was just that once-a-week thing. We never got caught. Never even came close to it. He'd write me love poems that I could read a couple of times, but I wasn't allowed to leave the house with them. He always took them back and set them on fire. You can guess why. Romantic teenage girls tend to blab. To teach me the lesson about how important it is not to blab, to never say anything to anyone, ever, he told me this fairy tale. Want to hear it?

There's a young prince consumed by greed. He wants to be king. He can't wait for his father to die so he can ascend to the throne and get what he thinks will be all the riches of Heaven and Earth. So, one night he puts poison in his father's wine and next day the king, who was old anyway, is found dead in his bed. The prince gets the throne. He's got it all. Being king soon proves to be better than he dreamed and unimaginable riches come his way. He even marries a beautiful and exotic princess from a neigh-bouring country, so now there's an even bigger kingdom for him to reign over, and even greater prosperity for his subjects who, of course, love their new king and queen.

And then this happens. The one thing he can't ignore is his conscience. He wants to admit what he did, get it off his chest, actually speak his crime because, despite everything, it's been building up in him and he's fit to explode. Can't tell the queen or a priest or a concubine. Sooner or later someone would let it slip and his life would fall apart. Even his poor innocent kingdom would go to ruin. He can't let that happen. What can he do?

So one day, holding his hand over his mouth to make sure the words won't spill out, he runs down the banks of a stream and, standing barefoot in the water, bending down, he lets the words tumble out in a rush. He tells the truth to the nodding reeds. Ah, that's all he needed to do, just unburden himself for one minute. Out it all pours. The truth gushes like that stream when it floods. There. The crisis has passed and his secret is still very safe.

But then. Ah, but then.

A group of travelling minstrels arrives by the stream and they've come to the kingdom for a very special occasion. So many years have passed since the murder of the old king that the new king and queen's only daughter is old enough to be married. Which is about to happen. There's to be a great celebration. Royalty, visitors, musicians and performers from all over have come to this most fortunate of countries in order to help make the festivities the most memorable ever witnessed.

One of these travelling minstrels wades into the water and carefully picks out the reeds he will make new musical pipes with, and he fashions them with all his love and skill. He wants to help create the most magnificent music the kingdom's ever heard.

The big day comes. The princess is married to a foreign prince. There's feasting and dancing. At the height of the celebrations the king throws up his hands and declares silence. His eyes pass over the jugglers, the jesters, the court musicians and all the minstrels who've gathered from near and far. Finally, his gaze falls upon one shy-looking young man. You there, play the most wondrous tune you can muster for my daughter. Play something full of life's truth.

Well, it wasn't exactly what the king meant, but it's exactly what he got. The minstrel stepped forward and with all his heart and all his skill he set to playing his new pipes.

What emerged wasn't music at all. Instead, clear as bells tolling across the kingdom, was this: I poisoned my father the king! I poisoned my father the king! Heaven forgive me, I poisoned my father the king! And in his voice too.

Well, soon enough, this horrible, worthless king was tried and hanged by the subjects who used to adore him. His body was quartered and fed to pigs, then the pigs were slaughtered and their remains thrown into the sea. All the royals were exiled to desert lands. They died the deaths of nomads and paupers. The kingdom disintegrated. Such was the effect of not being able to hold your tongue.

Now, he told me this story so that I'd know the value of secrets, and never, ever give my private thoughts away. He told me the future of our perfect little world was right in my hands. It was up to me if it ended up being destroyed or not.

For a while I was young enough to believe it really was a sort of perfection. I was young enough to believe that the attention a man gives says something about his heart. I didn't know how naïve it is to think this way. The day came when I learned my lesson, once and forever.

He always was a talker. During sex he liked to describe what he was doing to me, or what he was going to do to me. Soon enough he was whispering weird fantasies of what he'd like other men to do to me, or me to do to women. It did turn me on, but there's a difference between talk and action. One afternoon I went to his house in the usual way. He had visitors. I could tell they were friends of his from the city, not country types at all. They got down to it. Each man offered me fifty dollars to have sex with him.

At first I didn't know what to say, where to run, but then I looked at his face. At the expression in his face. I felt a rage rising up in me. Really, the sort of rage that could make you smash a mountain. That look in his face.

I took their money. I wasn't doing it because he wanted me to, but because I knew it would hurt him, really hurt him deep inside. And I was right. Soon his expression changed. It was like his own mind rebelled against him. Here was everything he'd set up, had planned and imagined, but he'd never really thought what the reality of it would be like. It didn't take too long before he got cold feet. He tried to stop it, but things were out of his control now. You know what it's like trying to call hungry dogs off fresh meat? That's how much hope he had of getting them away from me. And I didn't lift a finger or say a word that might make them want to forget it. I gave them what they wanted in exchange for their money. I wanted him to see it all and I wanted him to eat his own guts up.

Hurt, you bastard. Hurt bad.

So he stayed out of the way like a man witnessing a murder.

I went home with my one hundred dollars, more money than I'd ever seen in my life, but I was sick in my heart. I sat in the bathroom crying and then I tore the notes into confetti that I flushed down the toilet. Except it didn't all flush. My father came home and found some floating bits of cash. Now, there was a surprise. Well, I was in the world's worst trouble, and it was the only time I was close to getting caught. Then I thought, Why does this deserve to be a secret any more? How much have I really hurt him yet? Maybe not so much at all.

My father sat on the side of my bed, wanting to know where I'd got that money and why I'd destroyed it. So, it was like the king in the story. I was standing and I leaned down to my father's ear and whispered the truth. My father nodded gently, like a reed in a stream, and after I told it I knew that everything was ruined.

My father went to see his friend and he hurt him a lot. Three days later he left town. His wife stayed to sell the house then she moved away too, but in a completely different direction, taking Roxie.

That was my revenge, but in return I didn't have a home any more. I remember months of crying and staring out the window. I couldn't see anything and I didn't want to do anything. It was as if there had never been a farm, pets, livestock, or a single field of sorghum anywhere. One more thing was different too: my playing was better. All that anger, that vengeance, and my playing had improved. Huh. As soon as I turned sixteen I guess you could say I set out on the journey of my life. Some journey. I got as far as Thornberry and let myself be rescued by Phil the plumber. I am a fool, Max, an utter fool, and don't I know it.

But I'm telling you these things and you're smiling at me. What is it with you? The thing that gets me. What do you see in me that I don't? Or do you forgive every dumb step I took because each of them brought me closer to being here with you?

Whatever. I don't care, Max. This is where I'm staying. Right here. I'm sick of highways. I'm sick of doing wrong when I should be doing right. Here's a new secret that's bursting to come out. I have to say it. I'll whisper it. Lend me your ear.

You won't be getting rid of me, little drummer boy. Can you live with that?

III

I can live with that. Could have lived with that. And the answer
to what I saw in her that she didn't see was exactly what she'd
said: anger and vengeance coming out of that small frame, pouring from her violin and bow, transformed into music.

A birthday passed without her and another Christmas came
and went. During the day my rooms were sunny and at night
they were dark and nothing happened inside them. I was alone
and I had no friends left, not a single one. Sometimes I could con-
vince myself I was fine, then I'd start some simple activity, like
sweeping the floors or cutting down strangling vines in the front
entrance, and a wave would crash down on me out of nowhere. I
had a constant pain in my stomach and slept, at the most, two or
three hours at a time, then I'd walk around, then I'd try to get to
sleep again. When I couldn't stand the silence any more I played
records at top volume. None of them made me feel better. Each
piece of vinyl was tainted by a dream that hadn't come true; these
were the heroes I'd wanted to emulate and look instead at what
I'd become. Sometimes I tortured myself and played my copy of
DC; sometimes I hid the album under a stack of others.

Then the walls were too much for me and I started going out, to the lousiest drinking holes, to sit in bars with drunks and watch racing and boxing events on the television. That's when it started happening, just as Debbie Canova had told it to me. So much time had passed and still the truth was bubbling up, wanting to come out. I had to confess my crime, tell someone what I'd done. The first person I spilled it to was named Henry or Harry or something, but it didn't really matter who he was. All that was relevant was his hairy ear-hole, into which I poured the story of the breaking of Iron John's bones. For a few days after that I felt better, but it didn't last. So I told another drinker in another bar; then another night, someone else. It went on like this.

The thing is, these men I met wanted to listen. Their responses differed. One would say, 'Yeah, that's what I would have done if I had the guts,' while another would sigh, 'And you wonder why the world's so fucked, with people like you in it?' Many, more than I could have imagined, told me their own stories. Infidelities, acts of cruelty, petty betrayals and lives ruined by a split-second of unexpected violence. It struck me how these men seemed victims too, victims of nothing but themselves and the unbreakable cycles they'd created. At their core you found unhappiness, desperation and, more often than not, booze. These strangers and I would exchange our stories then need to move on; ashamed of ourselves, disgusted by the other, blindly seeking an absolution, or simple sense of brotherhood, that was impossible to find.

I told a stripper named Suzy Sunshine who'd taken a liking to me and wanted to take me home. 'Women need men like you. All this liberation stuff is bullshit. Men were made to stand up, and that's what you did.' I stood up all right, made an excuse and tried to escape. The last thing I wanted was to be thought of as some kind of champion. Suzy wasn't to be put off, at least not until she got me in her car and discovered my soft cock. I was definitely no champion to her after that and was kicked out of the passenger seat, left to stagger home.

My talking went beyond simply trying to get something off my chest. I wanted someone to punish me. The expected result finally arrived on my doorstep. One afternoon two men came to the house and showed me their identification. Someone had reported me. The two detectives drove me into the city watch-house and interrogated me for hours. Relieved, I confessed everything, probably the first time I'd done it sober. They kept looking at me like I was crazy; they checked my arms for track-marks.

'You're skinnier than Jesus Christ. What's your drug? It's really just booze?'

I agreed, yes, booze. Booze is my drug; alcohol is my Lord; my church is the lowest stinking bar you care to name.

It was clear they didn't believe me when I repeated my story as many times as they wanted to hear it. The confession just didn't wash. The weapon that might convict me was long gone — I'd thrown that mattock handle into the river. The detectives were annoyed at me for wasting their time.

'Says here, '75 you did six months in a prison farm for breaking into a bottle shop. They found you asleep on the floor. Psych report says you'd suffered a bereavement and were off your head with grief. Man who was your stepfather got killed in a single vehicle accident and you went on a binge. Lasted a week. In that store you drank the better part of a bottle of tequila then laid down. We were able to stick three break-and-enters that week on you. Now it's '82 and look at the shape you're in. What are you, going on twenty-six? You're a kid but your life's fucked. You tried to get any help for your problem?'

I said, 'I did it. I did it I did it I did it.'

His partner replied, 'Then tell us why the victim, Mr Tempest, supplied a very clear description of an individual who looks nothing like you. Not even your big toe matches. Why? Because his attacker is not Caucasian. So what makes you want to tell us this cock-and-bull story? You one of those people who likes to confess to crimes they didn't commit?'

I told them the reason I'd done it was because I didn't like the man.

'Anyone else you don't like who better watch out, Killer?'

I made sure there was nothing in what I divulged that could have hinted at a girl being a part of the tale. Debbie Canova had begged for it to be over. Wherever she was now, she was far away from all of this. I wasn't about to let her be coerced back to be questioned or to give evidence in court or something. So even I could understand how I must have sounded like I was off my head. Ravings of an alcoholic. They didn't even invite Iron John in to see if he'd pick me out of a line-up. Unlike the king Debbie told me about, I blabbed but received no punishment. That's the difference between fairy tales and life for you.

IV

The process of lifting me up started with two red stickers.

One was attached to the rates bill, another to the electricity bill. I'd missed their due dates and when I checked my bank balance to see if I could pay them, I saw I was a long way short. Even living frugally needs a certain amount of income. I could have sold Conny's prized EJ Holden Premier, of course, but even though he'd died in it I hadn't had the heart to get rid of it. He'd loved the thing, so instead the minor damage was repaired and it was always ready in the driveway. I even kept the radio tuned to the AM station he liked, the one that played his style of music all day and night. I rarely felt strange driving around in that vehicle; if anything, the leather interior with its musty, aged smell made me feel good. It was all Conny. I was going to keep it.

No one had shown any interest in buying my drum kit. Someone was missing out on making a smart purchase, it was a great setup. I'd have to find another way to make some money. First thing to do was get my expenses down even lower than they were now. I finished the last of the whisky in my house and swore off buying any more. The very thought of that made me sweat; those detectives had been right. I had a problem.

I was only doing two or at most three nightshifts a week at the supermarket, but really needed more. They didn't have the work so I went to a rival store further down the road. There they could give me seven graveyard shifts straight, if I wanted them. I signed up, barely thinking about it.

The work was as mind-numbing as ever, but I liked having a new purpose. It was a simple one: earn enough to pay my bills, otherwise lose the house – and that was one thing I would never allow to happen. So I spent my days and nights in blameless sobriety, but always with a gnawing hunger left in my belly, reason being that I still couldn't bring myself to eat properly. After the graveyard shifts, my daytime sleeps were short and jagged, a funk of sweaty twitches and bad dreams. Worse, the people who used to be close to me seemed hidden in the shadows and corners of every room, keeping me edgy.

Another great commercial occasion was about to arrive, so I signed up for double-shifts. That means I turned myself into the Phantom of the Supermarket, this black-eyed, pasty-faced ghoul always lurking somewhere, always stacking shelves, no better place to go.

Easter. There were gaudily wrapped eggs and bunnies of every size and description, all to be presented beautifully and sold as quickly as possible. Jesus Christ is rising from the dead so go buy yourself a chocolate egg. Just as soon, it was all over and the leftover eggs and presentation boxes were going into the discount bins. I remember picking up one of the largest bunnies, which must have been the size of a small child, and hurling it down, smashing it to pieces. The aisles were moving and the fluorescent lights seemed to be eating my skin. I thought I was about to faint. Then I did fall, cracking my skull on the floor.

What was it, three a.m.? I lay there blinking, feeling the lump on the back of my head. There were slow footsteps. Someone came around the corner of the aisle, which I remember clearly was number three: condiments, soups, canned vegetables and discounted Easter eggs. She looked at me lying there. Some middle-aged woman.

'Well, just look at you, Max. What the hell's happened – are you sick or something?'

Hey Patti, I tried to say. Good to see you again.

V

Well hello again, Max. What do we have to call this aisle, then? Aisle number one, I guess: coffins, cadavers and carnations. Hmm, no, that's wisteria you're adorned with. Well, you know what I mean anyway.

I'm so glad they've got the lid sealed. You go to any number of funerals these days and the departed is right there for you to see. Take a good long look at the dead face of the person you used to know and, believe me, you're seeing your own. Max, can you even imagine how old I am these days? I can't. But do you think I'm not counting the days till it's my turn to lie down in the big aisle?

Would never have thought you'd go first. Knowing you're in there really does remind me of that horrible morning I found you spread out with the condiments and leftover Easter eggs. Not to mention the big bunny smashed on the floor.

Well, just look at you, Max. What the hell's happened – are you sick or something?

Today I wish you were just a bit sick. Bet you do, too. And I wish I really could lift you up and take you home. Get you out of that box, look after you one more time.

I looked down at the way you were lying there and I could see there was madness in you. And to you I must have looked like an old woman worse for wear, but I was still recognisable, right? Maybe more recognisable than I am now. Do you see me, old friend? Do you know that I'm here for you? Back then it would have seemed as if some cruel clock had accelerated exponentially. I was a hag; I was a crone; the seven years since we last met were cruel. And I was fifty-two years of age. What's that make me now, Max? Do the terrible arithmetic.

'For God's sake,' I whispered down to you on the floor. The mad look in your eyes said I was standing twelve feet tall and five feet wide. 'Have you got this AIDS shit?'

'No,' you replied. 'Just a little tired. Too many shifts.'

I pulled you to your feet, then got you to lean against me.

'Tired? You're ill.' You stared at the crags of my face while I tried to figure out what was wrong with you. A floor superintendent came by, this twenty-year-old kid with a waist like an hourglass, name of Angus. 'Angus, you Goddamn twit,' I said. 'Don't you check the state of your night employees? Can't we be sued for making people sick like this?'

The poor kid looked like he'd been hit with a shovel. 'Yes, Mrs Baxter, do you want me to personally drive him home?'

'No, I want you to personally go fucking sign him off at the end of the shift. I'll look after the rest. This man needs care.' Outside the supermarket I threw you over my shoulder. Oh, to have the strength I used to take for granted in those days. Max, you were a doll and I was that Italian puppet-maker, Gepeto. I could have had you do anything. 'You weigh nothing,' I told you, getting furious. 'Nothing!' We were in my car. We were driving. You lolled in the passenger seat, but I made you direct me to your place.

'Let me guess. You're still single, but you don't live alone any more, you've got a houseful of deadbeats. You eat takeaway roast chicken off some greasy rotisserie and you all drink too much. Correct?' I pulled up outside the house that I thought was the one you meant. 'And you don't take care of yourself at all. You've picked up some autumn virus. I hope that's all you've got.'

You shook your head, Max. 'Not sick. Just not eating,' and you said it like it ought to make sense.

'Not eating? Why?' I had you at your front door. Guess what? It was unlocked. It was a wonder you could even dress yourself for the supermarket. 'Not over a woman,' I said. 'Please don't tell me you've got yourself into this state over a girl.'

But you had.

I staggered inside with you and let you fall into your bed, which was unmade and quite filthy. That would have to wait. I helped lay you straight and you were barely conscious of the way my hands arranged you so that you lay snug and safe. Shoes and socks off, shirt opening, the belt holding up your baggy jeans being unbuckled and whisked out from under you. Then I didn't even think about it, I crawled into your disgusting bed too, an old, big woman with a craggy face against a skinny young man with sickness under his skin. I left you alone a while, but you were mumbling, so very gently I lifted your head and laid it against the lumpy pillow of my chest.

'Whatever stupid girl it's all about,' I told you, 'she's just the trigger,' but I'm not sure you heard me. You were asleep with your mouth open on the sad remains of my breasts, the sort a woman like me used to be really, really proud of.

VI

I sure was asleep, Patti, and it was my deepest for months, and if you were to let me lay on your breast now I'd sleep with a smile on my face. Yes, you're a little on the mature side, and I know you feel positively ancient, but when you smile you're just like a girl, you know that?

The morning after, there was the smell of food in the house and I thought Conny had returned to create some Italian delicacy. I rolled out of bed and found Patti all right, and the breakfast feast she was making in the kitchen looked a lot less exotic than anything Conny would have put together.

'You could have slept more, but I hope you're feeling better,' she said in a raspy morning voice.

I sat at the dining table, one hand shading my eyes from a sun that seemed all the harsher for the disarray in my head. She put a plate of scrambled eggs, grilled tomatoes, crispy bacon and sautéed button mushrooms in front of me. Next came buttered wholemeal toast and fresh filter coffee.

'How do you have it, sir?'

'Black.' I stared at the stack of food in front of me. At such close quarters, I thought I might be sick.

'Don't turn your nose up at all that,' Patti said, sitting beside me. 'I went shopping while you were still asleep. Down to *my* supermarket. Managers get ten percent off.'

'You manage that place?'

'Parts of it. Deli, meats and customer complaints. I took one look at the food you *didn't* have here. A mouse wouldn't live on what you had. Now eat up.'

My hand was shaking as I picked up the cup and brought it to my lips. The coffee was good, but I couldn't face her breakfast. The look and smell of food were nauseating.

'What is it?' Patti asked. 'Come on, start small. Just taste a bit.'

I tried. In appreciation of her efforts, I really did, but there was a genuine physical resistance to the act of taking food off my fork, chewing it and swallowing.

'It's good,' Patti said. 'Don't you think?'

It was good and bad and the one forkful was all I could manage. She shook her head and finished the plate off herself, and with good gusto. As she did I kept sipping my coffee.

'You think you want to die, but you don't really. If you did, you would have jumped off a bridge or something. Not that I want to put ideas in your head. Dying by degrees is bullshit.'

'You know something about that?' I asked, a last act of self-defence. Patti shook her head, but it could have meant Yes and it could have meant No. She didn't want me to push it. Maybe she'd thought about a bridge or a rope plenty of times. 'So you stayed here after you brought me home?' I said instead.

'For a little while. I fell asleep too, but you woke me up with all your shouting and struggling.'

'Shouting?'

'Oh yes, but not words. Like as if you were trapped under a

rock or something. God knows how long you've been doing that, huh? Your neighbours, they give you strange looks?'

'I don't know. I never see them.' I tore a corner of toast and took the tiniest nibble of it. Patti observed this with some satisfaction.

'I did stay with you, but I've got a home to go to as well. I stopped by on my way to the supermarket and did some fast explaining. Got myself married since the last time we met, you know.'

'Oh?'

'Yes. To my Roger. Used to be a public servant in water resources, retired now. Old school, decent man. Ten years on me, but I bless his blue socks every day.' She cleared away the breakfast plates, then took some fresh cheese from the refrigerator, cut a wedge and gave it to me. I chewed it in small bites, just like the mouse Patti had referred to. 'Hmm,' she said. 'We really will have to start small. Bland might be best for a while.'

'We?' I asked.

'I'm not getting out of your hair until you've got a bit of flesh back on those bones.'

'You don't have to worry.'

'Max, you just leave it to Auntie Patti.'

'You weren't much like an aunt last time we got together.'

She grinned. It was a big, craggy smile on her face. 'And don't you forget it.'

'What happened,' I asked, 'last night when I woke you up?'

'You suspect foul play?'

'Something went on,' I said. 'Something Roger might not like.'

'Sure you want to know?'

I had that unmistakable feeling in the pit of my belly that comes after some sort of sex, no matter how odd or inappropriate. Patti smiled.

'Well, I tried to quiet you down. You were in a state and your heart was pounding like mad. Really scared me.' She was standing next to my chair. She leaned down and whispered, 'Something a girl learns. There are times when a little blowjob can save a young man's life. Sometimes even her own too, right?' She straightened. Slightly embarrassed, she went into the kitchen to get the dirty dishes and utensils done in the sink. 'Then,' she went on, 'I cleaned you up. Um, there was a lot. You still didn't wake up. That's when I left you and went home to Roger on my way down to the supermarket. Which is what I should be doing right now. I've got good stuff for you here, you make sure you eat today. There's orange juice waiting too. I'll see you tonight. I'll cook.'

'You don't need to come back.'

'Vegetables with chicken. You'll see, you'll have your appetite back in no time.' She poured me a fresh cup of coffee and left a little plate of cream biscuits. Patti walked down the dark corridor to the front door. 'Whatever's been going on with you, it's time to get over it. Tell yourself that.'

Your approach was simple, Patti, but my recuperation was underway. You never had to use your nocturnal ministration on me again. Still, I was glad that 'your Roger' never joined us for meals. It would have been difficult to face the friendly pensioner whose wife had kindly sucked me off. Instead, Roger would pull up outside, beep his horn, and you'd be on your way. He must have thought you were providing home-care for some hopeless invalid or something.

How long ago did that nice man die, Patti, only three years? Then at least you had some good time with him, hey?

And look at you on your own down there in row fifteen. You should be right up here next to me, where I can better share the way you're reliving your Florence Nightingale days.

One night, over another mostly wasted meal, you were curious about my parents, my family, so I told you about Conny.

'Your stepdad was Italian? Didn't he teach you to cook? Well, I've had enough of being your servant. When I come on Thursday night, I expect to be fed. Feed me something Italian and exotic. The shoe's on the other foot now.'

A day of panic. Conny, I asked, help me please. What the hell would you make?

It struck me that if he'd been with me, he would have been in a mood to make a special entrée of his that involved oysters. For a nice, healthy woman like Patti he would have followed it with braised swordfish steaks crowned with asparagus. Plus, on the side, rosemary-sprinkled steamed baby potatoes. I thanked the empty air; sometimes I didn't feel so alone at all.

Of everything I made that night, I liked preparing the oysters the best. I had sixteen of the plumpest and freshest Tasmanian specimens. I made a tomato and balsamic topping, crushed blue cheese over the top of each, and baked them in the oven till they were gold. Patti devoured each with gusto. When she saw my main course, I thought she was going to weep with delight. I prepared extra so that a warm plate could go home for Roger. When I started washing up, I realised all the dishes were clean. What I mean is, everything was gone, not only had Patti enjoyed the feast, but I'd eaten my portions too.

I looked around and you were standing there, Patti, and you knew your little homespun miracle had come to pass. You were so proud of yourself. What did you say to me?

Down in the long, crowded pew of row fifteen you remember it well, and you know you're about to say it again. With the smile that makes you look like a much younger woman:

'It was good, so for now, Max, it's gotta be goodbye.'

VII

Conny's old records lifted me out of myself even more. I'd kept them neatly stacked and covered for years, but on a rainy afternoon I dusted a few off and started spinning them again. Some of my stepfather's tastes I would never warm to, old big-band and trad Dixie in particular, but once I found his modern jazz, starting with John Coltrane's many records, particularly *Blue Train* but also *My Favourite Things* and *A Love Supreme*, it was going to be hard to step back to simple rock-and-roll.

The diamond-needle comes down.

Tenor sax intro, ratatat on the snare: here's me cooking in the kitchen, eating like a human, looking around and thinking, This place is the only thing that's stayed constant in my life. Even I'm different. What happened with Iron John and Debbie Canova and Tony Lester might have demolished me, okay, but maybe the upside is that I can put myself back together any way I want.

Hit a diminished chord on the upstroke, a major chord on the downstroke: so the first thing to do is to forget about the *me* inside every thought, inside every equation, right? How sick am I of sleepless nights and one-way conversations with Debbie, of staggering in and out of rooms at two and three a.m. wondering, Who's there? Why not show yourself? Who was there were the ghosts I'd created, so isn't it time to end this fruitless imagining?

Now change the key and improvise, let yourself go.

How many people's ownership had this house passed through? It was my turn to act like an owner. The easiest way to stop thinking was to start some hard work, and I'd never forgotten how good I'd felt helping Concetto San Filippo with his building project. My home needed fixing up all right, this poor old creaking, paint-peeling, timber-rotted mess of a place. There'd be a hundred things that needed doing once you got right down to it. So I made my plan: paint rooms, then attend to the carpentry outside, things I could maybe handle on my own.

It was all more expensive and complicated than I'd imagined. I needed more income to support the project, a whole lot more than what shelf-stacking would bring in. What do I look like sitting at a desk, facing a bank manager, asking for money? Maybe not so bad. With the bank's cash I bought myself a ute, then cleaned off my aunt's garden tools downstairs. Putting together an ad in the local paper, I called myself Your Local Gardener and had the telephone reinstalled. Within days I was so busy with other people's lawns that I had to find someone else to work on the house when I wasn't there.

Joss was a carpenter, plumber, electrician and builder combined, a grey-haired Dutchman going crazy in retirement. He whistled all day long and interspersed his labours with the odd, celebratory joint if something turned out particularly well. When I had money I paid him in cash and when I didn't have money he kept a running tab and went home with huge pots of Italian food. In return, his wife would send me *kartoffelpuffers*, *stamppot* and *snert*, the green pea soup that became my favourite.

One day, in the back of a bedroom closet that he was ripping out, Joss found a stinking, unwashed pile of my rock-pig clothes, left there from my last stage performance. That synth-pop-rock night Debbie moved out. Sweat- and beer-stained jeans, shirts, boots, socks – disgusting. He asked where he should put them. I told Joss to burn those clothes in the steel incinerator he'd set up in the yard.

'No. Putting your music clothes back when I am finished. This is your legend, yes?'

His sentences and word usage were sometimes more convoluted than Conny's had been, but I understood what he meant. Well, I could burn everything later, when we were finished. All in all the work took a year and a half, after which the house gleamed and I was brown as a berry. Just about every yard and garden within a radius of several kilometres was touched by my hands.

Pull the improv back now, let the notes do the talking and stretch them long, listen to how much space the ride cymbals are giving you.

I decided to try selling the Rogers kit again. Now that the upstairs of the house was complete, I thought I could put in an internal staircase down to what was currently the huge, unused, soundproof practice studio. Then I'd create some extra rooms there – maybe another set of bedrooms or a large private study. Anything, really, just to take up the space.

The kit was full of rust spots, dust and cobwebs. I remembered the way Conny used to keep his old drum kit protected with sheets and how he used to clean and polish it in preparation for his Sunday practice sessions. Ashamed, I crouched down and looked at dead spiders hanging off broken webs and the live spiders creeping back under the seat.

'Look here, the fittings. Really do look at them. See what holds this into this? This piece here, how it fits with this one there? This is quality.'

They still dancin' out there? I walked around the kit, then went and found all the cleaning products I'd need. If I was going to sell it, then I'd make sure it was in perfect shape. Sprucing it up took hours. Not only did I clean it, not only did I scrape every spot of rust away and touch up the bare metal, but I pulled apart each and every one of those heavy, beautifully tooled fittings and oiled them till they were smooth. This kit deserved nothing less. By the time I was finished it was dark and the bare overhead bulbs cast spidery shadows.

No, not really dancing, just hips sort of moving, couples swaying, this is an easy, easy beat: 'Take driver's seat.'

Then let's pick it up: I heard you then and I hear you now. And one day I overheard you say to my aunt, 'Emma, *mi tesora*, this boy he need help, yes? Is for us to do the help – who else can?'

Let's get cooking: I went upstairs, meditative as a monk, and slid a record out its sleeve. I cleaned it off and put the needle down on another of Conny's favourite records, a piece of vinyl he'd often made me drum alongside, Coltrane's *Blue Train*. I had a thought and went into my bedroom. The new clothes closets were large and covered in mirror doors. Joss's work was impeccable. I looked for the rock-pig clothes he wouldn't burn and, sure enough, there they were in a fetid pile. Boots, jeans, underwear, t-shirts and shirts – leftovers from a different life.

Kick it to the finish! I found what I was looking for with no trouble. The shirt I'd worn during that foul gig, my final show as a rock drummer. Even now the thing was rank with the smell of my own sweat, plus the stench of cigarette smoke and stale beer years old. In the top pocket was the piece of paper that skinny young guy had slipped into it, the cocky nineteen year old who'd claimed his grandfather had been a great friend of Conny's. The name and number were still intact. Coltrane's tenor saxophone hit a crescendo and I looked up and around at the shadows, suddenly staring.

Okay, you sweatin'? Better be. So let the fade come easy because we did great, boys, we did great. Wind it down, wind it down, and bye for now.

VIII

At the lectern beside the nave, our Baron of Burying, Mr Buddy Bettridge makes prefatory remarks, welcoming everyone to the celebration of my life, and gives a warm rundown of Max's human achievements. In a nutshell, I was a good, friendly guy of many talents. Drumming, audio technology and band management. Buddy would be beside himself if he knew that the latter description was so profoundly wrong, but no one is going to stand up from their pew and point it out. In the briefing about who and what I was, he must have misunderstood my relationship to the boys in Dirtybeat. Oh well, no matter. Buddy goes on to claim some kinship with me, a total stranger but a fellow musician, by telling an anecdote about how at the age of forty he purchased his first Fender Stratocaster, an American model of course, as these are the only ones that hold their value. The mourners titter politely, though they'd rather be getting drunk and stoned.

'Now we have a surprise – in fact, a special request.'

With a half-smile, because he enjoys the small oddities that tend to arise when dealing with the funerals of musicians, artists and assorted creative types on their way to their maker, Buddy nods toward a gangly, slightly stooped individual standing in the crowd at the back of the chapel.

Hard to surprise a dead man, believe me, but I never even knew Jamie Lazaroff was here. Fake leg and all, souvenir of a landmine in Somalia. So his Somali wife helps him along by carrying his instrument's case for him. Her skin is the darkest ebony and he is a little grey-haired but in no way is he old. You get the feeling a boy like him will never really age, not even as the venerable doctor and educator he will continue to become, already a veteran of umpteen medical campaigns in numerous African countries.

I can tell that he's extremely nervous. Not just because he's not quite used to his prosthetic leg – only had it eight months now, the explosion still rings in his one good ear, and probably always will; the other ear is inert as a stone – but because he has played so rarely since abandoning his fellow jazz aficionados in his collective and undertaking what turned out to be his true calling with Médecins Sans Frontières. Sometimes in makeshift medical tents and mess halls, sure he'd been known to play a few tunes to cheer people up, but you wouldn't call these performances, not by any stretch of the imagination. Now with only a bit of hearing left and little practice behind him he wonders whether he is going to embarrass himself in front of all these musically oriented mourners.

As Jamie passes my coffin, his hand touches the lid. There's warmth there, and a tremor. Good to have a little stage fright, right?

The scruffy boys from Dirtybeat get up and follow him to the front. They produce acoustic instruments from various hiding spots inside the chapel. The crowd oohs in delight. The boys grin sheepishly. Jamie opens the instrument case and takes out his signature instrument, the alto sax. It gleams; it shines. His eyes flick to the others. Wow, I get it. The special request came from them. Doesn't make much sense, though. Those rough and tumble young rockers asked a former virtuoso like Jamie to play with them?

Oh no. Oh no no no. I get it.

Da da daaa. Da da da-daaa. Da da daaa, da-da.

Performed at about 80 BPM, a super-slowed down 'Smoke on the Water', the song that synth-pop-rock group played in a jazz style just so this guy Jamie could hear my swing first hand. The Dirtybeat boys didn't ask him for this – he asked them. It's his little memento for me.

Jamie's breath, lips and fingers are ready to join in. His heart says, Dunno what it'll sound like, Max, but here's one for you. It's just for fun so if you want to laugh, go ahead.

The rhythm and melody is a little sluggish. My rock boys really don't have the first clue about how to swing at all.

But oh man, I am laughing. 'Smoke on the Water', bad-jazz style, yet with a trenchantly melodic alto saxophone soaring above it. Jamie, this has made my day.

IX

Was I surprised to hear from you after so long, Max? Well, yeah, you sat on that one a long time, that's for sure. But I guess I've learned that old musicians never give up and musicianship never goes away.

'What do you want to do?' was what I asked you the first time I tried to get you interested, and Max, that's what I asked you this time. You weren't so angry any more. Not sarcastic like back then. Instead you sounded shy. You answered, 'Play some real jazz. Really swing.'

Music to my ears.

I used to think – still do – today's drummers just don't have it in them. To swing's uncool, too laid back, but good jazz is all about cool even when expressing love, hate or the most misunderstood qualities of our type of music: grief and bewilderment. You've got to have lived a lot and be *old* inside yourself to get those emotions right. Anyone can crash and thump, as Pete Townshend once said, but the things I was looking for were in you all right. Just listen to Dirtybeat here beside me. Energetic kids, but let me give you another quote, this one courtesy of Satchmo and his manager Irving Mills: *It don't mean a thing if ain't got that swing*, right? Even Graham Parker had to use that line, because he knew too, and what these poor lads are doing today doesn't mean anything at all.

Sorry to subject you and everyone else to this, Max. Bad idea.

The pity of it is that if you could rise up out of that box and play right now, you'd really be something. You'd be best and fairest and most improved too. You've lived and died and that's what every good musician wants to do if their going to make memorable music.

Unfair, huh?

My mind shouldn't wander so, but maybe you prefer my thoughts to this trite little musical tribute I put together for you? No wonder I can't focus. Right now I'd rather be talking to you than playing. You used to agree that too many skin-men want to be the main man – they want their drumming to cut through all the other instruments and be *the* instrument. They're all about me, me, me. What do you end up with? A fight, and that ain't music. Unless you're Keith Moon or someone absolutely unique. Then it works, otherwise it *don't*. You never wanted to be centre stage, spotlight on you. You wanted, Max, to *set* the stage for the rest of us. The true Backroom Boiler. That's what made you so hot. Then, the fact that you could intuit what was inside the players you worked with, well, that's just what made you hotter.

Funny thing. Playing harmony, lead, now some syncopated sliding scales in this ditty about a gambling house burning down in Montreux, Switzerland, something's happening. What is it? Let me end my piece with a little flourish, then pass on to Greg the Dirtybeat guitarist so that he can give us a clever four bars of acoustic lead. *Nice, nice.*

Now I can think about it. Hmmm. Thing is, it's like I'm

standing here playing but what I hear is your voice giving me my old question back: Dr Jamie Lazaroff, specialist in triage and associate professor of surgery: What do you want to do?

Isn't there just a world of terror in a question like that? What does a man like me *want* to do as opposed to what *should* he do?

I've got a brand new leg and one quarter hearing. My young wife Dharka is pregnant with our first baby and I'm struggling to get through a song as simple as this. I've saved lives, but I could have saved more. I already run a discipline at university and still look for extra time to operate a private medical practice. Every year I donate six to eight weeks to MSF somewhere in the world. Often they're the best weeks out of any year, but I took a wrong step in a place I was warned about and I didn't die — but I've got a life that needs saving anyway, mine. I mean, look at you, Max. But for a whisker of luck I nearly beat you to the Pearly Gates.

What do I want to do or what do I *need* to do?

Old friends are the ones you can be honest with. Best estimate is I'm three-quarters deaf and rising. Well, while I've got time I need to teach myself something and it's something I used to know. If this kid in Dharka's belly is ever gonna have a real father, and not a nut-case progenitor good for nothing but professional achievement and longer and longer hours away from home, I've got to turn back the clock. Play some real jazz again, really swing. That's the sum of what I want. What I need. No more do-goodery.

There, I've said it. But I couldn't have said it before because I never even knew the shape of the question. Why'd I have to get up here to realise the truth?

What's that, old friend — this is all music to *your* ears?

Well, I don't think you mean this song Dirtybeat and me just murdered.

X

I told Jamie that like everyone else in his collective I didn't want attachment, only a good gig from time to time. His group of available musicians had settled into a core set of twelve and a wider, looser collection of about another fifteen. They were into jazz without labels, eschewing the names given to all the sub-genres. Big Band, Swing, Fusion, Bop, West Coast Cool, Continental Jazz, Progressive, Orchestral – not for Jamie and his friends. Our jams were free and fluid, a musical transition that felt natural to me, as if Concetto San Filippo had prepared me for this since the day he gave me my first lesson. What I didn't like was that my playing wasn't anywhere as clean as it used to be when I practised with him. So many years of rock drumming had narrowed my technique. Jamie asked for more colour and variation, more method and style – more grace, even. Sometimes as I set the groove I'd see Jamie watching me, a smile in the corner of his mouth. He was encouraging me, and seemed to be saying, Find it again, Max. It's not all gone.

Hey, it wasn't.

And Conny's old voice guided me as if he was right there. What was even better was that the click in my head in a thousand variations was still there too. The old metronome that becomes a part of your psyche: nothing would ever lose me that, not after Conny taught me so correctly. Whenever Jamie's musicians started off too fast or too slow I knew how to guide them back to the right click, no matter the tempo of the tune. I'd glance at our twenty-one-year-old leader and Jamie would be looking at me, the only one completely aware of what I'd done. His half-smile said he was watching a rebirth; the kid was right.

Then, one day, he said something that turned me upside-down. 'Your stepfather told my grandfather that you were one of the best drummers he'd seen. But you were going to have to follow a lot of side-roads before you got onto the right one. He knew you pretty well, huh?'

That night, for the first time in a long time, I walked around my house drinking too much. I missed him, wished we'd had more time together; I even wished he was my real father and had been my guide since the day I was born. Settling into the couch, I slept in exactly the place he'd fallen asleep so many times, the television's rippling hues bathing over him.

In a dream, we were walking down the local streets under a fat moon, and we were hand in hand. I looked at his olive-skinned face as he watched the stars; he was full of wonder. Then I was at his funeral. The look and feel of that day was exactly as it had been. Summer heat; scent of jasmine; sweat falling in droplets off my forehead. I hadn't had to do any of the organising. Friends I'd never even known he had did it all on my behalf. I was eighteen and I think already quite self-assured, but in the shock of his loss I could barely organise tying my shoe laces.

The thing was, before the funeral people started calling the house to speak to me. It wasn't just the old guys in the wedding band, but men I'd never heard of. They knew all about me, however, and would refer to me as 'Conny's son'. A small deputation finally came to visit, saying that if I'd allow them they would do everything needed for a decent funeral and wake. They were all Mediterranean like Conny and post-middle age. It soon dawned on me what was going on.

I quizzed Francesco, a large, sixty-five-year-old Neapolitan, about my stepfather's life and their connection. With the others drinking wine and watching us, Francesco explained that Conny had come to this country after he'd discovered the truth about his sexuality. Almost too late; he'd married young but at least had no children. In his country he'd trained as a master builder, and had liked women well enough, but the first time there was a man was not the last time. His wife found out and raised an unholy Hell. Conny escaped to this country for peace, quiet and a life he could lead without approbation. He found this circle of friends; some were musicians, some had trades, and by the time of the funeral most were retired. Not all of these men had lived completely open lives, but neither did those who were married hide very much from their families. I'd never imagined a world like this – or that it had existed inside my own home.

'You aunt Emma, she did know. She was not so happy for this,' Francesco spoke in his throaty accent, and I remembered what I'd sometimes heard and seen between Emma and Conny: affection, need, and once: 'Don't lie to me, you've gone back to it, haven't you?' or was it, 'Don't lie to me, you've gone back for more, haven't you?'

Francesco made sense. Seeing the surprise in my face, he said like a priest, 'Everyone they do have to find their way to live, right for them but no one else. *Figlio*, what man is made like a stone?'

Not you, Concetto. At his funeral his compatriots sat with me.

We were a group. In the vividness of my dream, as I slept in that couch, I could feel their arms again. Or was it Conny holding me? In the week following the funeral I drank myself into my own sort of oblivion, smashed my way into stores at midnight and stole more booze and ridiculous things I didn't need. I was never sober, but I kept wondering how I could have lived so close to this man and never bothered to know him. What effort did I make to understand why he would build me my own practice studio, buy me my drums and so tirelessly teach me how to be 'musician the finest'? What thanks did I ever offer him, what did I ever *do* for him? In that last bottle shop I drank their tequila and laid down on the floor, wanting to die. He'd had a big heart and mine was stone. It was almost a relief to end up in a prison farm, where others could do the thinking for me, and I could switch off, force myself to think nothing at all.

XI

Jamie's musicians had no illusions of hitting it big or making millions. They were well on the way to becoming doctors, lawyers, dentists and engineers. When we played we usually performed under different group names, things like Big Blue Jays, Smokey Leroy, The City Heat Quintet and the Three Horn Trio. Times were good. Bookings turned up at hotels, reception halls, bars, jazz clubs, restaurants, outdoor cafés and even street busking if the mood hit enough of them. I was one of four potential drummers. It remained unspoken, but I could tell I was the favourite.

Our equation worked to a canon Jamie Lazaroff had worked out for all of us. It was 'Be Cool'. We tried to be. If the telephone rang and I wanted to play somewhere for a night or two's pocket money and free drinks, then fine. If I didn't, no one pushed it. Under this arrangement I enjoyed playing more than I ever had, and in trying new styles alien to rock music, I moved from the musical plateau I'd been stuck on for decades into something a whole lot better.

Do people notice themselves growing older? I barely did, and I didn't pay much attention to the fact that my bank account was fattening month by month. The gardening business was a licence to print money, and, because I enjoyed the playing, I found myself saying yes to more and more gigs. I had untold energy; unless it was the height of summer, working outside all day hardly seemed to tire me at all. Running that on into late-night shows was natural enough. Nothing better to do anyway. I told myself that as soon as any of this felt like work, I would cut back, but it didn't happen. Gardens were full of sunlight and my flowers relished every new day. That could have been good enough, but playing with Jamie and his guys lifted me up even further.

Exhausted but happy one night in my living room, I told Conny, 'Thanks for teaching me the right way.' I fell into bed feeling light inside. At least I'd said something. My life was good; I'd been saved, but guess what, it was only a couple of whiskies, three shots of vodka and the blink of an eye before Jamie's musicians were graduates getting jobs, and turning those jobs into careers, and marrying and procreating too, eventually to fall into the endless loops and traps of young families.

Musicians dropped off the radar and Jamie Lazaroff was now a doctor specialising in accident and trauma care. The end of the Eighties came and he barely had time to scratch himself. At a practice session he gathered we leftovers and broke the news: he'd joined Médecins Sans Frontières and had signed up for a one year tour of duty in the Ivory Coast. Where? There was a new light in his eyes. Not yet thirty, but something told me Jamie had found his real road. He said, 'This'll be it, guys,' and it was. No farewell show to tug at the heartstrings, the look in his eyes and the determination in the set of his jaw said he was going *now*.

What a loss. I missed his skinny frame, his stoop, the almost spiritual air that he played his saxes with. There were many times I thought he was connected to something a lot bigger and darker than the sum of either himself or the musicians around him. Maybe it was what the Spanish call the *Duende*; if there really was such a thing, the person who reached into it was Jamie. His sets were exercises in the exploration of his spirit, and, with it, the spirits of others. No wonder audiences loved him. When I watched the way he played it made me realise how much Debbie Canova had been like this too: born with a magic unlearned and unlearnable.

The remnants of Jamie's collective got together and faced the reality of the coming decade. Our sort of music was largely out of fashion. The few of us that remained from the collective formed a permanent band because it was either give in to that or never find a way to play again, there was just so little work. We called our septet DoctorJay in honour of our absent leader, but there was even a bitter taste to that idea.

With me there was Stefan Ola on trumpet, Randal Ferguson on saxophone, Bobby Mitchell on rhythm guitar, Rodney Brand on lead guitar, Sam Wyvel on piano and Raf Santos on basses. Each of these guys was now married and had a good- or high-paying job, three already had kids. They'd arrive to gigs in their BMWs and Saabs while I parked Conny's Premier or my gardening ute between them.

Things never really worked out. Venues continued to close down and what new ones did open always failed in their first months. The wedding and twenty-first birthday circuit was terminal. Performing stopped being fun, but I didn't follow my vow to throw it in. Still, after trudging on for year after year with diminishing returns, DoctorJay was ready to call it quits. Well, that would be it then. Maybe I'd fall into line with what Conny had done; just keep my kit under the house and indulge in my own practice sessions, no one else around. Become a teacher maybe.

Or just stop.

Before we came to the point of making the final decision, one night I received a phone call. It was toward the end of 1994 and DoctorJay had managed three gigs the entire year. There was a venue in town called Club Marrakesh and it was one of the last of the jazz clubs to survive in this city. Funny thing was, we'd never played there, the owners keeping themselves going by always booking big. That meant they only imported name bands or artists from down south and overseas. Now things had changed. The Scottish-Italian brothers who owned the place, Joseph and Roland Sparks – Conny would have called them Giuseppe and Rolando – had been in a legal battle with the local council which was preparing to tear down the luxury hotel the club was in, not to mention the entire business precinct.

The caller was Joseph Sparks. Parkland near his club was to be redeveloped, and everything in the way would have to go. The Sparks brothers had joined a consortium in opposing the development and the rezoning that would close down their businesses, but it had been a losing battle and sort of half-hearted too. It's hard to say no to new greenery and open spaces, even when you're the one who has to take the fall. They soon threw in the towel.

'We might think about a pizzeria or something, somewhere we can't get fucked over again.' Joseph and Roland wanted to go out with a bang, really say thank you and farewell to their patrons. 'It's gonna be a big night. We're gonna get Misty Blue up from Sydney. Know them?'

I did, the quintet was one of the most in-demand jazz bands in the country.

'Well, I hear you guys can be pretty hot, too. Sorry we never had you, but we want to do a play-off, you against them. Alternating on stage, twenty- or thirty-minute brackets each until your fingers fall off or everyone goes home. But I'm thinking, a big finale, everyone together, the stage can handle it. The longest jam you can muster. What do you think?'

I thought it was pretty good. 'Most cool,' Jamie might have said.

'Consider yourself booked. October 31st, okay?'

'What are you going to call the show?'

'Call it? Haven't thought that far. It's Halloween night, right?' I heard him speak off from the telephone: 'Hey, Laetecia, is Roland around? No? Well, what do you think? What we gonna call this shit?' There was a pause, then a female's muffled reply. Joseph laughed. 'That could be it.' He returned to me. 'Max, I'll tell you later, but you're gonna like it.'

I received an invitation in the post. It wasn't signed with Joseph or Roland Sparks's names. Instead there was a fat red lipstick kiss that wasn't an imprint; I could smear it with my thumb. What that was supposed to mean, I didn't have a clue.

Club Marrakesh Presents
Halloween's
'End of the World Showdown'
feat.
Misty Blue vs. DoctorJay
31 October
And Then Bye Bye!

XII

It was Misty Blue's first bracket in Club Marrakesh's last night on Earth. If you had a pulse you were on that giant dance floor, rubbing your hips against everyone else's, getting touched up, toes squashed and you were dripping sweat before the first bracket was even over.

The Sparks brothers had planned a musical battle that we'd already lost. This interstate ensemble knew exactly how to play the crowd. They'd done all the jazz festivals in the world, including the meccas: Monterey, Montreux and the New Orleans' Mardi Gras. The band had thought the gig through and it wasn't going to be one of those quiet affairs with couples and lonely types leaning at the bar or nodding to the beat in darkened corners. It was all jump and jive and get everyone dancing right from the start.

On a stage that reached right into the dance floor, Misty Blue was set up a little to the left, DoctorJay a little to the right. The lightshow illuminated the band playing and cast the collection of opposing instruments into a sort of glittery darkness, promising even better things to come.

Our approach was different. Expecting that this club's patrons would be real jazz enthusiasts, we were going to dig deep into classic twentieth-century albums and play a lot of them in their entirety. I mean, both sides of well-loved vinyl records all the way through, starting at a side per bracket. What a bad idea. We came out and opened with side one of *Blue Train* – the ten-minute title track plus the nine minute 'Moment's Notice'. Our audience went into a sort of awed silence. It sounded good, but you could hardly dance to it. As soon as we finished, Misty Blue came out and got everyone moving again; we took to the stage and gave them side two: 'Locomotion', 'I'm Old-Fashioned' and 'Lazy Bird'.

Here was the difference between us. The crowd went wild for Misty Blue; the crowd really appreciated DoctorJay. Added to which, the Misty Blue singer, an African-American with the unlikely name of Nathaniel Prince, had a great bluesy voice and really looked the part in his all-white suit and electric blue shirt, not to mention that women were going weak at the knees every time he crooned in their direction.

During one of those breaks where our opposition murdered our memory, we smoked weed and swallowed all the free drinks we could. We decided it was either give in or try something different; we couldn't keep dampening that crowd just so our interstate rivals could move in and whip them into even greater frenzies. We decided to throw away our plan.

What would Jamie have told us? Boys, it's time to get loose. Be cool.

At the first few bars of 'Theme From Shaft' the crowd didn't know whether to tear us apart or dance. This wasn't jazz – but someone screamed, then someone else. That meant they liked it. From there it was plain sailing. We kept up the tempo and, on the spot, developed a sort of instinct for what this crowd really wanted. At the end of every tune someone in the band would call out the next song, picked on the spot. Everything from Curtis Mayfield's 'Superfly', to Gil Scott-Heron and James Brown. Rodney, our lead guitarist, definitely was not sexy, and his voice wouldn't challenge a professional like Nathaniel Prince, but he had this crazy way of duck-dancing while vocalising that made the crowd laugh and egg him on.

No one wanted either band to give in, to call it a night. We all did literally play until our fingers were ready to fall off. Misty Blue and DoctorJay had been going for hours, but, at the stroke of midnight, Joseph Sparks jumped the stage and shouted into a microphone, 'It's Halloween, isn't it — who wants to go home to the ghosts and gremlins?' The crowd let him know they didn't. Joseph yelled, 'Jam!' The crowd chanted back: 'Jam! Jam! Jam!'

The dozen of us got together. Misty Blue's drummer deferred to me and took up the congas, vibes and a glockenspiel. We started off with a slow groove, letting each soloing instrument weave in at will, then that turned into what everyone really wanted, an old-style cutting contest with each soloist trying to out-duel the next. The energy was up, then went higher and higher. I even got a turn, me soloing on the drums and Misty Blue's drummer replying on the congas. It was a blast. All of that burned for a good hour. Then, two girls, maybe on a dare, jumped the stage and ran through the musicians, alternately kissing us and tugging at our clothes. One tore her blouse as she tried to pull it over her head, but the other, a flaming redhead, had no trouble. Her shirt and bra went sailing into the air and she bounced her breasts in time to my beat. Joseph and Roland were in no hurry to get her off-stage. Eventually they had to, laughingly helping her down. The intrusion set the tone for our last hour. Not a soul in this place felt laid-back. We played hard and Nat Prince scat-sang his heart out. We hit a final ecstatic high and everyone knew that was it. You just couldn't go any further, couldn't get any happier.

Stage lights down. Applause like the end of the world. The night had lasted more than five hours and the place was still packed. No one had wandered off, except for one – and despite the high, I was mad with disappointment.

XIII

I noticed her while we were setting up. Outside, an unhappy twi-light was settling over the city and rain started to come down. Inside, Joseph and Roland Sparks conferred at a main bar long and deep enough for five bartenders. The brothers had enough Italian and black Scottish blood in their veins to look like a pair of curly-headed Moors. They were worried the bad weather would keep people away. While preparations were ongoing she entered the club shaking rain from her hair. The three kissed and I saw her call one of the bartenders, who stopped washing glasses and brought her a bottle of champagne. Knew her pretty well. She popped the cork and poured a glass. The brothers weren't having any; she sat on a stool and drank while Joseph and Roland went outside to fret at the storm-clouds. I didn't know who she was, but I couldn't take my eyes off the swing of her long black hair.

There was an aura about her. She was dressed well, but wasn't very relaxed, and instead seemed to be holding in a lot of nerv-ous energy. She sat, she drank, she got up and checked the rain with the others. If someone had told me she was preparing to do something like make her stage debut up here with one of the bands it would have made sense. I was fastening my kit's rivets. When I tried out the snare, giving a few rolls and a ratatat, she was back at the champagne bottle, this time watching what I was doing.

The boys in my band might all have been married, but they'd noticed her as soon as I did. Ronald asked a technician, 'Who is that?' but Nathaniel Prince, in a t-shirt and studiously ripped jeans, and sitting cross-legged on the stage as he went through his set-list, said in his deep Louisiana accent, 'The babe is the Sparks brothers' little sister. This has been a public safety warning.'

It was the 'Laetecia' Joseph Sparks had turned to when he'd first been on the telephone to me. So this was the person who'd given the 'End of the World' night its name – and it was her red kiss on the invitation, I knew it.

She finished a last drink and I lost sight of her until later in the night, during our second bracket, playing the flip side of *Blue Train*. From being nowhere to standing right at the front of our stage, she smiled up at me. My eyes locked not with hers but with those of the grinning Raf Santos, and his fun, rumbling bass runs were echoed by my foot-pedal and tom-tom.

Next time I looked she was gone. Didn't see her at all, not for the rest of the night, and that made the whole thing go a little sour for me. It was just part of being a player in this sort of an outfit; we were nobodies and six-sevenths of our septet was married anyway. Appreciative females were for the likes of Nat Prince, who probably ate them up with cream. Red kisses – all for him.

Three in the morning and we were nearly done packing. Staff finished cleaning up and I was making trips to the Premier to get the drum kit squared away into the boot and back seat. Rain and storms had kept no one home. The Sparks brothers were thrilled their night had been such a success. Thrilled – and full of gloom to see it all over. It seemed more than appropriate the weather was so foul. The boys in the band had taken turns holding borrowed umbrellas over one another as they crammed instruments and equipment into their cars. Roadies were one thing we lacked; Misty Blue had three of them and a decent-sized truck. I envied all of that. Then, as mementoes, Nat handed each of us a signed copy of the band's latest CD. I felt like I was a small dog and a Great Dane had just urinated on me.

The younger brother, Joseph Sparks, called me over.

'We're gonna finish all the champagne before the auditors get their hands on it. Drink up, okay?'

It was good stuff and he poured generously. Roland was quiet, resting his great, dark face in his hands. Joseph said, 'Don't mind him.' Roland nodded as if to mean that sooner or later he'd get over this great disappointment. He drank steadily and efficiently, on a mission to get plastered.

There were about twenty of us sitting in that funk of stale cigarette smoke and spilled drinks that creates the usual post-gig haze. Tonight the haze was deeper; soon bulldozers and wrecking balls would be moving in. Someone joked that the demolition company's motto read, 'All that's left are the memories,' but it wasn't a joke, that's exactly what it was.

The others in my band had families to get to and sports days to rise and shine for, all of it less than a few hours away. Misty Blue had also left, but for Nathaniel Prince, who'd been doing lines of coke since the witching hour and looked like he could keep going a week. Most of the female staff staying behind had their eye on him; he wouldn't need to go anywhere alone.

Exhaustion had the better of me. One or two drinks, then bed. My temples hurt. The funny thing is, I had no idea that I was about to lose the ability to choose whether I would play drums in a band again. I had no idea the turn my life was about to take. You never get the chance to get ready for change; you simply hurtle in, blind, lonesome and always ill-prepared.

Quiet, even-tempered Joseph picked up a bottle of Krug and threw it against a wall, where it smashed to pieces. Then he burst into tears. Roland grabbed his kid brother and the two hugged, forehead against forehead; they cried and cried. From there the dam was broken. It was on for young and old. Lines of coke were cut and prepared. The bartenders emptied all the champagne bottles from out of the refrigerators onto the counter. Everyone took one for themselves. Corks popped; coke was snorted; no one was going to be straight or sober for very much longer.

When Joseph noticed I was getting ready to go, he unlocked himself from his brother's embrace. 'Hey, you can't leave, our sister told us to get you to stay.'

Laetecia Sparks. It turned out she'd be the only one to remember me. I mean, really remember me.

I looked around and there she was. Nice red lips.

Roland moved out of his seat and went and sat beside one of his blonde waitresses, putting his arm around her. They started to kiss right in front of the rest of us. Nat Prince's eyes lit upon the Sparks' young sister and he said hello with easy familiarity, trying to get closer. He couldn't because she sat next to me on the stool Roland had vacated. Everyone was stale with the post three a.m. doldrums, yet she was as fresh as if she'd just stepped out of the shower. It looked like she'd changed her clothes. Her new attire was demure; she could have been ready to go teach a class of school kids. What was she, early twenties? Twenty-five?

'What took you so long, Lee?' Joseph asked.

His sister opened her shoulder-bag, which was a little too big for nights out in bars and clubs. She had packet after packet of hash, and flipped one each to Joseph, Roland, Nat Prince, the bartenders, other staff. She didn't keep any for herself, but looked at me and weighed the last one.

'Thanks, but I'm heading off. Gotta drive.'

'Hmm, Jamie said you didn't like to make a pig of yourself.'

'You know Jamie Lazaroff?'

'Until he went to Africa. One year becomes many, right?'

I couldn't think of what to say and she passed the bag to someone else.

Joseph was pulling himself together. 'Is this all of us?' There was general agreement. 'Then let's head up. Roland,' he said to his brother, 'want to lock up one last time?'

They went to do it, their staff spraying the bitter little door-locking ceremony with champagne.

'The boys've got some rooms upstairs. The hotel managers are friends. It's not just the club closing down, the whole building's going to be demolished.' Laetecia stood up. 'Are you really so sure you want to go home?'

'I guess not.'

She grinned and took my arm. Nathaniel Prince gave me a rueful smile. His top-dog attentions were going to have to shift elsewhere – and, the thing was, I still had no idea why.

XIV

They'd booked plenty of rooms, but one of them was the presidential suite, top floor, uninterrupted view of the world.

To room service Joseph rattled off a food order long as his arm. Roland filled the not-one, not-two, but three already-stacked, decent-sized bar fridges with all the booze taken from the club. Everyone drank and moved around, watching the random pattern of city-lights glitter through the rain. There was music. Television sets were on in every last gold-plated room. Big budget Hollywood movies and glossy porn films played. Images only, sound turned down. It was easy to see what sort of bacchanal this party was headed toward. The food arrived on a convoy of trolleys. Tokes were rolled, more coke was snorted, expensive drinks flowed like water. People came in and out; the entire hotel, or at least the top floors, was a movable feast. Suite to suite to suite; strangers arrived and disappeared, all celebrating the fact that soon this place was going to be one great big hole in the ground.

Roland's depression was lifting. He was all over a different blonde to the one he'd been kissing downstairs. Joseph assuaged

his own rage with a redhead sitting in his lap, the girl who'd
danced bare-chested on stage. Nathaniel Prince was telling stories
I couldn't hear, that deep, sexy voice of his rumbling like a bass.
No time passed before couples were swaying together, others yab-
bering over God-awful disco music that got louder and louder.
Adrenalin and blood seemed to pound. Now pills were going
around. Uppers, downers, who could even tell?

'So you missed the show tonight,' I said to Laetecia.

'Not everything. I liked the risk you took, playing Coltrane's
best album like that. Not everyone knew it but they liked it. I
came back in the middle of your "funk and soul" period. Sacri-
lege in a jazz club, still, you got away with it. Better than this.'

'Why did you have to go?'

She thought it over. 'Well, a lot of things are finishing today. I
promised myself this Halloween would be my special day too.'

'For what?'

'I don't know you, so let's leave it for now.' She looked at me
with an inquisitive smile. 'Do you know where Halloween comes
from?'

'No idea.'

'Two thousand years ago the Celts celebrated their new year
on November first. The night before was called Samhain, and
that was when the boundary between the worlds of the living and
the dead became blurred. So, for one night all these ghosts could
come back to Earth and wreak havoc with homes and crops.'

'I thought Halloween was just American trick-or-treat type
stuff.'

'It is now, but do you want to know how that part of Halloween got added? In England, the poor would beg for food and
people would give them things called "soul cakes" to eat, but
only if those beggars promised to pray long and hard for the

souls of the dear-departed. The church liked all the praying. They thought it was better than what people used to do, which was to leave food and wine out on doorsteps and in cemeteries for ghosts and ghouls to collect. So soul cakes and prayers were encouraged. Later, cakes in exchange for paupers' prayers turned into little treats for neighbourhood kids. Simple evolution.'

'You like these stories.'

'Well, ghosts are fun, don't you think?'

'Not for everyone.'

Some of the glossy group sex on the television sets was being turned into rawer, more vivid pleasures in this ridiculously well-appointed living room. Laetecia said, 'Want to find a place we don't have to be voyeurs?'

I looked at how open and bright her face was. 'All right.'

She crossed the room to the telephone and dialled an internal number. The lights were low, sugary music played too loud, and bodies moved in and out of shadows. Plates of food and bottles of champagne lay about. Outside it was storming, the windows regularly washed by gusts of rain.

She might have been fresh as a daisy, but my neck hurt and my eyes actually throbbed. Sleep, blessed sleep. I felt a sheen of perspiration, oil, on my face. While Laetecia used the phone I went to the main bathroom. Joseph Sparks and the redhead were in the shower. She was bending under the water spray and he was devouring her back and hips. I found another bathroom, its toilet bowl covered in fresh vomit. I held my breath and washed my face and hands with plenty of soap and hot water. When I was finished, Laetecia was waiting for me.

'Sure you want to come?'

Why me? I wanted to say. What did I do to get your attention?

'I'm sure.'

She picked two bottles of champagne from the refrigerator. We left the presidential suite and walked down the thickly carpeted corridor, bumping into totally ripped revellers like it was a wild new year's eve.

'How did you get us a room?'

'I know this place pretty well.'

'You work here?'

'Sort of.'

We stopped at the lift doors and she pressed the down button. The look in her face said she wondered if I finally realised.

In a second I did.

'Oh,' I said. 'So what about Jamie?'

'We go back quite a few years. Thing is, it's the work I *used* to do, finished as of tonight. While the party was going on I was attending to my last date. The real last. I've got the savings I've been aiming for. In three days I'll be in Thailand, one month of beaches. When I come back I'm going back to university.'

'To study what?'

'Psychology. You could say I'm quite interested in human nature.'

As the lift descended she didn't stand too near, probably wondering if I'd really want to be close to someone like her. I barely knew the answer myself. In this light she didn't look quite as young as I thought she was; still, she wouldn't have been over thirty. She had clear skin and the whites of her eyes were very white indeed, as if she was full of health. But she worked at something that was full of sickness and the potential for terminal disease, and not just of the body, but of the heart and soul too. Just like my mother.

It was odd. Why was I the one? Nothing about her made me think she might have been trying to set me up for some sort of elaborate sting, and I didn't think she was going through this entire production just to tell me that if I wanted to fuck her it would require a certain amount of cash.

Room 2602. Laetecia flicked a switch and locked the door behind her. Subdued wall-lighting illuminated a good suite of rooms far smaller than the presidential suite. This place was quieter and warmer, but I was nervous. I thought of all the paid sex Laetecia would have had with men who were hard and ramming, no second thoughts to make them soft and useless. That's the way I'd be, thinking too much, too tired, useless. But I still didn't want to go home. That red kiss on the invitation had hooked me before I even met her.

Room 2602 was designed like an apartment, with a kitchen and glass doors that you could open to a balcony. Below were railway tracks and the start of a great expanse of dirt that in some visionary's mind would be the new and improved lungs of our city. Laetecia turned off the air conditioning. She wanted the balcony doors open and the rain had let up a little. Lightning flashed in the distance. Dawn was close. She popped a fresh bottle and found two coffee cups; for some reason there were no glasses to be found, no cutlery of any form, no plates, no saucepans. Maybe staff had already started taking souvenirs.

'To All Saints and All Souls,' she said.

'I don't quite get your interest in Halloween.'

'Want to hear some mad stuff?'

'Mad stuff is okay.'

'I've always felt an attraction for what comes after you die. I like the idea of a door opening and there being a way to get between this world and the next. No religion has the entire afterlife story right, but as soon as you say to yourself that, yes, there is an afterlife, then anything goes. When you say, okay, there is life after death, then you must believe there is a human spirit, a soul. Something that lives on. If that's so, then souls might be able to do things we can barely imagine – or that have been imagined all through history: our ancestors stay with us after they die; there's a Heaven and a Hell; we become reincarnated around a karmic circle. And so on. The idea of hauntings doesn't become so silly. If the soul of a human being does go on then it has to be some-where, right?'

'Well, let's not talk about somewhere for a second. Let's talk about here. This suite.'

'There aren't any spirits here. This place is like a cardboard box. No other-worldly vibes, that's for sure.'

'No, I mean why am I here?'

Laetecia poured herself more champagne. I didn't want any, inside I was seedy and tired enough.

'Jamie spoke about you. I went to see him play and that's when I saw you.'

'But like you said, that was a long time ago. And I'm sure I never met you.'

'Hmm, I was younger, and Jamie didn't know I went to a show, not the first or any other time.'

I thought about what she said, trying to figure it out. 'How often did you see us play?'

'Maybe a half-dozen gigs. I used to do up my hair, wear heavy makeup and lots of kohl around the eyes, dress in black and stay up the back. It wouldn't have been right for Jamie to know I was following the band.'

'Because he was a client.'

'Correct. Jamie had problems with girls. All that talent, but women didn't find him attractive. He used to come see me every fortnight, sometimes weekly. I liked him, but he never knew how

228

much. This went on nearly two years. He's got something, you know. He's an *old* soul. It's such a pity we didn't meet in a different way.'

It was so strange to be having this conversation. It made me uncomfortable, but from Laetecia none of it sounded so impossible. 'You're really into this stuff.'

'Maybe. My mother was a professional mourner. So was my grandmother, and who knows, maybe my grandmother's mother too.'

'What the hell is a professional mourner?'

'Where my family came from, they believed that when people died the more mourners there were the better things would work out at the gates of Heaven.'

'You mean, lots of people crying means you must have been a good person?'

'And the more there are and the louder they wail, the more loved you were. So paid mourners like my mother were hired by the families of the deceased to really put on a show. Tears, prayers, grief – and the better the show a woman could put on, the more she was paid.'

'Huh, I like that idea. To have crazy women wailing at your funeral, it'd make everyone reconsider your worth.'

She laughed. The whole thing was funny, all right.

'But with your mother, that was just a paid gig, so it didn't have anything to do with souls or ghosts or anything.'

'No, it did. Some of those professional mourners used to be able to see the dead person amongst them. The louder they wailed, the more clearly they saw them. In the region my family came from, they believed wailing called the soul out of the corpse and set it free.'

'Pity when everyone's quiet, or if no one turns up.'

'It's just a superstition. But those women really did believe they could see the dead person, especially when the wailing reached fever pitch. In the old country they were professional mourners, but the really spiritual ones like my mother were also called *stregas* — sort of like witches. That's the streak that ran through the women in my family.'

'You're a witch.'

'A pretty useless one.'

'Where's this place your family came from?'

'The deep south of Italy. I left when I was six.'

'My stepfather said he came from the deep south too.'

'My father's name is Stefano and he's living in a beachside retirement village about two hours from here.'

'For a second I was thinking maybe you were my unknown stepsister or something. Why the move?'

'My parents split, a big thing in those days. *Papà* got me and we came to Australia. I can't explain why my mother gave me up, but people say she didn't want me following in her footsteps. Maybe sending me away was her trick for breaking the cycle.'

'Then what about your brothers? Roland and Joseph?'

'Okay, now you're getting the lot. The boys aren't my brothers. They run a half-dozen girls like me. Some of them are full-time, but I've always been a part-timer. I've had plenty of breaks from the biz. Travelled Eastern Europe once. Got my first degree. History and nineteenth-century literature, if you want to know. None of us ever used to work the club, but we did use this hotel.'

'"Sparks" isn't your real name then?'

'That's right.'

I thought it over. 'What about "Laetecia"?' Her reply was a smile. 'Then what is it?'

'That's classified.'

'You've got to be the strangest girl I've ever spoken to.'

'Isn't that a good thing?'

The exhaustion was lifting, that early morning jaded feeling going away too. I felt as if a door was opening. Crazy. But she was like a balm, this young woman with no real name any more, at least no real name for me. The rain resumed its steady beat and blew through the open doors. She started to unbutton my shirt, pushed some hair away from my eye.

'I've talked a lot,' she said. 'I don't think I've known a man who's wanted to listen so much.'

'Talk can be good.'

'Even with the crazy things I say?'

I nodded. Laetecia kissed the side of my face and snuggled into me, her head against my chest.

'How old are you, Max?'

'Thirty-eight in a couple of weeks. How about you?'

'Thirty-one.' I put my arms around her. She said, 'You know the mistake men make with the women they pay for? They think it has to be like hardcore movies. Women don't like to have their breasts squeezed like fruit. They don't like getting their nipples pinched and twisted. If you rub her clitoris too hard it will hurt. A woman doesn't like sperm in her hair or across her face. She doesn't like a man to ram her blindly, to force a finger or two into her anus, or to have her ear nearly bitten off.'

She hid her face. It was quite a speech. Despite all the things she must have done, she was still just as vulnerable as anyone. Fair enough, I thought, if I can do it then let this be for her.

My heart wasn't pounding. My anxiety had disappeared. Every time Laetecia looked at me I felt like someone better. The rain outside was getting even heavier. I undressed her piece by piece and under that sober clothing was a ripe woman's body. There was colour in her cheeks and her breasts were swollen. Even her nipples were large. I didn't have a condom and asked her if she did. Laetecia opened her handbag, but when she passed one over there was something strangely hesitant about her manner.

I kissed her all over, everything between us nice and gentle. It had to be because I could see the redness left in her skin from where someone had been not quite so tender. Her final client. I understood why she'd wanted to give me some instructions. I took it slow until it wasn't time to be slow any more.

'Wait, wait,' she said. Laetecia eased off the condom, then swallowed me deep inside.

'*Now.*' Then she held me while we listened to the rain.

XV

Next time I opened my eyes the sun was above the hori-
zon, but had to compete against rain patches and black
thunderclouds.

'Look at that,' Laetecia — real name unknown — said, and
walked out of the bedroom and across to the open balcony
doors.

She stood there a minute and I knew this would be with me
for a long time, because such moments are all too rare, even if
you spend your life straining and railing against death, which
is of course what good sex is — our rebellion against oblivion. I
couldn't recall a woman's silhouette that looked quite so powerful. Laetecia went into the rain and leaned naked over the railing.
No one in this gloomy dawn would see her but she didn't seem
the type to care anyway. When I followed her we hugged, two
people in nature's good grace — but even grace can be too cold
and too wet, and soon we were laughing and shivering. Laetecia's
teeth were chattering. Her skin was covered in goose pimples and
her nipples had become tight and hard. She wanted to stay there.
I held her tight, rubbing my face along her wet long hair.

She said, 'I talked my head off last night, but you haven't told me anything. So tell me something. Tell me something now.'

'Okay. Maybe some of the things you said weren't so mad. Once, I did something terrible. I mean, really bad. It lost me someone – and for a long time I thought I was going to die. I was sort of demolished, but instead of it being one thing or the next, I felt like I went through a door and spent too long half-in and half-out of the world. The boundary between being alive and being dead really was sort of blurred.'

'What happened then?'

'A woman by the name of Patti helped me. Things turned out all right.'

'Did you want to marry her?'

That made me grin. Me and old Patti. 'Yeah, that would have been fun.'

That was it. We couldn't take any more of the cold. We shut the rain out of the room and warmed ourselves. Wrapped in a towel, Laetecia sat in the armchair while I made coffee in the kitchen. At least the place hadn't been completely cannibalised.

She rubbed her hair with another towel. Then I was conscious of the fact that she'd stopped and was watching me. She said, 'So how do you know everything turned out all right?'

It felt as if I'd been awake a week, me all numb and silly in the head. The coffee had dripped into the pot and it smelled good. I started to pour two cups.

'Because I'm happy, Lee. Right now I'm really happy.'

XVI

Midday, and the Premier's doors rattled and the steering wheel shook before its cold engine would cough into life. The city streets were still hazy with showers as I drove off into the daytime shadows.

At the stroke of ten the suite's telephone had started ringing. We didn't answer it until they'd tried another seven times. Friends of the managers or not, the reception staff wanted everyone checking out. It was time for the hotel to empty one last time. We ignored the calls, sitting in front of the rain, drinking bottled orange juice. Then, when I was finally on my way, downstairs I'd seen that Joseph, Roland and some workmen were already ripping out fittings from the club. Joseph and Roland were in last night's clothes; they might still have been drunk and stoned because they worked with haphazard gusto, smashing more things than they were neatly removing.

I watched for a minute, but didn't go speak to them. That was because I wasn't sure I'd be able to talk anyway. First the intensity of that 'End of the World' play-off against Misty Blue, then the almost delirious ecstasy of being with Laetecia.

What I'd done before coming downstairs was to beg 'Laetecia Sparks' to come with me. I didn't want things to end in a hotel suite. Sex was the smallest part of it. Red lipstick kisses too. There was a moment when she'd been drinking a cup of coffee, tired, her long black hair straggling over her face. Watching her, that towel covering creamy breasts and dark nipples swollen with kisses, I thought, I'm going to know this girl for the rest of my life. I want to. I'll never be half-hearted again. She should be mine and I want to marry her. That's it. There's nothing else. That's exactly what I want.

'Come with me, come to my place. I'll make you breakfast. Then we can sleep the whole day, if you want.'

I liked the way a smile curled in the corner of her mouth, sleepy eyes crinkling up. 'You don't know me, Max, and I don't know you.'

'After all this?'

'It's just one night.'

'Sure,' I said, 'but we could get to know each other. You just have to give it the chance.'

'I don't go home with men.'

'Those days are over though, aren't they? This is your new life, right?'

'My last real boyfriend was Roland Sparks and that was more than three years ago. I just have to go slow now.' She smiled some more. 'The one thing I learned by being with so many men is that there's a price for being with any man. I'm not sure I really like a lot of what I saw.'

'But it's not fair to think of me that way too.'

'You're right.' She placed my hand against her cheek. 'Maybe when I do know you.'

'Okay. Then I'll give you a lift home. Let's at least leave together.'

She put her cup down and slowly got to her feet. Her towel fell away and she slipped naked into my lap. 'I'd really like to, but no, we can't do that either.'

'What's your real name, how can I contact you? "Laetecia". "Lee". What do I even call you?'

'Either of those is good. I'll make you a promise. You will see me again. Maybe when you're not expecting it, there I'll be.'

I found a square of notepaper and wrote down my full name, address and telephone number. 'You better be.'

Abject weariness finally had the better of her. And me too. We stopped talking when she turned her lips up to mine. Morning bad breath kisses. Something about that made me want her more. We were exhausted and raw, but for just a little while longer I was that boy Maree Kilmister taught everything she knew in front of stacks of vinyl records. Laetecia clung to me.

'Did I hurt you? Lee, what's the matter?'

'Oh God, you're sweet. Max, you're just so sweet.'

The Premier's engine sounded as shaky as a cheap motorbike. It didn't like the rain and neither did I. Conny used to say his car had more character than most of the people he met. Maybe one day I'd get a real job and make some money, really get this car fixed up properly. I'd drive Laetecia Sparks around in Conny's beautifully reconditioned Premier sedan, an acrylic lacquer job giving it back its old-world iridescent sheen, plus new narrow-band whitewall tyres, chrome wheel trim rings and all. That would be a laugh. We'd go to the beach and to movies and to clubs. What would life be like then? I'd enrol in some proper music conservatorium too, put myself through course after course of advanced drumming techniques. It was time to get serious. I'd been on a plateau in my rock band, had improved out of sight in Jamie Lazaroff's jazz ensembles, but now I'd well and truly plateaued again. There were parts of some of the more complex pieces DoctorJay played where I really fudged, really did some flashy things to hide the fact I couldn't quite follow the snap and zing of the records. I thought I got away with it, but someone like Jamie used to know; you couldn't fool a natural like him. So I'd better get ready. My band was dead, but one day a hot group like Misty Blue will need a new drummer and there I'll be, the best in the business.

I pulled away from the hotel and didn't like the fact that everything I'd experienced in there would soon fall under wrecking balls and jackhammers. Just before I left 2602 Laetecia had fallen asleep in the big bed. I didn't want to wake her, but didn't want to leave her like that either. Looking at her lying there naked wasn't enough. I wanted her. Again and again and again. I put my mouth on her breast, then moved down and parted her legs, lapping at her cunt. Reckless. Every single thing I'd done with her. Reckless. I thought of all the men who'd paid good money to be allowed to get on their knees and bury their faces in her; I thought of my mother strung out on smack, a skinny, scrawny, rag-doll of a toy for men full of wrath and self-justification, probably not so much unlike me.

So what? Laetecia tasted like honey and gold. What she'd done before was over and what was now was me.

I left her sleeping, but she would go on sleeping and when the demolition teams turned that place into memories she'd become only a memory too. Room 2602 was my door into another world and when the suite was gone there'd be no more door and Laetecia would be gone with it.

Too late a night, too much champagne, too much exertion. I shook my head. Crazy thoughts. Get yourself straight, Max. We'll meet again soon enough; she promised as much.

It was good there wasn't too much traffic around. The day was grey and those low thunderclouds made the city seem unreal, like the flats of a film set without depth or texture. The storms would continue, but I'd be home, showered and clean, and asleep in bed. But when *might* I see Laetecia again? What was the time I *might* least expect her? At my door, or in a club while I was playing another show, or would she contrive some accidental meeting in a supermarket, our trolleys banging into one another like those of absolute strangers?

A car horn resounded behind me. I'd let a red light turn green and then red again and I hadn't even moved. *Jesus.* Could have killed somebody.

I lifted my hand in apology to the yellow taxi in the rear-vision mirror. The driver might or might not have seen the gesture. When the light changed again he powered his vehicle past me with an angry slide of tyres. They kicked up muddy water that covered my windscreen. I didn't want to hold anyone else up, and as I fumbled at the wiper control the stupid things wouldn't work and, too late, I saw that I'd managed to drive straight through a stop sign. I was in an intersection and a truck of some sort was already swerving to avoid me.

Before it hit I saw Conny's neck snapping. Then the impact threw my head backwards and to the side. I felt a crunch go through my body as the driver's door crumpled in against me. My mouth filled with a rubble of teeth. The Holden slewed left, driven by the direct sideways smack of the truck, which could not stop, and without traction my car aquaplaned on and on, to finally bend with a shriek of metal around a power pole. The passenger seat where I'd wanted Laetecia Sparks to sit while we kept our story going just a little longer more or less ceased to exist. A secondary crash of what I didn't know smashed all the glass around me. The windows and the windscreen were gone, rain and glass were blinding in my face, and the Premier's roof caved in.

Whatever was happening I no longer understood any of it, and was pulled down like a flagging swimmer into the limitless black below.

XVII

Buddy Bettridge looks up into all the waiting faces. These good folk want to hear more of the Chronicles of Max, and he likes that, so much so that sometimes he thinks he's less the high priest of funerals and more a storyteller of old, fashioning tales that make sense of the peaks, troughs and blank, awfully bland spaces in people's lives. Maybe that's all any priest ever did anyway: Friends, it all didn't mean nothing, your good times and bad added up to something worthwhile. Trust me and I'll tell you how.

He hasn't needed to consult his notes and now folds them into his hand. When he was fourteen he broke his right arm falling out of a tree, so has no idea what it must have been like to be so — demolished. Now there's an interesting choice of word, he thinks, and what the hell made me come up with it? *Demolished.* Yes it's true, I tell him: people can believe that their emotional troubles can leave them in such a way, but it's not till you spend a couple of years in and out of hospitals, dealing with therapists, medicos and specialists of various types, and even the tea ladies who bring you meals made of cardboard and plastic, that you realise the true meaning of a word like that.

I wish I could make Buddy see something that actually does hurt as much as the physical agonies of being mended. A fully loaded bread delivery van was coming, and in blinding rain it T-boned my Holden Premier, pushing it diagonally down a city street until the car wrapped around a telephone pole. There was an agonising screech of metal made by a sedan skidding and slamming into the dead Premier, and actually jumping on top of the cabin, crushing it down like an eggshell. I was half-crushed, trapped inside, but what hurt more was the small voice that drifted through an endless drug-delirium — *Are you there, Max? Are you there?* — and the way I could never quite open my eyes to see her. Later, the answer from the nurses in the ward was that Laetecia visited on a number of occasions, maybe three or four, then they never saw her again.

Buddy, that was it. She's not even here today. I've been looking and hoping, believe me.

He arranges his features into a friendly smile and contemplates his next words.

Wait, Buddy, wait. You've been doing a sterling job, but listen to me a sec. It's no wonder she's not here. Once I was out and free you should have seen the way I petitioned Joseph and Roland Sparks. Really, with all my heart, but they didn't want to help. Said Laetecia was gone, whereabouts unknown. Sometimes I hung around university campuses. Psychology, remember? History, nineteenth-century literature. Nothing. Sometimes I went to jazz gigs and stayed up the back, looking for a young woman with her hair up, wearing heavy makeup and lots of kohl around the eyes, dressed in black.

The one thing I learned by being with so many men is that there's a price for being with any man.

And what about women, Laetecia, that's what I would have

liked to ask her. What price am I paying for the fact of a woman like you? The only answer I ever got came out of the mouths of therapists: 'Come on Max, let's make it nine, let's make it ten. Wow, that's enough for today. Eleven – just an unbelievable effort.'

They did their best all right, but I wasn't a drummer any more. Right shoulder and right elbow just couldn't be repaired to that extent. Physical therapy went on forever, but I stopped taking their pain-killers. That was my one sacrifice for the lucidity I wanted to keep. Go on, Buddy, tell them that. Tell them that Max said to himself, If I'm going to stay on this planet and live, then I'm not gonna be drug-fucked. I will be *here*.

On the anniversary of the crash, the first card arrived. A hand-printed Halloween card with no name and no return address. God sighed and a decade passed and now I had ten of them.

In the meantime, I could drive, I could walk, I could even run for a bus, if required. The problem was the shoulder and elbow, trying to lift them. The rest I could deal with. I couldn't drum, but I knew a few styles of music. I knew sound and there was a perfectly good studio under the house that musicians and bands could use to practise. I remembered how I envied Misty Blue's equipment and their van. Every up-and-comer in the business knows how that feels. In my bank account, all my years of gardening and frugal living had accumulated into something. I went to see six bank and building society managers in a row until I found one stupid enough to give me a fat loan. The repayments were okay. This would work.

My own van and hand-picked sound equipment. Spent a fortune, really. I took out ads and became a fixture of every good and bad club in the city, hiring out my new mixing desk and stack of PA equipment to anyone who needed them. They make up a fair portion of the people here today in the church. For bands I liked, I also made sure the lighting they were getting would show them off to their best advantage, that their instrument set-up was good enough, and gave impromptu music lessons and advice when needed. The business thrived. No more mowing. Young musicians just referred to me as 'the drummer' even though I only sat in on rare occasions, and when I did, could only manage simple time signatures and very little adornment. Maybe a minute's drumming, that was it. Anything else hurt too much, but sometimes it was worth the effort to try, especially when all some kid needed was a quick demonstration of what he should be doing.

None of the playing hurt as much as each and every Halloween. Whenever my next card arrived in the letter box I would let out a string of curses and wish she'd at least delivered it by hand. The postal stamps revealed nothing. Then I'd slit open the envelope and there would be a Jack O'Lantern, or a hand-drawn picture of a twelve-year-old witch with an eight-year-old werewolf, or a blurry doorway opening this world into the next. She had a sense of humour. Most times I managed to smile too. She wrote things like, *I don't forget you*, or, a couple of times, *Thank you, Max*.

Yeah, some thanks.

Well, Buddy, it's going fast now, and isn't that the way the last bits of a life go — fast?

So tell them we're on the road to that dance with a girl named Ash.

XVIII

No one was making much money or getting worthwhile work in the live music business. Jazz clubs were history and rock venues were becoming as rare as drive-in theatres. Their replacements were cheap and it made my teeth ache just to be inside their chintzy walls listening to the new corporate rock sound of computer-processed three-chord tunes. Weird how it all sounded alike to me, as if some factory in LA was using a cookie cutter to create rock group after rock group that relied on heavily over-produced riffs recycled from everything you'd ever heard before. In the Sixties Phil Spector created the wall of sound but the Nineties and the new noughts were all about some executive's idea of a slab of sound, and it was as exciting as getting pounded by a side of beef.

So now I was a dinosaur.

Most of my work went into setting-up in low-rent pubs with musicians who wanted the opposite of the new sound. Young bands heard about me and saved up their dollars to get the dirty feel of old. My equipment was good, it didn't much rely on the silicon chip and I knew what I was doing. Before long I was more than just 'the drummer' but a middle-aged guru — business took off. The truck and the gear even went interstate, often without me. If I trusted someone enough, I took their money and handed them the keys.

I told these kids, Shoot straight or don't shoot at all. Got it?

My hair thinned; my skin wrinkled. My legs lost meat and my belly got bigger. If musicians had kids I'd spend hours playing with them at sound-checks, fascinated by things like full cheeks, chubby arms, small white teeth — everything that's the opposite of decay.

When I hauled equipment I puffed a lot; tests found the problem. Atherosclerosis. Back into hospital I went, but they didn't even consider the procedure a major surgery. The surgeons gave me a balloon angioplasty because one of my arteries was strangulated by gunk. I got a lesson in bad living and the price you pay, but I went back to work feeling better than I had in years. My GP, Dr Bailey, told me I could live a normal life with normal exertion, no blood-thinning medicine required. Maybe lose a bit of weight; well, a lot.

I resumed work and forgot about it, because one of the new bands I was doing sound for was pretty good. They were called BeerGoggles but I pulled the manager aside and asked him if he was trying to kill them before they even started. Give them something catchy to be known as, let it ring in people's minds. Try Dirtybeat or maybe — no, it stuck. Dirtybeat's sort of raw rock-and-roll melded well with my anti-technology equipment so it was a marriage that just worked, then down the line an opportunity came when they needed my truck and PA in Sydney for a record company showcase. I told them to pay me a security deposit and look after the whole thing themselves, but no, they wanted me to travel with them and be there twiddling dials at the show. At the last minute their hassled and harangued manager came down with pleurisy and there was no one else to nursemaid them through their big shot at impressing the impresarios. It was time to give in.

I set off down the highway while they flew economy. When we met up in Sydney at the Sacré Coeur Theatre, which wasn't a religious auditorium, but a large, run-down music venue, the band played a monster of a show. It was good to have been there to see it after all. The record company plus its one hundred invitees went wild.

At the end of the night I left the Dirtybeat boys to the new, loving arms of the recording and management corps that had just discovered them. The lines of coke were running too long for my liking. In the darkness of the empty car park, while I unlocked the truck and climbed in, I couldn't help wondering if these so-called impresarios would turn out to be the real deal or just some modern incarnation of the likes of Iron John. I guess because of the record company attentions Iron John Tempest kept coming to mind. Maybe my job with the boys wasn't to nursemaid them through but to nursemaid them the fuck *out*.

Nah, I wasn't a manager. The boys had performed a great show and with luck they'd be stars one day. They'd have to grow up and think for themselves, fast.

The energy and excitement of their playing had rubbed off on me, but even though my blood was up it was time to get back to my hotel room. I was still about twenty kilos heavier than I'd been before the accident and these days my poorly mended body needed plenty of rest. My fingers touched the ignition key, but didn't turn it. I rolled my window down and enjoyed the quiet and solitude of the late hour. Music drifted from the back of the Sacré Coeur, as did the unmistakable odour of hash. Funny, that sound and smell hadn't travelled into the car park before. A minute ago the place had been closed up tight, all its doors shut, however the theatre's rear exit was now open – and someone was framed in that doorway, looking across the otherwise empty car park towards my truck and me.

Was it a woman? None of the boys had brought their girlfriends. None of the record company people was female. The bar staff had long since packed up and gone home. The theatre owner himself had been doling out the drinks and the drugs, some French guy by the fancy name of Etienne. I squinted, trying to see; something was up.

She crossed the gravel, footsteps crunching until she stopped in a sliver of yellow light. My mind went into a sort of spiral. Through the windscreen I saw she was thin and had a bird-like quality. Her hair was dark instead of blonde, not quite black but laced with strands of grey. She still liked it long. I could barely understand that there were lines etched around her eyes and mouth, and loose skin under her chin and jaw, but it was her, she remained unmistakable. Debbie Canova had lost her youth, but hadn't we all?

I got out of the cabin and climbed unsteadily down, keeping firm hold of the hand-grip. She stepped closer. I wanted to find someone who could explain why it should be that after decades of wishing for her, we had to meet in a car park that stank of last week's garbage and the unhappy marriage of human and animal urine. I'd been thinking about Iron John and who should be here but her.

'Hey, Max. How are you?'

I might have nodded a reply, unable to speak or let go of the side of the truck. Finally I said, 'What are you doing here?'

'Here? Etienne is my husband.'

'That guy inside?'

'Sure.'

'You've been here all night?'

'I stayed in the office,' Debbie replied, reaching into her hand-bag and taking out a fat and exquisitely hand-crafted joint. 'Shall we go up there?'

She meant the truck. I pulled myself back up as if entering a dream. When I looked behind me I saw the way worry lines in her forehead and between her eyebrows grew deeper. She was frown-ing, having noticed my weight and how painful the effort to get into the cabin. She climbed up after me and sat in the passenger seat. I was behind the wheel. We weren't going anywhere, but she pulled the door shut. I didn't like the way she noticed my crabbed way of moving, the obvious lack of motion in my right shoulder and arm.

'I was in an accident,' I said. 'Got a bit banged up.'

She used a lighter to get the weed going, then passed it to me. 'It's good to see you, Max, banged up or otherwise.'

My hand was shaking. Perspiration broke out on my forehead. My face was hot. I wondered if she could tell.

'Yes,' was all I could reply. 'Yes.'

We sat smoking in silence. With so much to say neither of us could get a word out. I swivelled around to look at the side of her face. How much despair had she caused me, how much heart-ache – and all I could do was wish I still had the right to touch her. Fuck it, why not. I've waited long enough.

The joint helped. She didn't flinch, so I caressed her thin, lined cheek with the backs of my fingers. In fact, she leaned into the touch, pressing to me. It was the best thing I could have done because she closed her eyes and then she spoke.

'Three children. Two girls and a boy. Eighteen, sixteen and eleven. The eleven-year-old is Jason, the light of my life. The girls too, but they're so independent now.'

'How — what happened?'

She rubbed her face against my arm, like a cat. She cuddled in to me, still keeping her eyes closed. 'I met Etienne when I was still playing. He was a musician a bit like you, very talented but unfocused. He found his forté in business. He runs three venues like this one and I do some of the accounts. I've heard you've done well too. You're a legend with these bands. The smashed-up drummer who's the audio man, the story keeps coming up. I knew you'd get here one day. I've been expecting you.'

'You've been expecting me?'

'Yes.'

'Don't you think you could have just called?'

She shook her head. 'No.' Her lines were quite harsh and she seemed much older than her years, as if she'd given more and suffered more than most.

'Fuck, I think about you, Debbie Canova.'

She liked that for about five seconds. Her eyes opened as I handed her the joint. She said, 'Debbie Canova? That takes me back.'

'What?'

'I haven't heard that name for a long time.' She kind of laughed and I had no idea what she meant. 'Debbie's a little girl's name. And Canova was my first husband's name. Remember Phil? These days people call me Mrs Deborah Debasque, or when we go back to Etienne's home in France it's Madame Debasque. *C'est chic, non?*'

I hated the lightness in her tone. Despised it. And Madame Debasque — it sounded like some harlot's idiot mother in a costume farce. I wanted to shake her, but said instead, 'So, what have you been doing, I mean, other than the kids?'

'Well, art college started me on the right road. I was able to combine art with my music when I went into therapy. That was Etienne's influence. I needed help very badly. I was approaching the point of not being able to function with other people, not trust anyone at all any more. You might remember a bit about why. But I was lucky. Things came together and I've been studying and working in music therapy. Mostly with abused children. It's been about twenty years now.'

'Twenty. Is that all?'

She didn't like the sarcasm in my tone, but it was a lot to swallow. In fact, it was a quarter century since she left me. I gasp, God sighs, and there you go, twenty-five years pass since the last time I held her. It didn't really change anything. I still wanted to kiss her. I still wanted to caress her body. I wanted to arch *Debbie Canova*'s stiff, old back over these seats and be the young man I used to be all over again.

And what did she want?

Debbie frowned, lips parted. She leaned toward me.

'I can't say. Max—'

My hand went around the back of her neck. I pulled her to me and bruised her lips with mine. I heard her sigh. I remembered that sigh. It still had the power to reach deep down into me; my cock was as hard as it used to be all those years ago. She was the one. The one. My body knew it, but I could barely believe it. Distance is nothing, time is immaterial, a sigh travels across decades and hits you in the same places.

Her hands were in my hair, pulling me to her mouth. She lay back and drew me over her. It was overwhelming, like being sucked down into the deepest, happiest dream you ever had. She felt the same, she kissed the same, her wandering hands grasped my erection through my trousers just the way I remembered.

Not a minute had passed since the last time she'd done that. Her breath, that panting in my ear, so familiar, so well-known. I was kissing her and tugging at her clothes.

Then her little gypsy shirt was open and I unsnapped the front clasp of her pink brassiere. How so like Debbie Canova – pink. I buried my face and lips into her breasts, but there's where the dream unravelled, because her breasts were relics of what I remembered. Debbie tried to push them up for me, but they were worn folds of skin, and when I ran my hands along her waistline there was no real sense of a waist at all, just a continuous line of thickened flesh. She pushed me onto my back and her fingers undid the buttons of my trousers. This was a teenagers' game, making out in a car. Or the cab of a truck; pretty much the same thing. Once upon a time we would have revelled in it.

Her mouth sought out my prick and though it was hard it wasn't as hard as it was one minute ago. I had time to say to myself, My dream's come true but I've got a huge belly and a new set of teeth, a balloon in my heart and a prick that thinks too much. Not only that, but in this cramped space my side hurts the way it hasn't hurt in a long time, and my arm, my elbow – God, in a second I might just have to cry out in agony.

Debbie's caressing hand gave up as my cock died in her mouth. She straightened herself and by that flickering yellow streetlamp I saw her eyes were wide, shocked and almost afraid. She said, 'Oh God, Max, I'm sorry.'

'Fuck,' I said. 'Me too.'

'What was I thinking? What was I thinking?' she breathed. Slowly she did up her bra and her blouse. 'For a lot of years I – I don't know how to say this.'

'Just say anything you want. It doesn't matter.'

'For a lot of years I wanted to throw everything away and have a life of mindless fucking with you, try to find happiness that way.'

It felt as if my guts were emptying, my stupid heart too. Maybe this was the sort of thing that should have made me feel good, but it didn't. Mindless fucking. Try to find happiness. She wouldn't come because she needed or loved me, not even because she liked me. Dreaming of my cock while I dreamed of her heart. Well, yes, and her tits, and her mouth, ass, and pussy, everything – but it was everything. Everything I thought that was in her. It was enough for me, all I wanted.

I was ill. The joint and Debbie Canova, too overwhelming in one dose. Things would never change: I'd always wish she loved me and she never had and never would. My old aunt Emma and Conny, so different and so apparently incompatible, but they'd been able to stand shoulder to shoulder, need against need. Debbie and I had never had that; maybe we could have but we'd given in too easily. Plenty of passion but passion burns and leaves ashes. I stopped myself from crying; I wasn't even sure she would comfort me.

'I have to go—'

'Debbie. Wait, please.'

'*Deborah.*'

'Okay. Deborah. Tell me. Aren't you happy?'

'I'm happy enough.'

'Kids, husband—?'

'Max, I love them with all my heart.'

'But you came here to me. To be with me. You could have just stayed hiding somewhere in there, couldn't you?'

'I was hiding,' she nodded, not looking in my direction. 'In the office with the accounts books.'

'Want me to drive you home?'

'My car's out the front. If I walk down that side-path Etienne won't even know I didn't go when I said.'

'Debbie—'

'*Deborah Debasque*. I'm a married woman with kids,' she said, pulling it out of herself, 'with kids I adore. I don't know what I was thinking. Seeing you again. I didn't plan to try and – I just thought a joint and a chat with Max. My old drummer. But it's like time has stood still. Butterflies, straight in my belly.'

'Butterflies.'

'Yes.'

'Even though I'm not much of the man I used to be?'

'I bet you have your moments, Max.'

Did I? Did I have my moments? And was that enough – just a few moments to fill up the rest of a life? I felt a wave rising, ready to break over me. 'I should never have hurt Iron John. You were right. You were, Debbie. A monster. Me. What did I do?'

'Stop it. Stop it, Max. Listen.' She caught her breath. 'I can't say this more than once. The truth. That day, when he did what he wanted, Iron John said I teased him, little playful looks, little flirts. Stringing him along so that I could get what I wanted. He was right. I did. That's exactly it. Since I was little I never trusted anyone would like my talent, see it as good enough, give me a chance, and as soon as I grew up I knew how to hook men, get their attention. Get them to like me and want me. I did that with Iron John. You can't touch but I'll let you follow me like a puppy, and here, I'll swish my little dress and let you see my panties, and you just follow, and then you give me what I want, but don't ever try to touch.'

'You can't say—'

'I don't. I don't say I deserved it but I knew what I was doing. Then—,' Debbie's breath caught again. 'Then I liked what you did to him. God I liked it. Yes, smash him. Yes, make him bleed. It appealed to the worst part of me. Maim him. *Hurt* him. I pictured it every waking minute and in my dreams too. Destroy a man the way you would squash a cockroach under your shoe and wipe the disgusting remains off on a brick. You did what I wanted to do and I couldn't look at that every day. Couldn't fuck with that every night. You did the blackest thing inside my soul, Max, as if I sent you to do it. You were the perfect other side of me. I was too scared to even look at that, but you weren't a monster, you were my mirror.'

She was crying and I tried to take hold of her; she pushed me away.

'I ran. I ran and ran and ran.'

All those deep lines, all that pain etched into her face. All those years of biting down on anger and resentment. Squashing down on something that wouldn't be squashed. When had it started, as soon as she was developing and men wanted her? Or later, when her dreams stayed always a step out of reach? I grabbed her hands and pulled them to my chest. She struggled but I wouldn't let go. I kissed her hands, her fingers, fighting her all the way. She had perfect fingernails on both hands, the left and the right. No more violin. No more music.

'One more thing. Then I have to go, okay?' I let go of her hands and she wiped her eyes. Everything went quiet and still. Soon, in the dark, a twenty-two-year-old Debbie Canova was looking at me, her brow creased with concern and just a little love. She took a breath, and another and another. 'You said it right. Fuck, I think of you, Max.'

Debbie opened the passenger door and climbed down. I watched her shadow lengthen as she hurried across the empty car park. I couldn't believe she was going. She disappeared into the black beside her husband's theatre. A dream.

I thought, this can't be. Is this what I get? Is this it?

XIX

So came the second time I paid for a woman's body.

I didn't turn the key in the ignition; couldn't. Left the truck and went back into the theatre. My boys were drunk and high as kites. The goodies supplied by Etienne and all those record executive types had their effect. Closer inspection seemed to show that these impresarios didn't seem all that impressive after all. There was the standard sort of talk about constant touring and cracking the United States. A fifteen year old would have said the same thing. The boys were probably already tasting wealth, fame and easy female companionship. Sex and tons of it. Still, it was a masculine affair in here. So much drinking and celebrating and not a woman in sight.

They were surprised to see me back, but were pleased too. Even cheered. Why did I decide not to go back to the hotel? I mumbled some reply. The truth is, I wanted a closer look at this guy, Etienne Debasque. I sat in a deep armchair and accepted a drink, heavy eyes on him. What's so special about you? What made you the right one? He was neither tall nor short; in a certain light you could see the scars left over from what must have been terrible adolescent acne. He was friendly, even courtly, but not particularly interesting. Only the faintest touch of a sexy accent too, nothing to write home about. In total, what? A solid father and husband? If so, why had Debbie Canova so easily bent to me in the truck — why, even, did she wait to see me?

Fuck, I think of you, Max.

Etienne was putting on a sophisticate's turn, now mixing martinis. A move wasted on Dirtybeat. And on me. Vodka and accoutrements flowed from his expert hands. He handed me a martini and when I gulped it down he didn't flinch, but made me another. I noticed he didn't drink. He didn't touch the lines of coke being snorted like fairy dust. No joints for him; he wasn't even smoking a cigarette. The martinis and marijuana made my brain sizzle. Fuck you, I was telling him — and he politely delivered snacks and speed on a tray. That's rock-and-roll for you.

One of the jerks passing for a music executive these days suddenly stated the obvious. We needed women. Etienne reeled off a shopping list of possibilities — Ocean Nights, Pussy Galore's, The Grotto, The Kasbah, Poison Ivy's, Casablanca — how nice he knew them all by heart. There was enthusiastic agreement and he used an expensive-looking mobile phone to call two taxis. His face was charming yet thoroughly inscrutable. I had no idea what he might be thinking.

By the time the taxis arrived every one of us was crazy with vodka slammers. We climbed six apiece into each cab. I grabbed the stone-cold-sober Etienne hard by the bicep and told him he just *had* to come with us. Without smiling he pulled his arm out of my grip and said nothing. Did he know my history with Debbie Canova or was he wordlessly telling me, Fuck you too you degenerate rock-and-roller, I've got a wife and kids to get home to?

He slammed the taxi doors and waved us goodbye, definitely

257

not coming. Whatever this night was supposed to be, it wasn't
for him. As my particular taxi pulled away I turned around and
through the window glass looked him full in the face. He made
his hands into fervent fists and his expression into one of suppli-
cation to heaven. Then he held those fists hard to his heart. The
meaning was clear: Good luck, Godspeed with your boys, let's
pray for a brilliant contract. Let's get them on their way.

A fan. How thoroughly deflating.

As I sat back into the uncomfortable press of those drunk and
excited masculine bodies I knew how wrong I was to feel this way.
Debbie Canova loved a nice man. A good guy. Maybe the mirror
to the good part of her. But me. Yeah, but me. I was the unlovable
anti-DC, huh?

My side didn't hurt and neither did my arm or my elbow, the
spots where the pain usually concentrated. My body was numb,
but my mind sizzled. I slumped in the seat anyway. So I'd finally
laid eyes on her again. I'd seen her, kissed her; my prick had even
been in that once-lovely mouth – and nothing. Instead I let myself
be affected by the shock of facing what she was, a middle-aged
woman with three children and a second husband. She didn't
make music any more – and every word of a confession she must
have bitten down on over twenty-five years was a blade that cut
more and more deeply inside of her.

And now inside of me.

The first place, Casablanca, didn't need two taxi-loads of drunks.
Similarly, Pussy Galore's seemed to prefer to wait for the more
James Bond-types of the world. The seedier Poison Ivy's received
our number gratefully. As everyone trooped inside I hung back.
The entrance door shut and I slipped away, drunker and much
more stoned than I'd realised, staggering down the quiet street
humming some popular glam-song from the Seventies. I knew

what it was: Alice Cooper singing, *God/I feel so strong/I feel so strong/I'm
so strong/I feel so strong*.

I'd been down this particular little avenue in 1973, during a
short trip to Sydney for a reason I'd forgotten. I wished it really
was 1973 and me a young man again, no belly to carry around and
no stupid stent in my artery.

A blue light was blinking; my vision was blurry. This place was
called either Ali Baba or Ali-Ali, or something else entirely. I went
in and leaned against a counter, took a deep breath and looked up
into the sallow cheeks of a fiftyish woman who conducted herself
with as much circumspection as a fishmonger. She was laughing,
braying really, at something on a portable television. It took her
a second to finish.

'What?'

'I want to choose,' I breathed.

She must have thought I was about to expire right there. She
flicked off the TV and came around the counter, helping me into
the next room. She put me onto a couch. As requested, there was
a short parade of the *carte du jour*.

'There, her.'

'Jezebel?'

I couldn't help laughing a little. 'Yes, Jezebel,' but she was
already Debbie Canova. Roughly the same height, roughly the
correct eye colour, and just about as firm and fresh as the day I
met her in Thornberry. In my coat was an envelope stuffed with
cash. Etienne had paid the band for the night's performance,
so I paid cash for my Jezebel and followed her into a clean, air-
conditioned room that had one purpose. Jezebel sat on the bed
after stripping off her blouse and miniskirt. She was in black linge-
rie. I wished it was white so she would seem as unsoiled as the
room – or pink, Debbie's colour. I remembered what Debbie, or

Madame Debasque, had said about flicking her skirt, letting men see her panties so that she could tease them into giving her what she wanted. I remembered the first day in Thornberry, her helping that ancient grandpa-in-law of hers, the way we salivating dogs had taken in her long, smooth legs, her miniskirt, her flash of pink underpants. She was playing with us, even then?

I thought I was going to fall down. Jezebel waited with her legs crossed while I showered in the ensuite.

Go home, crossed my mind. I did not at all feel strong. *Get out of here*; but the piss and vinegar in old stupid men is sometimes too powerful to conquer. As I emerged, towel wrapped around my fat waist, she gave a beautiful smile and flipped a condom in its silvery sealed packet to me. I shook my head.

'Not this time, not tonight.'

'Sweetie,' she said, 'it's illegal to ask for unprotected sex and illegal to offer it.' She kept looking at me and it was a very friendly gaze, but the beautiful smile was gone. I went to my coat and pulled out the fat envelope. A fifty had no effect. Neither did two or three, but a fourth was just fine. She took off her bra and her breasts were bigger than Debbie's had ever been; certainly a lot bigger than they were now.

She pulled away the towel and went onto her knees. 'All right,' she said, 'I'll suck you off skinless, but you can't fuck me skinless,' and she went to work while I looked down at her bobbing blonde head, that glimpse of her swaying breasts, and I thought Debbie, Debbie, Debbie, and for better or worse that's when it hit me, the truth, and it wasn't some sweet candy-coloured truth about neverending love and eternal longing, but was instead the horror of having Debbie Canova in my arms and wishing I didn't, wishing I didn't see that middle-aged woman's dried-up mouth and dried-up tits, wishing I'd never heard the words of such corrosive honesty that she'd finally spoken. And in turn, I wished she never touched my great hairy belly, or witnessed the ache in my right side and arm. I wished I hadn't let my one love see the sad semi-erection of a fat, banged-up forty-nine-year-old man, or felt it deflate like a child's balloon in her mouth.

This grizzled lion was no longer roaring. Not even a whimper. Silent, I spurted, one hard little shot that hit Jezebel in the shoulder. The silvery bead stayed there. She smiled up at me. Really, such a beautiful smile. Her work was done, she had her money. I wished I knew this kid. I wished I could take her by the hand and lead her to some nice restaurant, where we'd sit at a corner table and I could say, 'Now, Jezebel, tell me a bit about yourself,' then speak to her about my mother, and advise her not to stay in this shit too much longer, not to let herself become a skinny, scrawny, rag-doll toy for worthless men like me.

Jezebel used a warm, wet flannel to dry me off and wipe that lousy little spit off the hollow of her shoulder. She put on her bra and took me by the hand, and sat me on the side of the bed. She used a different flannel to wipe the stupid tears falling from my eyes.

'Give me another fifty and you can tell me, Sweetie, tell me what's going on.'

I gave it to her. The kid put her slender, fragrant arms around my thick shoulders. She stared at the wall as tears dropped salty and forlorn down the exposed parts of her breasts, like the powerful sperm of all those younger and stronger men who paid for the privilege of spurting on her.

I said, 'It was a dream. Just a dream.'

'Then that's good, isn't it, Sweetie? That's really good. Dreams are fantastic.'

After I stumbled out of there, I spent the rest of the night in a different hotel room to the one I'd been booked into. I didn't want the boys to see me this way. All the way to dawn I huddled in on myself, wondering who or what could save me. The dream had been Debbie Canova and it hadn't turned out to be real. Maybe I'd never loved her; maybe the only thing I'd really felt was the need that eats the insides of all lonely people.

The next morning I called Darren, the band's notional leader. I told him I'd decided to stay in town and catch up with some old friends. He could drive my van back home while the others, all sour-breathed and sleepy-eyed, caught their return flight. Darren was only too happy to oblige; he loved my van and hated flying.

Three nights in a room devoid of character staring at beige curtains, eating hotel hamburgers and fries, watching execrable pay-per-view movies on the television. I felt I was in the aftermath of some cataclysm, but what had it been, really? Nothing but a lousy meeting with an old flame, followed by a drunkard's visit to a brothel. Things, nevertheless, felt finished. I felt finished. Yet when I organised a flight back and dragged myself home, on the telephone answering machine were each of the boys with the great news: a fat, three-record contract, recording dates starting in six weeks, and tentative bookings for a support spot on the national tour of a big name US metal band.

The record execs hadn't been impresarios of fakery. It was all true and the offer was as good as it gets. Soon my boys would have photo shoots, new girlfriends and a stylist. I had to laugh. What was finished? Just another chapter of my life. Dirtybeat wouldn't need my sound equipment any more. I could either put it all up for sale or keep on keeping on, it didn't matter either way.

Alone with the ghosts of my house I took out *DC*, the long-player recorded by Xodus (featuring Ms Deborah Canova). I didn't play the record, but instead stared at the album cover. My face next to hers against a grainy image of the wretched and miserable of this world travelling a lousy road. What had Iron John meant to convey? Was it some inescapable nihilism or perhaps the hopefulness you feel whenever you look into such young and open faces? I didn't know – but we were so young, captured like that forever. It was the only picture of her or us I had.

I didn't play the record because instead I was playing the answer-tape over and over, just to listen to the way the voices of the Dirtybeat boys sounded. It was certainly the other side of the coin to how I felt. Well, good for them. Come on, I told myself, it's good the world marches on. People like me and Debbie get old, but she has three children with her and I've got boys like these watching their dreams come true. Whatever joy you lose yourself, it means less than nothing to the ones who come next.

The telephone never stopped ringing. Congratulations came from everywhere, as if I'd had anything to do with their success. So I let Dirtybeat's manager, who was still recovering from his pleurisy, talk me into doing the band's sound at an impromptu mid-week gig, hastily organised as a celebration for the great things happening to them.

And there, late at night, I let the sound mixing desk look after itself for ten minutes while I took the time to dance with this witch-eyed Ash, who seemed more interested in me than any young woman ought to. Her firm breasts every now and then pressing against my chest; her dark hair flicking across her eyes as she swung her head to a solid, dirty beat. I'd taught the drummer that beat, had tapped out the rhythm on his shoulder till he got it straight. Ash swayed, lips parting, a hint of pink tongue, then for some reason her hand went over my forearm – a young woman's impetuous promise to a man much too old for her.

Oh, Ash. You're too lovely for me and you should know it. The good in someone like you should go to someone more deserving. Let me dream about you, but don't waste your time, hey?

Ash caught her breath; the song's middle-eight was a heart-breaker. The boys had become so good they could stop on a penny and kick like a mule. I looked at that face and her wild hair, and caught my own breath, then from nowhere came the limitless fall and everything was nearly done.

XX

Buddy, my spruiker, has finished his spiel. He's said all he has to say except for one final thing: 'Happy birthday, Max.' Everyone repeats after him: 'Happy birthday, Max.'

When he closes his eyes, leading everyone in a minute's silent reflection, of what I don't know, maybe the big fiftieth party I should have had, his mind goes back to worrying over what his daughter's fate will be at her school later this afternoon. I tell him not to worry so much. If he's strong he can protect the girl from just about anything. His face hardens as he decides: I'm gonna be a rock for my Kelley. I'm gonna tell that school what I really think: *Fuck them.*

The minute's silence is interrupted by the last of the never-ending stream of late arrivals. I take a good look at her and whatever mouth I have twists into a slow grin. Happiness – it's always a welcome flame. It would have been too much to ask for Debbie Canova to appear, she in some terrible realisation that the only man she'd ever, could ever, love was gone – but Laetecia Sparks turning up, now this is something.

Up the back, Jamie Lazaroff's eyes widen. He has to look twice. Is that——?

She doesn't see him. Everyone is solemn and silent but what does 'Laetecia' care about sixty seconds' reflection? She pushes her way past the standing throng, sashays down the aisle and drapes herself over the lid of my coffin. She slides a card sealed in a mauve envelope underneath my flower arrangement. It's my annual Halloween memento, finally hand-delivered. Also late. Oh well.

Jamie's neck becomes rigid. I don't believe it. That's really her.

He watches the act, not quite comprehending how this can be, then vaguely recalls quiet moments so long ago in Laetecia's arms, talking to her about music and his musicians, and the one he liked best: the drummer, guy named Max, Lee, you should meet him sometime.

Well, I never, he thinks. *Laetecia.* Did I make him sound that good? He gives a small smile. God above, you and Max?

Jamie can't know that it was just one Halloween gone crazy followed by years of memorial cards. Instead, he feels a sort of jealousy growing in his still-lean chest, but he tightens his grip as he holds Dharka's hand. Tightens it very hard, and Dharka smiles up at him, pleased with the way her man wants to squeeze her so, wants to love her so. And she will please him when they go home, she will love him, over and over.

Sometimes I think misdirection and misunderstanding are most of what makes this world go round, it's just part of the human comedy, right?

Meanwhile, Laetecia's face is in the wisteria. She says in a sort of friendly *soto voce*, You're here, aren't you?

Yes, I am, but for how much longer?

She can't hear me. A useless *strega*, that's what she called herself. She'll just have to make whatever one-way conversation she can.

Max, do you want to know what I've been doing all these years? It's pretty simple, pretty boring, but it's called living, that's what, really living. I hope you don't blame me for that. The best years have been in a women's commune on the coast. Men, forget it, I saw enough of them to last me a lifetime, but the love of women, Honey, well, that opens your eyes. So now I'm a forty-something gypsy crazy who reads the tarot and tea leaves for money, but what I really care about is my garden and planting trees. Isn't that a scream? The opposite of a wild life, but hey, that's good. Then there's him, of course, I had to bring him up. The tall one there with your long arms and my hazel eyes.

So I take a look. A good, long look.

He's at the back, a boy, my unmistakable boy, wondering why the hell his ma has dragged him to a stranger's funeral. He's got floppy hair over one eye and looks like he'll need to be shaving in a year or two. His mother has given him a white suit to wear and he's uncomfortable in it, but at least his big feet are bare. That makes him feel better.

That's him, Max.

Did you know how infatuated I was with Jamie Lazaroff? But he joined those good doctors in the Ivory Coast. I missed the chance for what I wanted, which was to get him to plant a seed inside me. You think I'd take a baby out of any old gene pool? I was miserable when he took off so suddenly, but then there was you. I watched you playing and I liked what you were doing. You were serious and determined, but you knew how to relax into a groove too. And then in some numbers you were so playful. You were enjoying yourself. I thought to myself, I like a man like that. So I waited. I didn't mind it took years. You were worth waiting for.

I wanted to tell her, But Laetecia, that was just the stage-me.

Sssh, she says, as if comforting me. You didn't act and I liked

267

your quiet way. I liked your big arms and that strong profile. We were going to be right. So I settled back and made sure I was good and fertile before I took the chance to meet you. But now, Max, if you don't mind, there's something I want to do for you in exchange. It'll never repay you, but that night we were together, you did say this would be cool. Okay? So cover your ears.

Laetecia straightens and swallows a great gulp of air that lifts her hearty chest high, then she lets out a cry, a shriek, an *ululation* so extraordinary that it makes everyone's hair stand on end – those who have hair, that is. Those who don't feel their eyes widen, the skin at the back of their necks tighten, and a shiver spread right across their chests, nipple to nipple. That cry even seems to make me go all quivery. It's the wail of the *stregas* of old, all right, but it doesn't lift me out of my body and it doesn't make me rise into Laetecia's vision. What it does do, though, is make me feel good. Really good. Laetecia Sparks is some kind of power-house, no doubt about it.

At the back of the chapel, my boy rolls his eyes and gives a sheepish smile; his mother has told him to expect this, but not to be too upset by it, because it will all be play-acting, just a little game that grown-ups sometimes indulge in to make one another feel better.

Now she pounds weakly with her fist on the coffin lid and mutters loud enough for all to hear, 'Oh my love, my love. Why did you go?'

Laetecia knows not to pour it on too much thicker than this. The ancient superstitions of another country don't always translate. Her mascara has run; she's even made herself cry. She wipes her eyes with a tissue, snuffles a bit and longingly kisses the glossy wood under her nose. Her great breasts polish my coffin's lid. Up at the podium, Buddy is thinking he's never seen

anything like this. Wow, he tells himself, these musicians are
crazy.

One more thing, Max, she says. I never told you my name.

I wish I could let her know that she shouldn't worry; she'll
always be Laetecia Sparks to me. What does it matter what name
I use to remember her by? She's already in my soul and will be
there forever – both her and my boy. It's okay like this.

Of course she doesn't hear me. She's not half as fey as she
wishes she was. Laetecia says, Well, it's San Filippo. I think that
for some reason she's calling Conny – who, to be fair, is paying
a great deal of attention to these goings-on. In fact, he's smiling
like a loon.

Muxx, you better listen, eh?

It's nice that Conny's taken this opportunity to speak, his
warm smile of old drifting right inside my satin-lined box.

He says, Be quiet, let this woman speak. Then you do learn
something, ok?

Ok.

Then I get it. Laetecia. Laetecia San Filippo.

She slides away from the coffin lid and forces her now-matronly
frame into an adjacent pew, making Iron John have to practically
sit in the lap of Tony Lester beside him. Conny steps out of his seat
and goes to kneel before her. He bends his face down and kisses
his lovely niece's hand. When he'd come to Australia his travel
had been assisted by family already here; later, that same family
also helped his younger brother Stefano's emigration. Stefano San
Filippo, escaping the witch's streak in his wife's bloodline, him
with a daughter six years of age and a bitter crust of resentment
and anger at his elder brother, the dirty *finocchio*, that *omosessuale*. A
man he would never let his daughter even go near.

And, up the back, while the adults of this world go about

their mysterious business, my boy is worrying about a grumbling stomach. If there's a wake for this dead dude, he thinks, there'll be food, right?

Right, I'd like to tell him. You'll be looked after. You'll be looked after as well as your mother and all her women have looked after you, and as well as I would have liked to have looked after you if she'd trusted me to do so. Unfortunately, years of selling herself to men showed her all she wanted or needed to know about the species; now, of course, she contends with you, but it's a different thing. She thinks she can make you better than those who've gone before. Well, who knows, she may be right.

What can I say that would be useful? That I would have been a good father, though I dreamed all my life for a woman who wasn't your ma; or that I'd have taught you how to use a drum kit; or maybe just that you could have counted on me to be your friend?

No. It's time for what is, not what might have been.

The kid thinks, All these people, all these funny, dried-up musician people.

Yes, boy, all these funny dried-up musician people. And you, you're full of the juice of life. One day you'll understand how lucky you've been to have a mother who told you, I love your arms; I love how strong you've become; and your smile, you know, you'll drive the girls wild. She's already given you the confidence and bearing to face the world and shake the world, and you break the world if it suits you, boy, because that's what you're here for. Let the rotting rot and the old ways pass; make something new and do it soon. Don't be half-hearted. You shoot good and straight, or you don't shoot at all.

*　　*　　*

They've lifted me. Down the aisle and into the back of a glaringly white station wagon, and the drive to the waiting grave is short and sweet as a man's life. Out in the hot sun, that gaping maw is ready to receive its payment.

My friends carry me. My friends.

They're my boys doing well and then there's my real boy watching from a short distance, now wishing for something like a bowl of nachos or a falafel roll. An important matter, I know that, for a young man to fill the yearning in his belly.

And one more yearning that's starting to rise; he's noticed Ash. Ash standing in her silk dress, with the cooling mid-morning breeze making it cling to her long legs. She's leaning in to her father. My boy's too young yet to really focus on what he's feeling, but he understands there's the hunger you get when you need to eat and there's the yearning that grips both your belly and your heart when you see someone like her. I wish I could explain to him what this means, but he'll make a better fist of it on his own. I expect, in some matters, a father is truly just a pain in the ass.

Well, I can't help myself. It's the only patriarchal duty I'll get to fulfil.

I tell him, Go talk to her, boy, get her a drink at whatever sort of wake they're going to throw for me, make yourself known. Just stand next to her and see what it feels like. Smell her skin; see the way her hair falls; notice the way your heart starts to thump. It's life, kid, the best part of it.

Here it is. Lowering the dead weight on straps, shimmying it down into the earth. Laetecia sets up the tape player she's brought with her.

Oh God, let it not be more psychedelia to haunt me into eternity – but someone like her, with the things we did after the End of the World party, and our beautiful outcome standing by her side, surely she would be the one to know better, wouldn't she? So I wait for the music of *Blue Train* to rise into this lazy summer's day.

It doesn't and it won't.

There's another ghost present and its name is Debbie Canova. Her violin's notes peel out and soar, resurrected by Laetecia San Filippo, who's dug up a copy of that one LP of ours, committed it to tape, and pressed 'play' on the long, twisting song that features violin and drums only.

Tony Lester's head drops. Shit, what did I do to deserve this? I should have known.

What the poor guy really doesn't know is that when in a few days he puts up his hand for my collection of hundreds and hundreds of records, he'll not only inherit my rock albums, but Concetto San Filippo's comprehensive and thoroughly impressive jazz library as well. Worth a mint but he'll never sell it. He'll spin all that jazz for months, meanwhile discovering that between my rock records and his there is an almost exact duplication, though of course there'll be one amongst those massive piles of vinyl that he never wanted to own and now does. In his pink mansion he'll sit back in a black leather armchair and stare into young Debbie Canova's face, into her blue eyes, and our broken down truck rolling into a dusty town called Thornberry won't be yesterday but today, and none of it will seem so bad, in fact a major part of him will feel good to almost-but-not-quite have the girl back in his arms.

In the crowd, Iron John pricks up his old ears. *Is it?* It sure is. He feels something like a hot poker stick in his gut. That day. That day we made this, and his son Thomas sees him slump and has to come forward to take the old man's weight off his walking frame and help him sit in a plastic folding chair. Out here in the sun he keeps his hand on his father's shoulder while incomprehensible tears come pouring down.

Thankfully it's not all quite so terrible.

Patti takes a step forward with a walnut grin in those still-craggy features. She just can't keep that immense smile off her face. It even surprises a few people beside her. But she knows this music so well! It was her guilty, secret pleasure for so long. After all, her Roger might never have known why there were nights they had to listen to this record all the way through, but she did. Every other LP they owned was in the very pleasant fashion of Shirley Bassey, Perry Como and José Feliciano, but this raucous pounding? Still, she's sure he never really minded all that much, for whenever she laid that platter down they didn't relax in sedate contemplation of too-loud rock-and-roll but did actually fuck like minx.

So now a significant proportion of the gathered mourners hold their breath; of course they're familiar with this piece of music too; they know that after the violin's extended haunting solo at the start their absent friend's drums will come in with body and wings.

Wait, wait. Debbie Canova holds me back. Not yet, Max, not yet.

Wait, wait. Laetecia pulls me out of her and gently eases off the condom, then swallows me deep inside.

Wait, wait, Muxx, this is the beat, wait till you do feel it in you bones, then you join like this.

Now.

The flesh shivers and the air vibrates to a beat taught me by

273

a young woman's slender fingers tapping on my shoulder. That beat shoots straight, straight and true, until it's slowly silenced in the endless sky.

ACKNOWLEDGMENTS

The author would like to extend his sincere gratitude to Madonna Duffy, Katherine Howell, Fiona Inglis, Sarah Muirhead, Julia Stiles, Matt 'Tonne' Tucker and Alan Westacott. Also, never to forget a broken-down rock band called Paradox and its assortment of players, including Cyril Campbell, Alan and Rodney Westacott and Tony Widowski. Thanks Nic, thanks Rocco.

The lyrics quoted in Part One were ad-libbed by Alice Cooper during his recording of Rolf Kempf's 'Hello Hooray' on the album *Billion Dollar Babies* (Warner Bros. 1973). The song appears in *The Dirty Beat* with the kind permission of Rolf Kempf. www.woodysparks.com

For Cyril Campbell, drummer and friend.
1954–2005